IR

KISSING LESSONS

KISSING LESSONS

SOPHIE JORDAN

Houghton Mifflin Harcourt
Boston   New York

hmhbooks.com

The text was set in Adobe Jenson Pro.
Title hand-lettering and book design by Mary Claire Cruz

Library of Congress Cataloging-in-Publication Data
Names: Jordan, Sophie, author.
Title: Kissing lessons / Sophie Jordan.
Description: Boston : Houghton Mifflin Harcourt, [2020] |
Audience: Ages 14 and up. | Audience: Grades 10–12. |
Summary: Hayden Vargas is a girl with a bad reputation who really just
wants to finish high school and get away from her alcoholic mother and the
whole boring high school dating scene, so when Emmaline Martin offers
to pay her for lessons in attracting and managing boys it seems like a way
to pick up some easy money for her post-high school life — but she did not
count on the attraction she feels for her client's brother, Nolan,
who is not only gorgeous, but actually interesting.
Identifiers: LCCN 2019029208 (print) | LCCN 2019029209 (ebook) |
ISBN 9781328977076 (hardcover) | ISBN 9780358067412 (ebook)
Subjects: LCSH: High school students — Juvenile fiction. | Interpersonal
relations — Juvenile fiction. | Dating (Social customs) — Juvenile fiction. |
Reputation — Juvenile fiction. | Children of alcoholics — Juvenile fiction. |
Mothers and daughters — Juvenile fiction. | Young adult fiction. |
Romance fiction. | CYAC: High schools — Fiction. | Schools — Fiction. |
Interpersonal relations — Fiction. | Dating (Social customs) — Fiction. |
Love — Fiction. | Alcoholism—Fiction. |
Mothers and daughters — Fiction. | LCGFT: Romance fiction.
Classification: LCC PZ7.J76845 Ki 2020 (print) |
LCC PZ7.J76845 (ebook) | DDC 813.6 [Fic] — dc23
LC record available at https://lccn.loc.gov/2019029208
LC ebook record available at https://lccn.loc.gov/2019029209

Manufactured in the United States of America
DOC 10 9 8 7 6 5 4 3 2 1
4500794930

For Lily, my treasured compass throughout this book . . .

KISSING LESSONS

LESSON #1

PARTIES ARE THE PERFECT HUNTING GROUND.

x Hayden x

Hayden was having serious doubts about this party.

It was a big gathering, spilling out onto the front yard and into the cul-de-sac. The number of people on the lawn wouldn't even fit crammed inside her small house. Big parties likes this usually got shut down because someone called the police. It would be a shame if that happened. Her hair and makeup were on point tonight. If she went home early, it was a lot of effort for nothing.

Hayden stood on the sidewalk contemplating whether it was worth going inside, watching as girls stood shivering in their skirts and strappy tops. It was January and forty-five degrees, but hypothermia clearly didn't worry them.

High school parties (and parties in general) weren't usually her thing, but Dorian had begged her to come.

Dorian was a guy in her health class. Coach Alvarez teamed up students for a lot of the assignments and Dorian had appointed himself her partner in all things.

They'd made out a couple times in the east stairwell. He was cute and linebacker big, even though he played tennis. Good hair. Long on the top. High and tight on the sides. He smelled nice. Hayden appreciated a well-groomed guy who smelled of deodorant and mint toothpaste.

This week he had brought her a brownie. A *brownie* wrapped in foil. His mom made them. Dorian had a mom who baked brownies. God. As if that didn't scream they were from two different worlds. But Dorian was cute and into her, so hooking up was pretty inevitable. Dating, however, was *not*. Not even all the homemade brownies in the world could change that.

He'd been bugging her to hang out more outside of school. He asked her out on dates. Never mind that she didn't *date*. He even hinted about the winter formal in February. A dance. As if she would go to one of those.

She knew what it all meant. He was interested in taking their stairwell make-out sessions to the next level. And while there would never be anything serious between them, she'd caved and agreed to meet him at this party.

Her gaze swept over the scene spread out before her. The beautiful, popular people were in attendance. The people who had their own lunch tables and moms that made brownies. She didn't belong here. And she didn't think that with any amount of bitterness. She didn't *want* to belong here. High school was just this *thing* she had to get through to arrive at the next stage in life.

Hopefully, a better stage.

There had to be a *better* stage.

She only had to make it until June and she'd be out. Away. Free.

As Hayden turned off the sidewalk onto the front walkway, a gorilla of a guy ran out the front door chasing a girl with a pitcher of water. The girl shrieked delightedly and let herself get caught. One of his gorilla arms wrapped around her waist and lifted her off her feet. She squealed as he dumped the water down the front of her white shirt, soaking her. She laughed, spreading her arms wide and showcasing her boobs now on full display through her transparent tee. With a Tarzan shout, he tossed her over his shoulder and marched back into the house with her.

Hayden expelled a heavy breath. *Punch me. Hard.*

This was *not* her scene. She didn't get a lot of nights off from work, and this wasn't how she preferred to spend them. She should have agreed to meet Dorian somewhere else.

She should have known better. Boredom propelled her, she guessed. And avoidance. She really didn't want to deal with Mom, who apparently had no plans for the night and was staying in. So here she was.

Stepping inside the loud and crowded party, Hayden scanned faces for Dorian.

She spotted the majority of the football team along with its cheerleaders milling about. There were also the basketball players, baseball players, and soccer players. All the athletes. Funny how they mattered so much in high school. As though they would all grow up to compete in the Olympics instead of being ordinary people living ordinary lives. Less than ordinary, if her mother was any indication of a Travis High School star athlete.

Mom still held the district record for the eight hundred meters, and last week Hayden found her passed out in the driveway, still sitting in the driver's seat with the car running. Her snores could be heard through the glass. Hayden almost had to break the window to rouse her.

"Hey! Hayden!"

She turned sharply, the sound of her name startling over the din of music and voices. She didn't expect to know many people here. That was the benefit of attending a large school. You could be a stranger among your own classmates. A ghost in the halls. Faces were familiar but names unknown.

Her gaze landed on a skinny kid. She didn't know his name, but she'd seen him with Dorian before.

"You looking for Dorian?" he called. Apparently he knew more about her than her name if he knew she was here for Dorian.

She nodded and he jerked a thumb behind him, toward a hallway. "That way. Through the mudroom and into the garage."

"Thanks." She passed him, heading in the direction he'd motioned, ignoring a drunken guy stumbling across her path. Beer sloshed over the rim of his cup, soaking the front of his sweater, but he didn't care.

He stopped hard at the sight of her. "Hey, girl." His chest puffed out, drawing attention to the dark beer stain that resembled the shape of Florida. "You looking for me? You must be." He belched and gave a smile she knew he thought was seductive and not total ridiculousness.

Sidestepping him, she debated whether to continue on to the mudroom. The night wasn't off to a great start. Except she'd come all this way, so she might as well let Dorian know she'd made the effort.

She was almost to the mudroom when her phone started vibrating. Hayden paused and pulled it from her pocket, sighing when she read her mom's name. She could ignore her, but she would just keep calling. Or worse. Her mom might even get in her car and track her down using the app she'd installed on Hayden's phone. She'd done it before. Sharon loathed being ignored.

"Hey, Mom." She couldn't hide the lack of enthusiasm in her voice.

"*Hayden*, I need you to bring home some pizzas. Three. No! Four. I invited some friends over." From the slur of her mom's words, she could tell she didn't have to worry about her mom noticing her lack of enthusiasm. She was well on her way to forgetting her own name.

"I'm not at work, Mom." She worked at the Tasty Freeze, but they shared a building with Tony's Pizza. It worked out well for the two businesses. People loved to grab a cone after their pizza.

"Oh. Well, so what? Swing by and get a few pepperonis."

"Mom, I don't have any cash on me —"

"Oh, your boss likes you —"

"I don't get free food, Mom." She'd explained to her mother before that she didn't work at Tony's and that even if she did, the manager there didn't give free food to employees either.

"Look, I put a roof over your head, don't I?" Her voice turned shrill in her ear. "Pick up some pizzas or there will be hell to pay."

There was always hell to pay. Even when she did what her mom wanted. Of course, it wouldn't do any good to say something like that. Those were fighting words, and Sharon loved nothing more than a fight.

Hayden closed her eyes. *Just one more semester. Just one more semester.* "I'll do what I can."

Because there was no use arguing with her. It never helped.

"Good." Mom gave a happy gasp. "Oh! They're here." The phone went dead in her ear. She wasn't even worth a goodbye. Her friends had arrived.

Hayden shoved the phone back in her pocket with a sigh that made her feel old. Her mom would probably get caught up in her friends and a bottle of Tito's and forget she had even called Hayden in the first place. She didn't need to bother with the pizzas. There was that at least.

She studied the closed door leading to the garage. She was close enough she could hear shouting and cheering coming from the other side. Any party was better than going home at this point.

With that happy thought, she stepped inside the garage.

LESSON #2

LEAVE ROOM FOR THE UNEXPECTED.

x   Nolan   x

Nolan was getting his ass kicked.

He bounced on the balls of his feet, swinging the paddle at the ball as though he was trying to launch it into outer space.

His opponent never missed, smacking the ball back at him again and again and again until, inevitably, Nolan was breathing raggedly and swinging and missing more than he liked.

Priscilla sidled close to him, as close as she dared while he was whacking the ball with his paddle like a madman. "You know Dorian is like a tennis god, right?"

He was well aware of the fact that the guy he was playing happened to be their school's best tennis player and had a decided advantage over him. It didn't matter. When Nolan played a game, he played to win.

He didn't know how *not* to give his all to win. Although losing did feel inevitable in this situation. Dorian played with a cocky grin on his face, not even out of breath. Nolan swung his paddle like he was trying to murder the ball.

Then Dorian did the unexpected and quit.

He didn't set his paddle down or anything, but his head definitely left the game. His gaze strayed away from the table somewhere beyond Nolan's shoulder just as Nolan landed the ball in the corner of the table, sending it launching across the garage.

Dorian's friends hissed and booed.

Dorian himself didn't seem to care. He didn't even look at the table or Nolan or his friends. No, he was looking toward the door.

Nolan swung around to see what had snared Dorian's attention. The object of his friend's sudden interest was — shocker! — a girl.

She strode through the garage by herself — but there wasn't the slightest bit of insecurity in her. She wore skinny jeans and a crop top that showed off her flat gold-skinned belly. His gaze traveled up, skimming over perky breasts. Her dark hair fell in ribbons of rippling ink over her shoulders and down her back.

He'd seen her before. She was kind of hard to miss in the halls. Even in a school as big as Travis, she definitely stood out. She was the type of girl who got noticed. The type guys talked about. There were always stories. Rumors. He never paid too much attention to them, but he recalled snippets of gossip about her.

She reached Dorian and turned so that he had a view of her from behind. The things those jeans did to her body . . . He swallowed hard. He hated noticing. Hated to be that leering guy. He had a girlfriend. He shouldn't stare at her. He knew that.

He looked away, uncomfortable.

Nolan's girlfriend was smart and pretty and nice and happened to be an extremely popular cheerleader. He didn't need to gaze at some other girl, no matter how much he liked the way she looked.

And it appeared that Nolan wasn't the only one who liked the way she looked. Most of the guys in the garage were drooling after her.

7

A quick glance around verified their glassy-eyed stares fixed on her. Though some of it was probably the beer.

Dorian said something to her and left her alone for a moment. He joined Nolan, slapping his paddle against his chest, forcing him to take the paddle or let it drop between them. "Sorry, Nol. You're gonna have to find another partner to crush you. I'm out of here."

"You leaving? I thought we were all going to head to Whataburger."

"Nah, man. Hayden just showed up. She's all the meal I need." Dorian winked and nodded at the girl where she stood across the garage. Nolan rolled his eyes at the awfulness of that line. Fortunately for Dorian no one else overheard.

The girl nodded back at Dorian in acknowledgment, her lips curving in a slight smile. "I invited her tonight, but I didn't think she would show." Again, a wink. "Guess my charm and persistence finally paid off."

"Lucky you," Nolan murmured, trying not to stare at the girl. He didn't know what it was about her that affected him, but she did. She was beautiful, but so were a lot of girls. His girlfriend included.

Dorian winked and brushed his knuckles against the front of his shirt in an overexaggerated gesture. "Guess she couldn't resist this."

Nolan couldn't help but roll his eyes again.

Priscilla moved in and wrapped an arm around Nolan's waist. "Hayden Vargas? Really, Dorian?" Her voice rang with disapproval. "Does your mother know?" Dorian's mother was a teacher at the high school.

"I'm my own man," Dorian replied, still grinning.

"Be careful," Priscilla warned.

"He's not going to war," Nolan snapped. He couldn't help it. This was a girl. Not the Terminator, and Priscilla didn't need to warn Dorian away from her like she was something dangerous. Sometimes she could be so judgmental.

A flicker of hurt flashed across Priscilla's eyes and Nolan felt bad then. To make up for it, he pulled her in closer to his side.

Dorian chuckled. "I don't know about that. I hear she leave marks."

That produced an image that Nolan promptly shoved from his mind.

"You laugh, but watch yourself," Priscilla warned, and then glanced over at Hayden Vargas again, her gaze narrowing slightly in speculation. "I hear she's a man eater."

Hayden was no longer alone. Several guys surrounded her.

Dorian laughed harder. "That's what I'm hoping for, Pris."

Priscilla clucked in disapproval and swatted Dorian on the arm. "You're so gross." She looked at Nolan. "I'm going to get my coat."

Priscilla walked away, her hips doing that natural roll of hers. Nolan turned back to look at Dorian ... only to find him admiring her departure.

"Hey, man. Mind not checking out my girlfriend?"

Dorian glanced back at Nolan and shrugged without apology. "She's nice to check out."

"Well, have some respect. Besides. You're here with someone else."

"Yeah, but Pris has it all ... she's the kind of girl you can bring home to your mom." Dorian glanced back over to Hayden Vargas. He wasn't saying the words, but it was understood. Hayden was *not* the kind of girl you brought home to Mom. That's what he meant.

Dorian lifted one shoulder in a shrug and added, "Hayden will do for now. She'll do just fine."

With a nod goodbye, Dorian wove his way toward Hayden, sliding up beside her and resting his hand on the small of her back. She smiled up at him and it didn't take long for the other guys to scatter. Dorian was too much competition for the faint of heart. On and off the Ping-Pong table.

Nolan stared at them for a moment longer, almost feeling sorry for the girl. The words ran on repeat through his mind. *Hayden will do for now.* Did she know that was Dorian's attitude? That he only considered her good enough for the moment?

No one deserved to be used like that.

Nolan had been looking after his mother and two sisters since he was thirteen years old. He knew that made him a little different than others his age. Hell, just the fact that he'd experienced the death of someone close to him made him different from his entire peer group, but most guys his age didn't usually have to act as a surrogate father to two younger sisters.

Nolan didn't take a breath or make a move without thinking about the welfare and feelings of his sisters and mother. His father left him with that responsibility. He'd instructed Nolan to be the man of the house and take care of them. At age thirteen, he had given his word that he would do that.

He knew he wasn't like Dorian. Not even like his best friend, Beau. They had no problem hooking up with a girl one night and then forgetting about her the next day.

Nolan, on the other hand, had been dating Priscilla since his sophomore year. She'd applied to all the same colleges he had. She was preparing for them to go to university together, and then after hitting all the proper dating milestones, Priscilla assumed they'd eventually get married. She didn't talk about her future without him in it.

Usually, it felt good to have order and plans — his future all set. Usually.

There had been enough chaos in his past. He craved stability. Now and in his life to come.

Priscilla returned wearing her coat, flipping her auburn waves out from inside the collar. "Ready?"

He nodded. "Let's go find my sister first."

"She might want to stay. Her friends are here."

He frowned at the suggestion. The party was a little rowdy and there was alcohol on the premises. He wasn't leaving Emmaline here. He hadn't even wanted her to come at all. But she rarely went to parties, and since she wanted to come for once, he didn't fight her on it. "Emmaline will leave with us," he insisted. He doubted she was enjoying herself anyway. He knew his sister. This wasn't her scene.

Priscilla gave him a look. He knew what the look meant. It meant, *You're being too protective.*

He didn't care.

Taking Priscilla's hand, he led her back inside the house.

The inside was even more crowded than it had been half an hour ago.

"Do you see her?" Priscilla stood on her tiptoes and tried to peer through the mass of people.

"Not yet. Come on, we'll find her."

They pushed ahead, getting stopped, it seemed, every other moment by someone they knew, which didn't do much for their progress. Nolan finally had to start ignoring people to get anywhere.

At last, he found some of Emmaline's friends. They stood huddled in a small group, looking like they weren't having any fun, which was heartening even if it made him a bit of a jerk.

He should want his sister to enjoy herself, and he did . . . but if she was miserable here, maybe he wouldn't have to convince Emmaline to leave at all. Maybe she was ready to go. Maybe she had learned her lesson and wouldn't want to come to parties like this anymore.

"Hey, seen my sister?"

"No," Monica replied a little testily. "We lost sight of her and we're ready to go." She motioned to the hallway. "She went off that way with Beau."

"Oh. Okay." Immediately, he breathed a little easier. He felt better knowing Beau was with her. Beau was more than a friend. He was like a brother. A brother to Nolan and his sisters. He was maybe even more protective than Nolan because he trusted people a whole lot less.

Nolan dug out his keys and handed them to Priscilla. He addressed the group. "Go wait in the truck. I'll find Emmaline and then we can head to Whataburger." Whataburger was a staple in these parts. An institution. Friday and Saturday nights it was jam-packed full of high school kids who were there as much for the socialization as for the food.

Her friends looked relieved to be leaving and immediately turned to make their way to the door.

"I can come with you," Priscilla said, clasping his arm.

"Nah, go on. I'll find her faster on my own. Warm the car up and we'll meet you out there."

She hesitated and then gave him a peck. "Okay. Hurry up though." She patted his chest. "I'm starving. If you don't find her, I'm sure Beau can bring her home." With a decisive nod, she spun around. People stepped aside, parting for her and sending admiring and envying glances as she passed. Nothing new there.

He watched her go for a moment longer and then headed back into the horde himself.

No matter what Priscilla said, he wasn't leaving this party without his sister.

LESSON #3

SOMETIMES HOLDING HANDS
IS THE MOST INTIMATE ACT OF ALL.

x Hayden x

Dorian guided Hayden from the garage, one hand on her elbow in a very proprietary manner. She didn't know how she felt about that.

Okay, yes she did.

She didn't need help or guiding. She could walk just fine, if not better, without his sweaty paw grasping her. She bit back her dislike and the urge to pull her arm away, telling herself not to be so prickly.

The hand on her elbow didn't mean anything. She came here because she had a rare night off and she didn't want to spend it at home with Mom, who was having her own rowdy night with friends. Hayden deserved some fun, and Dorian promised they would have a good time. That's all there was to it.

His fingers slid down from her elbow to her hand, holding it as he tugged her through the crowd. This handholding business was a foreign sensation and she didn't like that either.

Holding hands was pretty intimate stuff. She would much rather make out with a guy than hold his hand. Holding hands meant invest-ment and commitment, and she didn't allow herself to get invested in any guy. She wasn't like her mom, looking for someone to save her or pay her bills or make her feel better about herself. No, for those things she relied on herself. For everything she relied on herself.

He stopped before a group of jocks and did the whole fist-bump-and-lean-in kind of thing. Man-hugging. She mentally rolled her eyes. So the party was light on the fun. Hayden scanned the room, looking for the nearest exit. She'd give Dorian another five minutes to fulfill his promise and then she was out of here.

A couple of girls hung on the jocks. They looked Hayden up and down and then exchanged telling looks with each other that conveyed she was deficient in some way.

Undaunted, Hayden smiled back at each of them, letting them know they didn't affect her. High school was full of mean girls, but so was the world. She was way tougher than any of them. She knew what they thought of her, and she didn't care. She'd endured worse. Life with her mother had thickened her skin.

"Um. I'm gonna go find a bathroom." While the girls did not make her uncomfortable, she couldn't deal with the handholding anymore. Time to end it.

Not waiting for Dorian's response, Hayden dived into the crowd without a glance back. She got some stares, but no one talked to her as she passed. These weren't her people, after all. Not that she technically had people.

Washing her hands with expensive-looking hand wash that smelled of cucumber and mint, she assessed herself in the mirror of the bath-room she had just barricaded herself in. Staring at her reflection, she ignored the knocking at the door and instead propped her hands on the edge of the sink. "What are you doing here?" she asked her reflection, as though the person looking back at her was someone else. Someone who could give her an explanation.

So far she wasn't having a good time, and that had been the goal.

She didn't owe Dorian anything. She didn't owe *any* guy anything. She put herself first because if she didn't, no one else would. She'd learned that lesson when most kids had been learning to ride a bike.

No guy took priority in her life. She'd watched her mother get lost down that rabbit hole ever since she could remember, chasing after men and their false promises only to end up tossed aside at the end, a pile of broken pieces that Hayden had to gather up and patch back together. *Enough.*

Turning away from the mirror, she exited the bathroom. As she moved down the hall, a guy rounded the corner and his eyes lit up when he saw her. He walked an uneven line toward her, indicating he'd had more than a few drinks. "Heyyy there." He stopped in front of her, his shoulder falling against the wall. He wagged a finger at her. "I know you."

"Yeah?" She didn't know him.

"You're the hummer queen."

She released a gust of breath and crossed her arms over her chest. She knew people called her that. Guys. Girls. Everyone. Ever since eighth grade, when the rumors started about her giving some guy a BJ in the back of the school bus, it had been uttered indiscreetly behind her back and even directly to her face.

"That so?"

"Yeah." His gaze dropped, rolling down her body. "How about you show me your skills, baby?"

Ugh. Gross.

"How about I show you what else I'm good at?" She didn't even care that her agreement with him was tacit — that she *was* the "hummer queen." It just spoke to how little she cared what people thought about her. She knew rumors could destroy lives. If one let them. If one cared. Lucky for her, the opinions of others never mattered to her. Why should she care what people she didn't care about thought?

He jerked his chin in invitation, licking his lips obscenely, his gaze fixating on her chest. "Yeah. Show me. What else you good at, baby?"

"Castration."

His gaze shot back to hers. His swagger deflated as the single word sank in.

Without another glance, she walked into the party, searching for the nearest exit, ready to bail. There had to be a back door out of this place. Away from this party with its beautiful, carefree . . . and increasingly drunk people.

She found a way out through a set of French doors leading onto a patio with a burbling fountain. A fountain. Actual people lived like this. Unbelievable. It really was astonishing to think that she went to school with people who had fountains in their backyard. Crazy stuff. In her neighborhood, there were no fancy lawn fountains. She couldn't even keep someone from stealing the rickety lawn chair off the tiny slab of concrete that served as her front porch.

Hayden marched past the fountain, searching for a way out, but then stopped and backed up a few steps.

Crossing her arms over her chest, she squared off in front of it and grudgingly admired it, wondering if it was one of those wishing fountains. It seemed unlucky to walk past a fountain without tossing a coin in it, just in case. She didn't need bad luck in life. She'd been born under an unlucky star. Her mother told her that plenty of times.

Apologized for it, in fact — as though *that* were to blame for her lot in life. As though her mother might not bear any responsibility.

Hayden didn't have money to toss away, but she didn't need to risk bad luck either. Or rather . . . *worse* luck. You know, in case her mom was right and her stars really were that unlucky.

She dug around in her pocket. She'd bought a burrito for two dollars and fifty cents from the corner store for dinner, but she must have left the change in her car. She checked her wrist wallet. No change there either. Not so surprising. Money was always tight. A coveted thing. People said money couldn't buy happiness, but that was usually people who had plenty of it. Or at least enough.

Not people like her.

Not people who knew what it felt like to go to bed without dinner.

As soon as Hayden had turned fourteen, she got a job. She'd been working ever since.

She didn't do it so she could have extra money to shop for shoes at the mall. She did it for food, gas, car insurance, groceries. Last month she actually took herself to the dentist. If she wanted tampons or toothpaste, she had to buy them herself.

Sometimes Mom would surprise her and bring home groceries, but Hayden knew better than to rely on her for those things. Whoever said the best things in life were free never had to scrape off the moldy edges on bread just so they could have something to eat.

Hayden lingered in front of the fountain. She never counted herself as superstitious. That was her mother — reading her horoscope every day, driving into a ditch to avoid a black cat, and throwing spilled salt over her shoulder. Still, in some secret, buried part of her, Hayden hated to pass up the opportunity to improve her fortune.

A sound caught her attention, breaking the spell. The scratch of something over loose gravel. Hayden shifted on her feet, looked around, and then spotted a shoe peeking out from the other side of the fountain.

She inched around, following the shoe up to its owner — a girl sitting on the ground with her back propped against the stone base of the fountain. Her wide Bambi-brown eyes stared straight ahead into the night. She looked young, but she probably wasn't much younger than Hayden. Then again, Hayden thought every girl in high school looked young. Because Hayden *felt* so very old. She'd lived too much, seen too much. Hayden was eighteen, but she didn't feel young.

The girl's lips were moving, but her words were an inaudible whisper.

"Hey there," Hayden greeted. "You got a penny?"

Bambi stopped her muttering and blinked up at Hayden like an owl, evidently seeing her for the first time. "A penny?"

"Yeah." She wasn't above bumming a penny off someone. Not if there was even a remote chance it could improve her fate.

After a second of hesitation the girl searched through the small handbag at her side. "Here you go." She extended a coin to Hayden.

Hayden accepted it with a nod of thanks and stepped back several feet. Hayden could feel the girl's eyes watching her.

Taking a bracing breath, she made her wish. She kept it simple. General. Nothing too specific. No sense being greedy. *For my life to suck a little less.*

Not that wishes ever came true. She knew that.

When she was young she used to wish for big things. She didn't waste wishes on small things like a winter coat or art supplies, no matter how much she might want them. She wished for specific things like for Mom to stop drinking and get a good job that she wouldn't lose five minutes later. Things like a new house. Or for her father to suddenly materialize and be like one of those TV dads. The last one was absurd, she knew. The guy had bailed before she was even born. No way was he suddenly going to stroll back into her life and be a responsible father now.

"What did you wish for?"

Hayden looked down at the mumbling girl. If she went to Travis High School, Hayden had never seen her before, but that wasn't very surprising. Big school. Lots of faces.

"Come on," she pressed from where she sat on the ground. "You can tell me."

"I can't. You know the rules. If I tell it won't come true."

"Rules." The girl sneered, her top lip curling. The look didn't seem natural on her. She seemed like the kind of girl who was wearing bows up until recently. "So tired of rules."

Hayden thought about that for a moment. There weren't too many rules in her life. Her mom wasn't the kind of parent that enforced them.

"Yeah?" Hayden really looked at the girl, trying to determine if she was drunk. Her cheeks were flushed and her eyes were as bright as sunlit glass, but Hayden didn't think it had anything to do with alcohol or other substances. And given who her mother was, Hayden knew the signs.

"Yeah." She straightened her bent leg in a sudden move, almost as though she was kicking at something invisible in front of her. "I mean, it's bad enough my mom has rules, but then I have my brother breathing down my neck, watching my every move, telling me what to do. He's there to stop me if I want to step out of line even a teeny bit — which would only be a natural expression of adolescence, am I right?" Her gaze landed on Hayden in hot accusation. "Right?"

A natural expression of adolescence? Who talked like that?

"Right," Hayden replied, because it seemed the girl wasn't going to stop until Hayden agreed with her.

"Right." She nodded, satisfied but still full of fire. "But even when I step out of line just a little bit and decide to have some fun for myself, I can't. And you know why? Because I'm too green. *I* run away like a scared little girl. Turns out *I* am the one standing in my own way of living the life I want."

Hayden had no idea what was happening. She eyed the gate, ready to dive through and escape.

The girl wasn't done, however. Still in full rant mode, she stabbed a finger at the house in livid accusation. "I mean, I'm not even considering doing anything as extreme as some people. Did you know there are people at this party right now watching porn in the media room? It's a porn-watching party!"

The fact that people had a media room was actually more surprising to Hayden than the porn-watching scenario.

"Do you see me doing that?" the girl added, her voice gaining in shrillness.

Hayden shook her head. "No. I see you sitting right here." She motioned to the area where the girl sat.

"That's right. I ran from the room like some guy in a ski mask was after me." The girl sighed deeply and seemed to regain some of her composure. She looked Hayden over for a long moment. "You're Hayden Vargas," she said, as though it just dawned on her.

Hayden blinked at the strangeness of this girl knowing *her*, but Hayden not reciprocating in that knowing. "Uh. Yeah."

The girl nodded. "I've seen you around school. You've got a cool look." She gestured up and down at Hayden.

And that's why she knew her name? Because she noticed her look? A look that mostly consisted of clothes found at a thrift store?

"Thanks." What else should she say?

"I'm Emmaline Martin. You don't know me." She shrugged. "It's okay." She said it like people not knowing her was a long-accustomed condition of her life.

This might go down as one of the strangest conversations she'd ever had, and considering the colorful personalities that drifted in and out of her mother's life (and thereby her life), that was saying something.

She was about to say goodbye and end it when —

"Emmaline!"

At the sound of her name, the girl on the ground groaned. "Great. He found me."

From her position, Hayden could still see around the fountain to the house. The king of Travis High himself stood there, hands propped on his hips like he was squared off on the prow of a ship. She'd seen him in the garage when she first arrived, playing Ping-Pong with Dorian like a man possessed. His face had been intense, his body a thing of beauty in motion.

Of course she knew who he was. You couldn't attend Travis and not know. He was always on the morning news — either for sports or as homecoming king or as a featured member of some club.

He hadn't given her so much as a glance in the garage earlier tonight or any time before then, but of course she had noticed him. Her pulse always picked up at the sight of him. Her body betrayed her in that regard. Apparently she responded to guys who looked like the lead of some cheesy teen movie. Ugh. She was such a cliché.

He was tall and broad-shouldered, with lush thick hair, smoldering eyes, and a square jaw. That damn square jaw.

Girls drooled over him, and it was entirely justifiable, but she kept her admiration secret. She wadded it up into a ball and stuffed it way down deep. A guy like him would never go for a girl like her. Not that she wanted him to like her.

She forced her gaze off him and looked back to Emmaline. Suddenly it clicked.

Nolan Martin. Emmaline Martin. They were related. As in, siblings.

Hayden stared down at Emmaline again, noting the slight similarities. The rich brown hair. The shape and position of their eyes. The contour of their eyebrows.

Emmaline was looking up at her with a near-panicked expression on her face. "Is he coming this way?"

No doubt *he* was her brother.

Hayden looked up again. He was staring directly at her now, his head cocked at an angle. She realized he probably saw her talking to the ground.

Still staring at him, she answered Emmaline, "Yeah. Um. He's looking right at me and . . . yeah, now he's headed over here."

His long strides ate up the ground. She crossed her arms and watched him advance, only mildly affected over the display of hotness headed her way. She'd been around plenty of good-looking guys before. Dorian, with his two-percent-body-fat tennis bod, was in the house right now waiting for her. True, Dorian was not Nolan Martin hot, but he was hot, nonetheless.

Emmaline groaned again, dropping her face into her hands. "Tell him to go away."

He stopped beside Hayden, giving her a terse nod of acknowledgment before focusing his attention on his sister.

"Emmaline, we're going to Whataburger." He stared down at his sister expectantly. When she made no move to get up, he added, "Everybody is ready and waiting."

She huffed out a breath. "Fiiiiine." She clambered to her feet, shooting Hayden an apologetic look. "It was nice talking with you, Hayden. Maybe I'll see you around at school."

Hayden smiled and nodded, even though she doubted they would be seeing each other around. It was a big school, and they didn't travel in the same circles. A five-minute conversation wasn't suddenly going to change that.

Emmaline headed back inside.

Nolan hung behind, looking at Hayden as though he wanted to say something. He'd never said anything to her before, so she couldn't imagine what he had to say now.

Arms still crossed over her chest, Hayden arched both eyebrows at him. "Yes?"

"I think Dorian is inside looking for you."

Ah. He was looking out for his boy. He probably thought his buddy was going to get laid tonight and he wanted to help him along. "Well, aren't you helpful?"

He blinked, clearly picking up on her sarcastic tone and not knowing what to make of her.

"Nolan?"

They both turned at the sound of his name.

There, standing framed in the light of the patio, was the captain of the cheerleading team and this year's homecoming queen.

She and Nolan Martin were together often. On the morning announcements. In the halls at school. Hayden had never cared enough to gain confirmation on their status before. It was none of her business. She had her own life. Her own problems.

But she now knew. One look at the girl's face, at the impatience of her body language, and she knew. Of course they were a real-life couple. The queen and the king. Hayden laughed lightly.

"What's so funny?" Nolan looked back at her, his expression unreadable. Those deep-set eyes fixed on her, staring intently. She stopped laughing, uncomfortable under his scrutiny.

Butterflies took flight in her stomach.

Her body failed her. Again. She hated that. It reminded her of her mother. How often did Mom talk about some guy with beautiful eyes and magic hands only to end up wrecked by him weeks later?

"Is that your girlfriend?" Hayden asked what she already knew.

He looked back to where the homecoming queen stood near the house. "Yeah."

"I thought so." She gave another snort of laughter. "Well, she's waiting." Hayden waved toward the house. "You better get going."

He didn't move. "What's so funny?"

"It's kind of amusing."

"What is?"

She looked back and forth between him and his girlfriend. "It's just typical."

"Typical how?" he pressed, looking so serious she regretted ever saying anything to him. She didn't want to get into it with this guy. If he didn't know he was a walking cliché, then who was she to inform him?

"You're the homecoming king *and* queen. Both beautiful. Both popular. You're like the leads of a predictable teen movie."

He looked puzzled. "Are we? We're pretty rare, I would think."

Clearly he didn't like being called typical. He thought he was rare? *That* was funny. "I didn't mean to offend you."

"Well, it doesn't feel like you're complimenting me."

She guessed she wasn't.

He continued, "Wouldn't we have to be opposites for us to be typical for a teen movie? You know ... the school nerd and head cheerleader?"

"*Can't Buy Me Love*," she cited. "You know your teen rom-coms."

"I have a sister, remember?"

Emmaline Martin seemed like the kind of girl who would know her vintage adolescent rom-coms. "Yes. I know."

His eyes narrowed thoughtfully. "I didn't realize you two knew each other."

Maybe she was reading too much into it, but she got the impression that he didn't approve of her *knowing* his sister. Rather than explain that they had just met, she said, "Maybe you're right. You don't exactly fit the role."

"Nolan!" The girlfriend's voice lifted in a whine.

He glanced at her and then looked back to Hayden, seemingly in no hurry.

"And what's your role?" he asked.

"What do you mean?"

"You're not the school nerd. Not the head cheerleader."

"Oh." She shrugged. "I don't have one."

"You don't play a role?" he asked, an edge of challenge to his voice.

"No. No role here. Guess that makes me atypical."

"You sound ... proud of that."

It was just a fact. She knew herself. She didn't have a group. She didn't fit into any cliques. She didn't play roles. She was too busy surviving.

"I'll meet you at the car," Girlfriend called out, her voice the height of exasperation. She marched back inside.

For some reason Nolan remained behind.

He was still looking at her and waiting for her answer. "Pride has nothing to do with it," she replied at last, wondering if she sounded defensive and why she should.

"*You* play a role," he pointed out calmly, but she detected an undercurrent of judgment in his voice. "We all do."

Judgment was something she was very familiar with. She'd learned how to detect it in others at an early age . . . when someone from the state started dropping by for home visits because a well-meaning teacher reported her — or because she missed one too many days of school because Mom couldn't get her on the bus and she was reported for truancy. The state hadn't been by to check on her in years. Not since Hayden started taking care of herself.

He looked her up and down and she resisted fidgeting, but his eyes were scouring, reminding her of the ladies with their clipboards as they assessed her, scribbling notes as they walked through her house.

She shoved the memory away. "Then what's my role?" She stared at him, tensing all over, hating that she had asked, regretting it instantly because it made it seem like she cared.

He stared back at her, not answering. His silence was telling. Deafening.

It told her everything she needed to know.

She knew what he thought of her. How *little* he thought of her. She'd sensed it from him the moment he walked up on her talking with his sister.

He wouldn't put it into words. He wouldn't be impolite enough to say it, but he thought she was wild. A bad influence. A bad girl.

A slut.

That was her *role*, as far as he was concerned.

She'd heard it all before. Every ugly word. She had never cared.

They were just labels and usually uttered by people whose opinion she did not value.

So why did it sting a little right now? He was a stranger. His opinion meant nothing.

"You think you know me?" She stepped forward and stretched out a hand toward his chest, determined to shake his composure, to deflect. She brushed an invisible speck of lint away from his long-sleeved henley. Damn, his chest was solid. His pecs were outlined against the fitted fabric.

He grabbed her wrist, his fingers loose around her bones, but the contact made her breath hiss . . . and those butterflies. They were back with a vengeance.

She could easily twist free, but she felt frozen as she looked up at his dark eyes. "You like playing guys," he said, his voice whisper soft.

She liked *playing* guys? Is that what he thought? That was laughable.

Ever since she started high school, guys had been trying to play her. They looked at her mom, her house, her secondhand clothes, and thought they could use her. That she mattered less somehow.

"Is that what you've heard?" she asked.

"No." There was no crack in his expression as he uttered this.

"No?" she echoed, crossing her arms. "Fascinating. Tell me. How did you come to know this about me then?"

"I have eyes . . ." His voice trailed off.

Meaning he'd noticed her before? He never gave any indication of that. Whenever she'd observed him, he had never been looking her way.

She smiled thinly, letting it mask her turbulent feelings. "You think you know me because I wear a lot of makeup, because of the way I dress, because I have a tattoo . . . because I live in *Peasant Ranch*."

He jerked as though her words were a physical slap.

Hayden lived in *Pleasant Ranch*, but the joke around town was that it was really *Peasant Ranch*.

Once affordable housing in the 1970s, it was now a poorly maintained neighborhood full of dead lawns and houses with bars on the windows. Cops often patrolled the streets, giving in to the inevitability that they would be called into the neighborhood sometime during their shift — pulled in on some call or another. Domestic disturbance. Drugs. Truancy checks.

"Oh," she added. "And your friends want to fuck me." Hayden held her smile, fighting down a tremor of emotion. "And, yeah, I swear when I feel like it, too."

Nolan exhaled and glanced away, color rising in his cheeks. She'd embarrassed him.

Good.

She laughed harshly. "What's the matter?" Clearly he wasn't used to girls like her who talked so bluntly. "Does my language offend you . . . or is it because I'm aware that guys want to get in my pants? Am I not supposed to notice that?"

He shook his head, looking a little stunned.

She actually felt a little stunned, too. How had she ended up in this conversation with him?

"Nolan!" His girlfriend was back. Guess she decided not to wait at the car, after all. Hayden hid a smirk. Naturally she wouldn't like leaving him alone with the likes of her.

Hayden nodded in her direction. "You better go. You're being summoned."

His lips flattened into a thin line. He didn't like that.

Nolan didn't glance back to his waiting princess. No, sorry, she mentally amended, his waiting *queen*.

His stare was fixed steadily on Hayden, and she couldn't help marveling that this was the first time he had ever really looked at her. *Really looked at her.*

This was their first conversation. Now he would have a memory, an experience to go with her when he did see her in the halls. For some reason she thought he would definitely notice her now. This, weirdly, maybe wrongly, gave her some sense of satisfaction.

"Well, uh. Good night," he said.

Such manners, and after their borderline uncivil conversation, no less.

She didn't say anything as he turned away, but she couldn't help admiring his solid length, the way his henley stretched across the back of his broad shoulders. He really was a rare specimen. Fit and strong. The kind of guy who would do well in a zombie apocalypse. She nodded. *Yeah.* She thought about such things. She watched anything and everything zombie. Not just the obvious, like *The Walking Dead.* The classics, too. *Night of the Living Dead. Dawn of the Dead.* And her personal favorite, *Land of the Dead.*

It was normal behavior for her to walk around considering the nearest and most convenient escape route. She even had a go bag in the back of her closet. A zombie breakout wasn't the only thing that could happen, after all. There were things like angry ex-boyfriends of Mom. Or friends of Mom that suddenly weren't friends anymore. Angry individuals in general. Mom managed to piss off a lot of people.

The door shut behind Nolan and his cheerleader girlfriend. Hayden stood alone outside in the dark and cold, the sounds of the party a dim hum on the air.

She liked being alone. She was comfortable with it. It was safe. When you were alone, there was no one around to hurt you.

Wrapping her arms around her middle, she squeezed, hugging

herself against the chilly night. Right now, she was hard-pressed to even remember why she had wanted to come here tonight. A Netflix marathon and some microwave popcorn sounded far more tempting than this. Then again, Mom was at home with her friends. Hayden would only be alone as long as no one invaded her space. Unfortunately, Mom's get-togethers usually got rowdy, so that was unlikely. The thin barrier of her bedroom door offered little protection.

She studied the fountain for a moment, enjoying the soft sound of burbling water. It had a calming influence. She understood it now. She understood why rich people had them. If she had money, a fountain wouldn't have made it to the top of her list before, but she might have to readjust that list now.

That's the way of it for people who had nothing, she supposed. They always fantasized and played the *what if* game.

She turned and exited out the back gate, walking down the street until she reached her car, an old clunker. Her manager at the Tasty Freeze sold it to her last year dirt cheap, claiming it wouldn't bring her much money. Hayden knew the truth, though. Leticia had done it out of generosity.

At the time, Hayden had teased Leticia that she had done it so Hayden would stop being late to work. Hayden was always on time now, but before, she had to beg a ride off someone — her mother couldn't be relied on — or walk the three miles to the Tasty Freeze. More often than not, she walked. In heat. In cold. In rain. It didn't matter.

Hayden slid behind her steering wheel and turned the ignition. It sputtered and choked before coming to life. One day, it was going to quit on her for good. She knew it was inevitable. She didn't worry about it though.

Everything quit on her eventually, and she still found a way to go on.

LESSON #4

KNOW YOUR LIMITS AND SET REASONABLE GOALS.

x   Emmaline   x

Emmaline sat in mute frustration as they headed to Whataburger.

Frustration with her brother.

Frustration with her friends, who were too in awe of Nolan to stand up to him and side with her when she wanted to stay at the party. They were glad Nolan had called it quits for the night. Maybe a part of her had been glad, too. It's not like she was having a good time. The highlight of her night had been her conversation with Hayden Vargas.

Mostly, though, she was frustrated with herself. Because why couldn't she have a good time at a party? Why couldn't she be like everyone else?

When she'd walked into that media room where an adult film had been playing, she'd lost her composure. Maybe it wouldn't have been so bad if Beau hadn't been standing beside her — Beau, who she'd had a crazy stupid crush on since she was thirteen.

Maybe then she wouldn't have blushed like a schoolgirl.

It had been so awkward. For a moment she had thought Beau

looked from the naked, writhing bodies on the screen to her boobs. Not that she had been flaunting them or anything in her simple sweater.

Of course, she had to be wrong. He hadn't looked *there*. Not at her. He would never do that. She was Nolan's kid sister. She couldn't get any unsexier than that.

Beau had not been checking her out. Guys did *not* check her out in general.

When they got to Whataburger they all lined up at the counter, placed their orders, and then went their separate ways. Emmaline with her friends. Nolan with his.

There was never any question of this. They slid into different booths. It was the usual way of things. It was like Thanksgiving, when she was stuck at the kiddie table with her little cousins. Not that she wanted to sit with Nolan and his friends. He only made her feel small and insignificant, just like a child not yet ready for the grown-up table.

Nolan would be graduating at the end of the school year and off to college in the fall, but they would be living together for another eight months. And she'd decided that she wasn't going to sit idle, waiting for him to leave to begin doing what she wanted to do.

She was done waiting. Emmaline was ready to start living. She didn't want to be the girl to run from the room with her face on fire anymore, easily embarrassed and nervous around guys.

Emmaline expelled a heavy breath and interrupted her friends' conversation. "What are we doing?" She looked searchingly into each of their faces, her frustration spilling over.

Her friends blinked. Clearly they felt none of Emmaline's torment.

"Uh, eating?" Lia waved a chicken tender.

"That's not what I mean," Emmaline snapped.

"What are you talking about?" Sanjana asked.

"It's Friday night and we're at Whataburger. Again."

"I like Whataburger." Sanjana bit into a fry, her dark eyes as wide and guileless as a Disney princess.

"We were at a party tonight and we left early." Emmaline propped her elbows on the table. "We're juniors. And Lia, you're a senior. Don't you want to do something in high school besides study and —"

"I would rather not do anything that affects my getting into Stanford," Monica cut in.

"There were plenty of kids at that party who are going to college," Emmaline argued.

Monica considered that for a moment before nodding. "Some of them, yeah, but I didn't seen any kids from my AP classes, so I doubt anyone else at that party is aiming for Stanford."

Emmaline flung her hands wide. "You guys are hopeless."

"What do you want from us, Em?" Lia asked, slurping loudly from her straw. "We went with you tonight."

"I want things to change! I don't want to be seventeen and never-been-kissed anymore."

Everyone fell silent, and she knew why. She knew their experience did not amount to much more than hers.

"Well, what are you going to do then?" Lia asked slowly, wariness all over her face.

She shook her head. "I don't know."

Hayden Vargas flashed across her mind. Emmaline wished she could be like her. Even just a little bit. If she had one fraction of that girl's confidence, her life would be so much different. So much *better*.

Maybe she could get Hayden to give her lessons.

With a snort, Emmaline foraged into one of the bags on the table for more fries. She stuffed a bunch in her mouth, savoring the salty tastiness.

Priscilla laughed shrilly from the other booth and Emmaline rolled her eyes, stuffing even more fries in her mouth.

Then the thought came again. *Maybe she could get Hayden to give her lessons.*

Emmaline stopped chewing, her pulse picking up speed at her throat.

Lessons on how to be more like Hayden. Confident. Irresistible. A magnet for guys. Someone who didn't sit around regretting lost opportunities and run from the guy she liked with embarrassment.

"Emmaline?" Sanjana asked. "You okay? You have a funny look on your face."

"I'm fine. More than fine." She looked at Lia. "And to answer your question, I know exactly what I'm going to do now."

INSPIRATION CAN COME FROM SURPRISING SOURCES.

x   Nolan   x

"You going to eat those fries?"

Nolan didn't even blink as Priscilla reached a hand in his basket.

A discarded bun sat in front of her. She'd eaten her cheeseburger and left the bread. Too many carbs, she claimed.

As for fries, she never ordered them for herself. She contented herself with stealing his.

It wasn't logical, but he didn't point that out to her.

It's not like he was that protective of his fries anyway. He didn't mind. Especially tonight. He wasn't that hungry. He was . . . distracted.

That encounter with Hayden Vargas had to count for one of the weirdest conversations of his life. He couldn't help playing it over and over in his mind. He'd never talked to her before and he didn't know what he expected — but not *that*. Not what he got. She was bold and rude and blunt.

Fortunately, Nora and Reed sat with them. Nora was Pris's best friend and Nolan played football with Reed. He was an okay guy, but

Nora loved the sound of her own voice. At least he assumed she did, because she hardly ever took a breath between words. Even if he wanted to talk, it would be a challenge to get a word in, and tonight that was fine with him. They could chat. He didn't have to participate.

He sat quietly, zoning out of the two-sided conversation between the girls. Reed sipped from a milkshake and scrolled through his phone.

His sister and her friends sat a couple booths over, lost in their own conversation. Emmaline cast him several scowls. She wasn't happy with him. Usually they got along, but lately . . .

Lately, she had been short-tempered with him. He wasn't certain what had changed, but something had shifted between them. It would pass. They'd always been close.

"Nolan?" At the sound of his name, he jerked his attention back to the people at his table, leaning forward.

Nora was staring at him, dragging her fry through a disgusting mixture of mayonnaise, ketchup, and mustard. "Did you hear back from Notre Dame yet?"

He opened his mouth to answer, but Priscilla chimed in, covering her hand over his. "They accepted him in December. We're just waiting on their full offer. It's doubtful they can beat the package UT offered him"

Nora nodded as though she agreed.

We.

He wondered when he had become a *we*. When had he lost his individuality?

He gave himself a mental shake. It was fine. He had a good girlfriend. The prettiest girl in school. Everyone said so. And she was sweet. Goodhearted. Only a jerk would complain.

The girls continued to talk and he glanced over to his sister's booth again. She and her friends were gathering up their trash.

"Ready to go?" he asked the table.

"Already?" Priscilla glanced at the time on her phone. "But it's not even eleven yet."

He gathered his and Priscilla's trash, wadding up the orange wrapping. "I told Beau I'd run with him in the morning."

Priscilla's lips thinned, but she didn't say anything. Nora sent her a swift, meaningful look. Nolan knew the significance behind that look. Priscilla did not care for Beau. She did not say it in words — she was too sensitive of Nolan's feelings for that — but she didn't need to say anything. It was evident in how she shut down whenever he was around. Really, she shut down even when Beau's name was even mentioned. He couldn't blame her.

A year and a half ago, at Priscilla's sixteenth birthday party, Beau disappeared into the gardening shed with her cousin. Yeah, that had *not* been a good idea.

Beau had only kissed the girl, but that didn't stop a very one-sided infatuation from developing. Priscilla's cousin called, texted, and even drove over to Beau's house. It got awkward. Priscilla had to step in and break it to her cousin that Beau wasn't boyfriend material. She'd never forgiven Beau for that.

Beau liked girls. He liked kissing them. He played the field. He would never change.

Nolan might not agree with everything Beau did, and Priscilla might be right about him, but the guy had stuck by Nolan when he lost his father. He'd been there for him. The least Nolan could do was accept him for who he was.

Nolan could envision Beau when they were forty years old — unchanged, the eternal playboy. Nolan would be married with children and Uncle Beau would come over on Sundays to eat pot roast and play in the yard with his kids.

"I thought we were going to study together tomorrow," Priscilla reminded in a singsong voice, as though that would somehow lessen her judgment.

"We will," he promised.

She nodded and sipped from her straw as they headed outside.

His sister and friends walked ahead of them. Nora and Reed waved good night and headed for their car.

Priscilla started talking about everything they needed to review, and it all felt so very safe and uninteresting. Like most of his nights.

He wondered if Hayden Vargas wasn't maybe a little right about him. If he wasn't typical. Predictable. *Boring.*

LESSON #6

ANYTHING CAN HAPPEN AT A PARTY . . .
AND IT USUALLY DOES.

x Beau x

Beau lifted his lips from the girl he was kissing. He brushed his fingers over her cheek and spoke quietly, kindly. "Hey, I'm going to head downstairs, Chloe." A gentle voice always softened the sting. She was cute, but she tasted of cigarettes, and he didn't smoke . . . and he didn't like kissing girls who did.

"Caroline," she corrected with a pout, her fingers crawling up his chest like a spider. "I'll come with you."

When he'd gone upstairs it hadn't been to hook up with anyone, but then he'd bumped into Chloe — er, Caroline. She was a sophomore in his health class and she plastered herself to him and one thing led to another, and now he was under her in a giant beanbag chair in the rec room.

Not that the distraction was unwelcome.

He'd taken himself upstairs after the awkwardness of the media room. He wanted some space from Emmaline. He couldn't believe he'd walked in there with her. With *Emmaline* of all people. He shuddered.

He might be known for his exploits, but he wasn't the kind of guy who watched porn at a party. That kind of thing didn't strike him as a collective activity, and he definitely didn't want to watch something like that in the company of his best friend's little sister. That was just gross.

To add to the creepy factor, he'd looked from bouncing boobs on the big screen to Emmaline's cleavage.

It had been a knee-jerk reaction. He blamed it on the shock of walking in on hot, writhing, naked bodies. That big screen was bigger than his bedroom wall. It was a lot to take in. And there was Emmaline . . . wearing that snug sweater. That was a lot to take in as well. He'd never seen her wear anything like that . . . anything so . . . fitted. At least, he had never noticed before.

He'd noticed tonight.

Emmaline's face had turned beet red and she'd run from the room, proving it wasn't just an awkward moment for him. She'd been mortified, too.

She didn't go to many parties and mostly stayed in with her friends. He shook his head. That would probably keep her from venturing out for a while. Not a bad thing. Emmaline was good. Too good. She didn't need to be tainted by all this.

Caroline latched onto his hand as they descended the stairs, Beau leading the way. He guessed she hadn't gotten the hint. When he said he wanted to go downstairs, he'd meant he wanted to go downstairs without her.

"Hey, Beau!" Dorian waved at him as soon as he touched down on the first floor.

Beau wound his way through, extricated his hand from Caroline's, and fist-bumped Dorian. "Hey, man."

"Hey." Dorian's gaze skimmed over Caroline appraisingly. "Who's your friend?"

"Hey, I'm Caroline." She stepped forward, smiling widely as she put herself between Beau and Dorian.

"Caroline." Dorian looked down at her with interest. "Are you a freshman? Haven't seen you around."

"Sophomore." She pulled back her shoulders indignantly. "I'm not a baby."

"I can see that." Dorian lifted his cup and drank. His eyes met Beau's questioningly over the rim. It was Dorian's way of asking if Beau and Caroline were a thing . . . if he was crossing a line in flirting with her.

Beau answered with a shrug.

Dorian didn't have to worry. Beau flirted and fooled around, but he didn't feel possessive or overly attached to any single girl. He was young. Too young to be in a relationship. He didn't want to tie himself down like that. He saw the way Nolan was chained to Priscilla . . . accountable to her for everything he did. No thanks. Beau wanted no part of that.

"Cops! Cops out front!" someone yelled, and the house broke into instant chaos. Cups of beer hit the floor.

Beau shook his head. He thought the party had at least another hour before it got shut down. Everyone pushed toward the front door, shouting like they were a bunch of swimmers in shark-infested waters.

Still shaking his head, Beau turned for the double French doors that opened out into the backyard. Fewer bodies headed in that direction. It was the path of least resistance and it made the most sense. Panicked teenagers under the influence of alcohol weren't known for good decisions.

He strolled outside and located the back gate. Beau always knew how to avoid tricky situations.

Soon he was headed down the street, hands buried in his pockets, leaving a house full of teenagers and several flashing cop cars behind.

ALWAYS HAVE A PLAN, BUT KNOW THAT NO PLAN IS ETCHED IN STONE.

x   Hayden   x

Hayden's morning started out normal enough. Like any other Monday. She woke up at her usual time, showered, dressed, and grabbed a Pop-Tart from the box she kept in her room — definitely *not* in the kitchen where any one of her mom's friends could help themselves.

It was the same as any other morning.

Except when she stepped outside, she immediately saw that her car was blocked.

Joann, one of her mom's friends, had crashed at their place, and it was impossible to rouse either one of them from their alcohol-induced comas. God knew what they'd done. Copious amounts of alcohol, definitely. Possibly more than that.

Hayden had heard them come in last night. Or rather, this morning. The clock read 3:57 a.m. when she'd glanced up at it. They hadn't exactly been quiet. Knocking into furniture. Laughing uproariously.

Hayden had fallen back asleep. Just another day — or night — in her house.

Maybe if she hadn't been so groggy at four in the morning, it would have occurred to her that they had likely pulled in behind her in the driveway.

She shook her mom's shoulder. Hard. "Mom!"

Nothing. For a moment, she debated tossing a glass of water in her face, but decided she valued her life too much.

She turned to Joann, who was passed out on the mattress with her feet at the head of the bed. "Joann!"

Mom stirred for half a minute, lifting her hand. She was hanging half off the bed, the ends of her hair brushing the flattened carpet. She fumbled around on the floor until she came in contact with a shoe. Seizing it, she launched it at Hayden, striking her in the hip.

"G'way!" Mom mumbled. "Sleepin'."

With a sigh of disgust, she searched the house until she unearthed Joann's keys. Rushing outside, she pulled the little hatchback out of the driveway, all the while holding her breath inside the car. It smelled like an ashtray.

She parked along the curb and darted back inside, cursing the fifteen minutes she'd taken trying to wake Joann and Mom, hunt for the keys, and move Joann's car.

Despite her rush, Hayden was careful not to speed. She stopped fully at every stop sign and went slowly through the school zones. The last thing she needed was a ticket. She was almost to the school when she realized she'd left her mostly uneaten Pop-Tart on her dresser. Ugh. Now she'd be starving by third period, and she never bought lunch at school. Sometimes she packed a lunch, but not today, of course. No time.

The parking lot was devoid of bodies; everyone was in first period.

She'd already accumulated a couple tardies this semester. Another one would land her in detention, and she didn't have time for that. Kids who didn't have jobs to get to could waste afternoons in detention. Not Hayden.

First period was health class. Coach Alvarez wasn't going to let her slide in late. Some teachers were cool like that. Not him. Excuses didn't matter. It was black and white. Unless she had a doctor's note, a tardy was a tardy.

He was counting the days until retirement and wanted to be here even less than his students. He wasn't inclined to do anyone any favors.

Coach was partial to his athletes, but even they couldn't get in without a tardy slip or note from another teacher. He definitely wasn't going to let Hayden in, of all people.

There was only one possibility. She hurried down the hall with one hope, one objective in mind. Get to Ms. Mendez's class. If any teacher liked her well enough to help her out, it was her art teacher.

"You there," a voice called sharply.

She froze, closing her eyes in a slow blink.

Hayden turned, dread making her limbs suddenly heavy and sluggish.

A teacher advanced on her. The grumpy sort. Middle-aged. Permanently etched frown lines. Eyes that looked her over with disapproval. As though there was something inherently wrong with her ripped jeans and T-shirt that showed a sliver of belly. "You there," she said again. "Where are you supposed to be?"

That was always the question they asked.

Where are you supposed to be? She'd like to know the answer to that too. It was the one thing she chronically asked herself.

Not here.

She knew that much. She'd known that since elementary school, when her classmates started leaving her off the invite lists to their birthdays. Her peers didn't want her at their parties . . . and their moms definitely didn't want Hayden's mom coming around either.

Too many temptations for her mother. Too many things her mom might help herself to. Things like husbands.

Mom had a penchant for other people's husbands. Well, her penchant was for men in general. But especially for husbands of women who had more than she had. Which was pretty much everyone, considering they had next to nothing.

Natalie had been her best friend in kindergarten. Back then, at the very start of school, not everyone thought she was trash.

Hayden had a flashback of walking in on her mom making out with Natalie Washington's dad. Actually, the flashback was of Hayden, Natalie, *and* Mrs. Washington walking in on them.

Best friend no more.

Unsurprisingly, Hayden had never been invited over to Natalie's house again. Not after she had to flee it with Mom hastily shrugging back into her clothes and Mrs. Washington screaming behind them.

Hayden had cried in the car as they drove away. Great snotty tears had rolled down her face, knowing she'd lost her friend. Mom had just laughed, her unbuttoned shirt gaping open as she drove. *You don't need that stuck-up bitch or her daughter. You can do better, Hayden.*

She never did better.

Sometimes she spotted Natalie in the hall.

Whenever their eyes met, Hayden saw that Natalie still remembered and she felt the same shame and embarrassment all over again.

Nat was a cheerleader now. Pretty and popular, with lots of friends. That was her life. Hayden's life was different. No escaping that. At least not while she was still in high school and living with Mom.

Soon though. Soon.

The teacher stopped before her. "You're late."

"Yes, I realize —"

"Office. Now," she cut in, without giving Hayden a chance to even say anything. It was grossly unfair. What if she had something important to say? Something life-and-death important?

That was the thing that sucked most about being a teenager. So many adults thought they didn't have to listen. They thought they didn't *need* to listen, that youth negated one's voice. Made them "less than."

In Hayden's situation, she was also poor. Poor and female and without anyone to stick up for her. That made it easy for grownups to trample over her. No outraged parent was ever going to bat on her behalf. Sure, this woman didn't know all those details about her, but Hayden knew. Hayden knew herself and was aware of the obstacles.

"I just came from Ms. Mendez's class. I forgot to get a pass."

Yeah, it was a lie, but it was also her only hope.

The teacher stared with pinched lips, considering Hayden's explanation.

Hayden jerked a thumb behind her in the direction of the art room. "I can go get a pass now to show —"

"Yeah, I'll go with you." The lady nodded with sudden resolution, looking a little smug, as though she knew she was going to bust Hayden in a lie.

Great.

It wouldn't be the first time some self-righteous adult nailed her for a real or imagined infraction.

Heaving an internal sigh, Hayden forced a bright smile. "Okay."

They turned and walked toward the art room. She knew she should probably be nervous. As close as she was to her art teacher, it was a lot to ask her to cover for her.

Ms. Mendez was about to confirm this woman's suspicions that

Hayden was tardy. Then Hayden would probably be sent to the assistant principal's office, because it wouldn't just be about a tardy anymore. She'd lied to this teacher and the teacher knew it. Hayden could feel the woman's righteousness vibrating from her in waves. She wanted Hayden punished.

The teacher stepped ahead of her and rapped sharply on Ms. Mendez's door before pushing it open.

"Ms. Mendez, I found this girl loitering in the halls —" Hayden rolled her eyes at the use of the word *loitering*. She'd been marching very quickly and very purposefully. "She claims you forget to write her a pass."

Ms. Mendez paused at the front of the room, where she had presumably been giving instruction before the other teacher interrupted her.

Mr. Mendez's gaze flitted back and forth between Hayden and the woman. The art teacher's bright purple glasses did nothing to take away from the look in her wide dark eyes. Those sharp eyes missed nothing.

Hayden gazed at her in silent entreaty. She was the one teacher who got her . . . the one person in this building who cared about her and took any interest in her and her future.

"Ahhh," Ms. Mendez began. "Yes, yes, of course. I forgot." She moved to her cluttered desk. "I'll do that right now."

The other teacher huffed and sent a suspicious glance between the two of them. Clearly she did not buy the story. It probably didn't help that Ms. Mendez looked so young. She was actually thirty years old, but other teachers mistook her for a student. She once told Hayden that she got stopped in the hall during her off period on the regular and was often asked if she had a pass.

Ms. Mendez finished scrawling on the pass and held up an orange slip of paper with a flourish. "Here you go, Hayden. Hurry on to class." Her gaze settled meaningfully on Hayden. She would want an explanation later. She might be in Hayden's corner, but she wasn't a pushover.

Hayden smiled her thanks and slipped from the room, leaving Ms. Mendez to deal with the dragon.

She felt bad about that, but she was relieved she wasn't being dragged into the office. By seventh period, she was especially glad she hadn't been smacked with a detention. Hayden was so hungry, she was feeling faintly ill and her concentration was off. She was counting down the final minutes until the bell rang, anxious to get home and grab something to eat before she headed to work. She tried to take notes on what Mrs. Burke was copying onto the board, hardly noticing the girl who walked into the room with a slip of paper in her hand for the teacher.

Mrs. Burke looked out, scanning the classroom until her gaze landed on her. "Ms. Vargas. You're wanted in the principal's office."

Hayden snapped to attention.

The boy behind her made an *ooooh* sound. "What'd you do?" he taunted.

She didn't know his name. She didn't know any of their names. She only knew that he always picked his ears with the end of his pen.

"More like *who did she do*," the kid behind him whispered, inciting a chorus of laughter. Ear-picker turned to high-five him.

Hayden rolled her eyes and gathered her things. As she stood, she bent down toward the boys and said in the most seductive voice she could manage, "Well, it's never going to be you, is it?"

The boys around the kid laughed.

One slapped the desk. "Oh, she burned you, man."

The deliverer of the oh-so-clever sexist quips suddenly didn't look nearly so proud of himself, if his red face was any indication.

Hayden advanced to the front of the room, pausing when she noticed that the girl who had come to fetch her to the principal was none other than Emmaline Martin. The Bambi girl from the party the other night.

Chalking it up to coincidence, she pressed on and followed her from the room.

The moment they stepped out into the hall and the door shut behind them, Emmaline grabbed Hayden by the arm like they were old friends. "Hope you don't mind me getting you out of class."

"Wait. *You* got me out of class?"

She nodded cheerfully. She wore her hair in twin braids. They bounced over her shoulder, making her look more like a middle-schooler than someone in high school. "Yeah."

"Why?"

"I wanted to talk to you."

She shook her head, her hunger pangs suddenly resurfacing. "Look, I'm kind of in a mood. I haven't eaten all day and —"

"Oh, I've got some snacks in my locker. C'mon. You can have them."

Emmaline skipped ahead down the hall and Hayden followed, the temptation of food too much to resist.

Once at her locker, Emmaline pulled out her lunch bag and then glanced around. "Where should we go?"

Hayden plucked the bag from her hands. "It was your idea to bust me out of science. You didn't have a plan?"

She shook her head. "I just really wanted to talk to you. Thought we might go to the bathroom, but that's kind of a gross place to eat . . ."

Agreed. "You always have to have a plan. C'mon, amateur," she said teasingly. "I know where we can go."

This time, it was her turn to lead Emmaline through the halls.

They crossed the campus and exited the doors toward the athletic fields. Hayden led her toward the bleachers, keeping an eye out for teachers.

When they were close enough, she cast one furtive look over her shoulder and ducked underneath the stands.

It was a universal truth that nothing good ever happened under the bleachers.

The administration and staff knew this, too, which is why they did regular checks, but that didn't stop kids from risking it and going under there to skip out on a test, vape, get high, or make out. Lots of firsts happened under those bleachers.

She'd spent her fair share of time there during her tenure at Travis High School, but she never thought she'd have the likes of someone as innocent as Emmaline for company.

From the way the girl looked around, Hayden could tell she had never been under the bleachers before.

There was an almost hushed quality to the shadowed space, like when you entered a church. Not that she had much experience with churches, but Mom's friend Claudia had been a lapsed Catholic.

Once, after a night of partying with her mom, she took Hayden with her on a run to the grocery store to get them some food, pulling over on the way at a church. Hayden had settled into a wooden pew in the far back, watching the solemn scene of Claudia genuflecting before the altar and then slipping inside a confessional to talk to a priest, presumably hoping to exorcise her ghosts.

It mustn't have helped. Claudia had died less than a year later. Mom didn't say much about it except that Claudia got in over her head. Hayden could imagine what that meant. She could imagine all kinds of things, but she tried not to.

Strips of sunlight landed on the ground, marking the breaks in the bleachers. They walked along the ribbons of light until they found a place to sit. Somewhere far enough down where they would have a chance to run away if a teacher decided to look under the bleachers.

They sat side by side. An unlikely duo. There was a reason for that. They weren't friends.

It was windy and brisk. Snow was even rumored in the forecast for the coming weekend. Snow was a rarity, so when it happened the entire city shut down.

Hayden stretched her legs out in front of her. A breeze ruffled the loose threads edging the holes of her jeans. "What did you want to talk about?"

Emmaline eyed the food wrappers and bits of trash littering the ground, tucking her knees close to her chest. "Lots of kids come here?" she asked, wrinkling her nose.

Hayden nodded. It felt as though she were putting something off. The thing that she wanted to tell her. The thing she'd gotten her out of class to discuss.

"Emmaline. What did you want to talk about?"

"Yeah. Um." She stopped and cleared her throat. "So I've been thinking since we talked the other night. By the way, thanks for that."

"Thanks?"

"I wasn't having the best night and it was really nice to talk to you."

Hayden nodded, still wondering what she had done or said to make this girl's night *better* in any way. She couldn't imagine having the words to make anyone feel better.

There was a scuffing of loose gravel, and she jerked her gaze off Emmaline, ready to bolt at the sight of an advancing teacher.

It wasn't a teacher.

Beau Sanders approached, sweaty in his gym clothes, but still hot. How was it guys could look good after working out?

Shaking off his surprise, he approached, loose gravel scuffing under his sneakers. "Hey there, Pigeon," he said to Emmaline. "Vargas." He nodded to her.

Emmaline's head jerked up, her expression startled. She almost looked . . . guilty. "Beau."

She was definitely up to something. Whatever she wanted to tell Hayden, she didn't want him to hear.

His gaze tracked over Emmaline, in her sweater and hole-free jeans.

Beau looked unaffected by the cold. His blood was probably pumping hot from his workout. They had to look as chilled as they felt huddled on the ground. The tip of Emmaline's nose was bright pink.

"What are you guys doing out here?" he asked.

Emmaline's eyes narrowed slightly. "Nothing." The defensiveness was there, plain to hear.

Hayden smirked.

"You need a ride home today, Pigeon?" Beau asked her, using that stupid nickname again.

"Hayden here is giving me a ride home," she quickly supplied.

Hayden blinked, glancing at her in surprise for a split second before she masked it. "Um. Yeah. I got her covered, Sanders."

"I didn't know you two were friends."

This time Hayden narrowed her eyes on him. "Why so shocked?"

"Did I say I was shocked?"

"You're sure acting like it," she accused. "What's the matter? Afraid I will be a bad influence?"

Clearly he was. Because yeah. She was.

Hayden might be only a year older than Emmaline, but she felt like she had miles on her, and Beau knew that.

Beau lived one street over from Hayden in Pleasant Ranch.

They had similar backgrounds, both being raised by single moms, living in crapped-out, shoebox-small ranch-style homes. Although her place was probably more run-down than his. Who was she kidding? It definitely was. She lived in a shithole.

Beau made obvious efforts. She'd spotted him mowing his yard over the years, cleaning the gutters and doing all manner of maintenance and upkeep on his house. She never worried about that kind of thing. Food, clothing, her future. That's what she cared about.

Hayden had fooled around with Beau back in eighth grade. He was the first boy she French-kissed. They both took the school bus back then and got dropped off at the same stop. Two latchkey kids left to their own devices with stirring hormones. Making out was inevitable.

Once Beau started ninth grade and made varsity football, he never took the bus again. Upperclassmen with cars were always willing to give Beau a ride until he turned sixteen and got his own wheels.

After that, Beau and Hayden moved in different circles. They never hooked up again.

She used to see him drive past her as she waited at the bus stop. In the cold, in the rain, she'd wait for the bus and watch him drive past with one friend or another. Never a glance. Never a wave. She wasn't spared taking the bus until she got her own car last year.

"You're driving her home?" he asked again, needing that clarification.

Emmaline looked at him in exasperation. "Yes."

"Sure your brother is okay with that?"

Okay with that? He meant okay with her being with Emmaline.

The moment he said the words, he looked nervous. Clearly he knew he'd overstepped.

Emmaline pushed to her feet, her hands balled up into tiny fists at her sides. "Nolan is not my keeper. He's not my father. My father is buried in a cemetery across town."

Hayden whistled between her teeth and shook her head. "Nice, Sanders."

Still glaring at him, Emmaline addressed Hayden. "You want to skip the rest of seventh period, Hayden? I need to get out of here."

"Skip class?" Beau looked incredulous, like she'd just suggested they go kick a bunch of puppies or make out with a bunch of bikers. "Whoa. Hold on. Wait a second." He held up a hand as though the gesture might get her to stay.

Emmaline shook her head, her lips pressed into a mutinous line. "No, *you* hold on," she snapped. "You don't get to tell me what to do, Beau Sanders."

Hayden pushed to her feet, dusting off the back of her jeans. "Let's go then." Before things got ugly and Emmaline really went after Beau.

Emmaline cast him one last fulminating glare and fell in beside Hayden. "Can you believe that guy?" she asked as they marched away. "Acting like he's my brother."

Hayden shrugged, keeping an eye out for teachers. She'd avoided detention earlier today by the skin of her teeth. She didn't want to get in trouble now. "I wouldn't know. I don't have a brother."

"Well, I have one in my life already and I don't need another one. Especially not Beau. The nerve of that guy, judging what I do! Do you know his reputation? He's far from a saint."

"No, he's definitely not a saint." His exploits were more infamous than Hayden's. Except no one called him names for anything he did. Such was the sorry dichotomy of life. Girls were sluts and guys were merely players. "So, Emmaline. Are you ever going to tell me what you wanted to talk to me about?"

"Uh, yeah. Let's get out of here first." She cast another glance behind her, as though she feared Beau was following them.

Even though she really didn't have time for this — she needed to be at work soon — her interest was piqued. Emmaline Martin not only got her out of class, but she wouldn't dare say what she wanted in front of someone else.

As though the reason was too scandalous. Or criminal. Or embarrassing.

Hayden was dying to find out.

LESSON #8

THERE'S NOTHING WRONG WITH AVOIDING CONFLICT. IT'S CALLED SURVIVAL.

x Nolan x

Nolan was walking out to the parking lot with Priscilla, keeping one eye out for his sister, when his phone vibrated in his pocket. He pulled it out to see that it was a text from Emmaline.

"What's wrong?" Priscilla asked.

He didn't even notice he was frowning until she repeated the question.

"Nol? What's wrong?"

He shook his head and started typing back, staring down at the screen as he answered, "Emmaline already left. She got a ride home."

"But the bell just rang." Priscilla peered out at the parking lot. "She already left then? Did she skip out early?"

"That's what I'm finding out."

He and Priscilla had seventh period in the east wing, right beside the parking lot they stood in now. His sister was an office aide last period and had to hike it all the way from the west side of campus to reach the parking lot. They usually had to wait a good fifteen minutes in the car before she made it out to them. If his sister had already left with someone, that meant she took off well before the bell.

It meant she skipped.

"What did she say?" Priscilla asked, clearly anxious to find out the story.

Impatient for Emmaline's less-than-speedy reply, he went ahead and dialed her number. After a few rings it went to her voicemail. "She's not picking up."

Priscilla looked annoyed, which actually annoyed him.

Emmaline was *his* sister. His responsibility. Why was Priscilla so annoyed? He kept those feelings to himself though. He didn't want to pick a fight with her. Especially not right now. They didn't fight often, but when they did it was exhausting. She talked in circles and went over every little thing he said . . . every little thing he *didn't* say. It was better just to avoid a fight altogether. Yes, in the back of his mind he wondered if that avoidance was healthy.

He glanced back down at his phone as though it would give him the answers he sought.

His sister was usually quick to respond. This wasn't like her at all. At least, it wasn't like how she used to be. It was just more of this new Emmaline with her scowls.

"Oh, look." Priscilla pointed across the parking lot. "There's Lia."

His gaze followed the direction she pointed, and he spotted his sister's best friend, walking with her gaze down.

"Lia," he called.

The girl looked up and froze.

He strolled over to her, wondering why she looked like a cornered animal. "You seen my sister?"

"Uhhh." Her gaze darted back and forth between Priscilla and him. "She already . . . left," she replied haltingly as her hands tightened their grip on the straps of her backpack.

"Not with you?" He angled his head, studying her. If he didn't give Emmaline a ride home, then Lia did. It had always been him or Lia.

"Uhhh."

Priscilla sighed with exasperation. "Who is she with, Lia? Did she skip class? Do you know where she is or not?"

Lia's knuckles turned white where they clutched her straps. "She might have mentioned something at lunch about needing to talk to . . . someone."

The way Lia's eyes avoided his sent up a flag. She was being deliberately evasive.

Priscilla's fingers tightened ever so slightly on his arm. "Someone, who?"

"Hey, I really need to go. My mom is expecting me at home. I need to watch my little brother."

"Come on, Lia. This is ridiculous. What's going on?" Priscilla demanded.

He'd been relatively silent up until now, letting Priscilla do the talking. "Lia." It was all Nolan said. He let her name drop as he looked at her, letting her see the concern in his eyes and compelling her to speak the truth.

She released a heavy breath. "Fine. She wanted to talk to Hayden Vargas." Her shoulders slumped in defeat.

Instantly, he had flash of the party last Saturday, of Hayden Vargas with her heavily lashed eyes peering up at him. What was it she called herself? Oh yeah. *Atypical.*

She was certainly that. Until Saturday night, he hadn't fully understood that.

His face went hot just thinking about the other things she had said. *All your friends want to —*

He cut off the thought. Because it led to other thoughts about her. Thoughts that led him into thinking about her in ways he shouldn't.

"What does she want with Hayden Vargas?" he demanded. Evidently Lia knew what was going on with his sister. More than he did . . . which wasn't saying much, since it didn't seem he knew anything about his sister anymore.

Lia's gaze shot longingly toward her car. "I really don't know."

Nolan figured that was a lie, but he wasn't sticking around for the truth. It wasn't Lia's job to keep him up to date on his sister.

He turned away and started walking toward his own vehicle. Priscilla stuck close to his side. "Why would your sister need to talk to Hayden Vargas?"

He shook his head, not bothering to point out that he just asked Lia that very question with no success. "I have no idea."

First his sister was talking with Hayden at the party this weekend and now this? It seemed far too coincidental. Had something happened between them that night? As far as he knew, it was the only time they had ever talked. They weren't in the same grade or any of the same classes and they didn't run in the same crowd. What could possibly motivate this . . . whatever it was?

"Well, you better nip that in the bud. Hayden Vargas is not someone you want hanging out with your sister," Priscilla chirped beside him.

"What do you know about Hayden?"

"I know she has a reputation."

Irritation coursed through him, and he wasn't sure why. He'd thought the same thing when he saw her at the party the other night. Hayden Vargas . . . *the girl had a reputation.*

He'd thought those words, so how could he be so offended over Priscilla thinking the same?

Why should *he* feel offended?

"So you mean you've heard rumors?" he clarified.

"Well, yeah, and you know what they say. There's a kernel of truth to every rumor."

"Is that what they say?" He stopped and faced her. "And who are *they*? Jerks? Assholes?"

Himself. He suppressed a wince at the truth of that. He'd been that guy.

She looked at him in bewilderment. "What's gotten into you, Nolan?" Shaking her head, she flattened her hand over his chest, directly over his heart. "Hey, I didn't make the world the way it is, but if a girl is like her, then yeah, people are going to talk. It might not be right, but it's true." She shrugged. "You should want to keep your sister away from that kind of ugliness is all I'm saying."

He turned and unlocked his truck, his chest tight and uncomfortable.

Pris was spot-on. It definitely was not right.

It wasn't right and he had to wonder about her meaning. Was the ugliness she referred to just about people talking? Or Hayden Vargas specifically?

"My sister is smart. I'm sure I don't need to worry about her," he said as he started the ignition.

"Really?" She looked skeptical as she settled in beside him. "I'm just saying, if it was my little sister, I wouldn't want her anywhere near that girl."

"Yeah, she's not your sister though. She's mine." His words came out sharper than he intended, but he couldn't help it. He knew they had been together a long time, but sometimes he felt smothered. Like there was no boundary, no space between the two of them. As though there was no *him* anymore at all. Just them.

A quick glance verified that his words had been harsh. Hot color spotted Priscilla's cheeks.

He turned his attention back to the road. "Sorry," he murmured, hating that he hurt her.

She sniffed and looked ahead with a nod, but her eyes were overly bright. "It's okay. I would be testy too if the school sl —" She stopped herself from saying the rest, but he knew what she intended to say. It was another jab at Hayden Vargas. He snorted a little. Hayden had been right. People did say ugly things about her. His own girlfriend just proved that.

He didn't like the judgment and he didn't like Hayden being vilified, but he didn't love the idea of his sister hanging out with Hayden either. Call him a hypocrite.

"So, did you understand the physics assignment?" It was a deliberate change of topic. He didn't want to talk about his sister with Priscilla anymore. They were already dangerously close to an argument, and he wasn't in the mood.

His sister was his business. She always had been. Just like his entire family was his business, his responsibility. He would take care of it like he always did. Like he always would.

LESSON #9

YOUR COMFORT SHOULD ALWAYS BE A PRIORITY.

x   Hayden   x

Hayden's curiosity grew as she drove Emmaline home.

Emmaline sat beside her, only speaking up to give directions when required. The girl rubbed her palms over the knees of her jeans in clear nervousness.

"Want to stop at Sonic?" Emmaline blurted, spotting the sign ahead.

"I really don't have time." They'd left school early, but taking Emmaline home was costing her.

Emmaline nodded but looked disappointed, and damn if that didn't stab Hayden with guilt. She didn't owe this girl anything, but there was something about her that Hayden liked.

Before she knew what she was doing, she was pulling into the drive-through.

Emmaline beamed and bounced in her seat. "My treat!" She dug through the outer pocket of her backpack.

Hayden felt lighter, happy that she'd made Emmaline smile. It didn't take much.

"That's okay. I'm fine." Hayden wasn't planning on getting anything. Yes, she was hungry, but she was accustomed to deprivation. Besides, there was a peanut butter sandwich waiting for her at home. She'd bought a fresh loaf of bread and a jar of Skippy yesterday and stashed them in her bedroom. It would get her through the week.

"I insist. You're going out of your way and giving me a ride home. Least I can do, since I kind of forced you." She thrust a five dollar bill at Hayden like it was no big deal. "Sour green apple slush for me, please."

Nodding, Hayden accepted the money and turned to speak their orders into the intercom.

"This is fun," Emmaline declared.

Fun. That was a word. Not a word Hayden would use to describe this encounter, but a word.

Emmaline faced forward again and continued, "You have a lot of homework tonight?"

"Not much. I have study hall second period. I can usually get it all done in there."

"Lucky you. I have a truck-ton of homework."

"I'm guessing you're in all AP classes."

"You're not in any AP?" Emmaline asked.

"No. What would be the point?" She couldn't juggle such rigorous courses and work thirty to forty hours a week during the school year.

"It looks good on your transcript. Where are you going to college?"

Their drinks arrived. Hayden took a sip of her peach iced tea and secured it in her cup holder, wondering if Emmaline was ever going to get around to the reason she was sitting in Hayden's car. "I'm not going to college," she answered as she pulled out of the Sonic parking lot.

"You're not?"

She rolled her eyes. "There are alternatives to college, you know."

Emmaline fell silent for a few moments and Hayden shot her a quick glance. The girl looked so deep in thought that Hayden knew this must be a revelation to her. She was one of the privileged who had honestly never considered a future that did not consist of attending college. She'd probably been told she would go to college ever since she left the womb.

"Like what?" she finally asked.

"Lots of things." She had a list of possibilities. Too many things to rattle off. She had options upon graduation. She'd researched several possibilities if her first goal didn't work out, but she had her heart set on becoming a tattoo artist. She appreciated the skill that went into crafting and etching ink onto a person's skin. It was transformative — living art that lasted forever, or at least for a person's lifetime — and she wanted to do that.

She'd taken some design classes as electives — and art, of course. She'd been working hard on building an impressive portfolio, all the while corresponding with a couple of tattoo artists in Austin, emailing them samples of her work. They were willing to meet with her and discuss a potential apprenticeship.

Sure, if she was another kid who had been raised differently, by parents who took an interest in her education and future, she might have applied to design schools, but those places were so expensive. Apprenticing for a reputable, established tattoo artist could lead to a serious career — and in less time than it would take to attend a costly design college.

She'd never be rich, but she could be comfortable. She could be independent and in a creative profession, working as an artist. It's all she had ever wanted.

As soon as she graduated, she was packing up, getting in her car, and going. She had saved what money she could. Just a couple grand so far. Not a lot to most people, but it was huge for her. It was everything. It would get her there. Give her a start. She could find a place and get a job while she completed her apprenticeship. She'd work two jobs if she had to. She'd do whatever necessary. She was going to make it happen.

Emmaline slid her a dubious look and pointed for her to take a right turn. "You're not considering a career in something illegal, are you?"

She laughed and shook her head. "No." She didn't add anything else. The only person who knew of her goal was Ms. Mendez, her art teacher. Even her mother didn't know. Her mother had no clue of her plans. It was Hayden's dream, her goal, and it was personal.

"My house is the third on the left," Emmaline directed.

Hayden pulled up and parked in her driveway, but kept the car running. The house was typical middle-class for the area. A two-story brick colonial very similar to every other house on the street, but still nice. Where nice people lived. Nice families with moms who baked brownies.

"Well, here you are."

"Would you like to come inside?"

Hayden grimaced. There was nothing she would like to do less than step inside this girl's cookie-cutter house. There was probably a mantel full of figurines and family portraits on the walls. "No," she answered. "That's okay. I need to get going." Back to Hayden's own neighborhood. To her side of town, where there might be bars on the window, but she felt safer there. More at home. More herself.

"I'd really like you to come inside. So we can talk."

Hayden flexed her hands on the steering well. "Look. You seem nice, but I can't imagine what we have to talk about that you can't just say right here."

Emmaline visibly swallowed and Hayden felt a pang of sympathy. Apparently whatever she wanted to say wasn't easy.

"Okay." She sucked in a big breath. "I want you to teach me how to seduce a guy."

Hayden had not seen that one coming. "Seduce a guy?"

"Yeah."

Her mind raced. "Okay . . . there are so many things I want to ask, but let's just start with this: What makes you think I know how to seduce a guy?"

"Well, guys find you irresistible."

Hayden laughed. She laughed so hard tears pricked her ears. She actually held on to her aching sides. She couldn't help herself. It was the most ridiculous statement she had ever heard. Sure, she knew a lot of guys were into her, but she did absolutely nothing to encourage them. Most of the time she was rude. Indifferent at best. Her clothes came from thrift shops and couldn't be called the height of fashion by a long shot. The makeup she wore came from the dollar store. Her hair had never seen the inside of a salon. Her mom attended two weeks of cosmetology school and she'd learned enough to perform a decent haircut when Hayden needed one.

Hayden knew nothing about seduction. When she was with a guy, instinct led her. How could she teach this girl when she didn't really know the tricks herself? "I'm not —"

"Don't deny it. You are. All kind of guys . . . you attract them all. You have this look . . . this style." She waved a hand at Hayden.

Hayden snorted. "It's called thrift shop, honey."

Emmaline continued like she had not spoken. "You ooze confidence. You're just cool and sexy and you have this edge and — and I want you to teach me how to be more like that. More like you." She exhaled and gulped a fresh breath, her eyes shining hopefully.

"I'm not popular."

"Oh, I'm not looking for popularity." Emmaline made a sound of disgust. "I live in the same house and share the same DNA as Nolan Martin. That hasn't helped me." She nodded with conviction. "I don't want you to teach me to be like my brother."

"Well, that's good, since I can't."

"*You* . . . you're better than popular."

Better than popular? Hayden gaped at the girl next to her, convinced she had lost her mind. If there was something better than popular, it sure wasn't Hayden.

"Okay, you've piqued my interest. What's better than popular?"

"You're . . . legendary."

Legendary?

A long pause fell between them. For some reason, Hayden's palms felt clammy on the steering wheel. "I'm not sure what even to say right now . . . I don't know how to teach you anything. Whatever I am is just what I am."

"Then just let me spend some time with you so that I can pick up on your . . . you-ness."

Hayden shook her head in rejection of this. "This is crazy."

Emmaline stared bleakly ahead, looking through the windshield at her house. "Just hang out with me and let me observe you."

"I'm not some freak for you to ogle over," Hayden snapped.

"That's not what I mean!" Bright color spotted Emmaline's cheeks.

Right then a truck pulled up in the driveway alongside Hayden's car. She leaned forward slightly to peer around Emmaline at the driver, and her gaze collided with Nolan Martin's.

Great.

His expression revealed nothing, but just the same, she felt displeasure radiating from him. He didn't like her. He didn't like her talking to his sister. She didn't need to be a rocket scientist to know that.

Well, she didn't like him either. Judgmental jocks weren't her cup of tea.

"The police just arrived," she muttered sarcastically.

Emmaline rolled her eyes. "No kidding."

Nolan climbed out of the truck. Another door slammed shut, attracting her notice. It was the homecoming queen from the other night. Hayden really should know her name . . . but the information never stuck. Clearly, they were a match made in heaven. They'd probably be engaged in their second year of college and married immediately after they graduated. Kids before thirty. *Vomit.*

"Well, this is my cue," Hayden announced. "My time to go."

"No! Don't go. Come inside."

"Uh. That's okay. I've got to get to work." Even if she wanted to come inside, which she did not, Nolan Martin and his girlfriend did not look especially keen on her proximity to them. The girlfriend stopped in front of the hood of Hayden's car, propping her tiny hands on her hips.

"Ugh." Emmaline groaned. "Too bad it's illegal."

"What is?"

"Running her over."

Laughter bubbled out of Hayden. She couldn't help it. Emmaline Martin was feisty. "Yeah, probably not a good idea. I like living the life of a free woman. You don't like her?"

Emmaline shrugged. "She's okay. I mean, everyone loves her. So."

"So," Hayden echoed, understanding that even if she never much cared what other people thought. It was hard to go against what everyone else liked. She tapped her fingers on the steering wheel and glanced pointedly at the passenger door. "So. You gonna get out of the car or what?"

Nolan moved past his girlfriend, stopping in the front walkway and turning when the cheerleader said something to him. She gestured to where Hayden and Emmaline sat inside the car. It was clearly in reference to Hayden. Homecoming Queen didn't even bother pretending otherwise, sending a pointed glare at Hayden.

"Okay," Hayden began. "This has been fun and all, but I've really got to get to work."

Emmaline looked desperately between her brother and his girlfriend, and Hayden had the weird and unwelcome sensation that she was throwing the girl to the wolves by pushing her out of the car. "What can I say to convince you to help me?" Emmaline asked hurriedly, an undercurrent of desperation in her voice.

Hayden shook her head. "Nothing. Nothing at all. Please, get out of my car. I can't be late for work. I need this job. I don't get an allowance, okay?"

"I'll pay you," Emmaline blurted out.

Hayden pulled back slightly. "Excuse me?"

"You don't know me. You don't owe me anything. I get it. I will pay you for your time. It's only fair. I *do* get an allowance, and I've hardly touched it. I get birthday money and Christmas money from multiple grandparents, aunts, uncles. They're generous." She snorted. "It's like their generosity is going to make up for the fact that my dad is dead."

Hayden stared at her, marveling at what it must be like to have relatives sending you cold hard cash for things like your birthday and Christmas. Her mom's parents were dead and who knew if she even had grandparents on her father's side. That entire branch of her family tree was a mystery.

"Hello. You in there?" Emmaline waved a hand in front of her face. "Will you do it? Will you let me hire you?"

Hayden was torn. It might be the easiest money she ever made. She thought about her meager stash she was saving for after graduation. She needed money. She always needed money, but it would be especially nice to grow her little nest egg. The more she had when she moved to Austin, the better.

Still, it meant she was going to have to spend time with a girl who she wouldn't normally even talk to. "I don't know."

Emmaline plucked her phone out of her bag and unlocked it with a couple of taps. "What's your phone number?"

Hayden hesitated.

Emmaline looked up at her impatiently. "Number?"

Hayden took a breath and decided giving Emmaline her number wasn't a commitment. It wasn't like she was entering into a contract with the girl. Hayden rattled off the digits and watched as Emmaline typed them into her phone with speedy fingers. Almost immediately her phone pinged from inside her backpack on the floorboard behind her seat.

"There," Emmaline said. "You have my number now. Think it over. Let me know."

Hayden released a huff of laughter. The girl was determined. "Okay," she agreed, although she doubted it would ever happen. Right now she just wanted to get to work on time.

Emmaline beamed, her cheeks as round as apples. She was pretty
— and amusing. She shouldn't need any tips on attracting boys.

"You're funny," Hayden declared. "Are you like this with everyone?"

"You mean with boys? No, I tend to clam up around them." She
nodded solemnly. "I turn into a mannequin if I'm around a boy I find
even remotely interesting. And if he's cute? Oh my God." She rolled her
eyes. "Forget about it. I'm a mess."

"Hm." Maybe she was right then. Maybe she just needed to learn
a few tricks to be more confident. Hayden gave herself a mental kick.
She wasn't doing this. It was ridiculous. She wasn't an authority on anything, much less an expert on being irresistible.

Emmaline snatched up her stuff from the floorboard, her brown
braids bouncing. "I'm going to hear from you. I know it." With a small
giggle, she exited the car, slipping past her brother and his girlfriend,
who lingered in the driveway, still staring at Hayden in her car. Emmaline sent a jaunty little farewell wave behind her and disappeared
inside her house.

Hayden started to shift into reverse when she noticed that Nolan
was approaching her car. Fabulous.

Homecoming Queen called out to him. He turned back to look at
her and gave her a swift shake of his head. Pouting, she turned abruptly
on her heels and disappeared inside the house.

Then he was at Hayden's window, giving it a light tap with his
knuckles.

She manually rolled the window down. That's right. She didn't
even have automatic windows. She had to crank down her window with
a creaking lever that stuck on every upswing. She was embarrassingly
aware of the long moments until the glass slid far enough down.

"Hey," she finally said, placing her hands back on the steering wheel.

"Did you skip school with my sister?"

All right then. Straight to the point. "Yes, we skipped last period."

"Why?"

"What do you mean, why?" She felt like she was being grilled by a parent or school administrator and not a guy in her own grade. "I thought she might like to test out my new crack pipe with me."

His expression remained unchanged. "Not funny."

She cocked her head to the side. "It's kind of funny," she disagreed.

"My little sister is a good kid."

Her hands tightened where they gripped the wheel. So what was she then? Anger bubbled inside her chest.

"Well, your good *little* sister . . ." Really. They were just one grade apart. "Is the one who wants to hang out with *me*." She paused, letting that sink in. "So maybe you should interrogate her and leave me the hell alone."

He narrowed his dark eyes on her. "Why does she want to hang out with you all of a sudden?" He bent at the waist so that his face was close to hers. He settled a hand on her windowsill, revealing the sinewy underside of his bicep. The guy worked out. She fought back a grimace. That's what privileged guys did. At least the jocks. They worked out at gyms full of shiny equipment, ate lots of fast food, went to parties, and applied for colleges the rest of their time.

"I don't know. Maybe that's something you should ask her." Her gaze drifted to where his big hand gripped the peeling interior vinyl of her car. "Can I go now?"

He held her gaze, a muscle ticking in his cheek. "I'm not stopping you."

No. No, he wasn't.

He stepped away, his arms falling to his sides. She put the car into reverse and backed out, wondering what it was about that guy that got under her skin. She watched from the corner of her eye as he stood there, watching her leave.

Perfect people living their perfect lives.

No wonder she didn't like him.

THE BEST FOREPLAY STARTS WITH CONVERSATION.

x   Nolan   x

Nolan's stomach grumbled, alerting him that it was almost time for dinner.

He lifted his head from his notes and shut his laptop. Rubbing the bridge of his nose, he stood and stretched the kinks from his back, glad the week was almost over.

Calculus wasn't his friend, but at least it took his mind off other stuff. Stuff like Priscilla. Stuff like his sister and whatever was happening between her and Hayden Vargas. After that little standoff with Hayden outside his house the other day, his sister had been weird. He wanted — *needed* — things to go back to being unweird between them.

He glanced down at his phone and read the texts he had been ignoring. Priscilla wanted to start talking about prom plans. Already. He shoved his phone into his pocket. He was going to ignore those messages for a little longer.

As soon as he stepped out of his room, he could smell dinner on the air.

When he entered the kitchen, he spotted Mom at the stove, her back to him as she stirred the contents of a pot.

He must have made a sound because she glanced over her shoulder. "Hey there. Dinner's almost ready. I'm about to plate the pasta."

"Smells good." He approached and peered at the bubbling tomato sauce swimming with meatballs and slices of Italian sausage. Just the way Dad had made it. A carnivore's dream. Nolan's chest squeezed at the thought. He tried not to think about Dad too often. At least not in any lingering way. He was usually so busy that it was an easy enough task. Between sports and school and looking after his sisters and Priscilla, he hardly had time to think. He was go-go-go all the time, and the minute his head hit the pillow at night, he was out.

His youngest sister walked in the room. "What are we having?" she asked, tugging the buds from her ears.

"Spaghetti," Mom answered.

Savannah's eyes brightened. "With Dad's sauce?"

"You bet." Mom slid the garlic bread into the oven to warm.

Nolan fixed his smile in place. Faking happy was something he'd been doing for a while now. He wouldn't be the lone voice to ruin the moment by saying that his stomach cramped every time he tasted Dad's sauce.

Mom slid off the oven mitts and moved back to the fridge, pulling out the salad dressing. "Now, I'll never make it as good as Dad, but I'll keep trying. Can one of you fetch Emmaline?" Mom asked, oblivious to Nolan's less-than-kind thoughts.

Savannah plucked a carrot out of the salad bowl. "She's not here."

"What do you mean, she's not here?" Mom frowned as she set the dressing on the counter. "I thought she was in her room."

Savannah shook her head. "She left about an hour ago. You didn't hear her call out? She took your car."

"Oh." Mom looked confused. Not concerned, though, because she trusted Emmaline. She trusted all of them. They never gave her cause to worry. They never got into trouble. She told them all the time how lucky she was to have such great kids.

As always, Nolan stopped himself from reminding her that she couldn't be *that* lucky. She'd lost her husband at forty-one.

Nolan wasn't one of those kids who thought anyone over thirty was old. He wasn't that shortsighted. People could live to ninety these days. He knew forty-one was young. Too young to lose a spouse.

Which was maybe why he tried so hard to be good. It was like an unspoken rule among all three of them. Do not add to Mom's grief.

"Where is she?" he asked.

"I think she mentioned Sanjana."

Mom picked up her phone, presumably to call Emmaline.

A few seconds later Emmaline's phone jingled from the couch cushions.

Savannah retrieved it from beneath a cushion and waved it in the air. "Guess who forgot her phone?"

Mom tsked and shook her head.

"I'll go get her," Nolan volunteered. Sanjana only lived a few streets away in a neighboring subdivision.

Mom nodded. "I'll keep everything warm."

He snatched his keys from the hall table and his hoodie from the peg near the door, pulling it over his head as he stepped outside.

Less than five minutes later he was knocking on Sanjana's door.

She answered, even as she was chewing something. Evidently he'd interrupted her dinner. "Hey, Nolan."

"Sanjana," he greeted. "Is my sister here?"

Sanjana seemed confused "Um. No. She hasn't been here today." Suddenly, she got a cagey look. It reminded him of the way Lia had looked in the parking lot the other day. "There was a study group at Ihop," she quickly said. "She might have gone to that."

"A study group?"

"Yeah."

She was covering for Emmaline. He suddenly felt tired. Tired of being kept in the dark. Tired of feeling like he didn't even know his sister anymore — and that really worried him. He'd made a promise to his father, and she was making it very difficult to keep. "What's going on, Sanjana? Where is she?"

"Uhhh —"

"She's with her, isn't she?" He nodded. "Hayden Vargas."

Hayden. His sister's new friend.

She gave a single shake of her head. "N-no."

"She's at Ihop? You're still sticking with that story?"

Sanjana exhaled, her shoulders slumping. "I actually don't know where she is."

He gave a snort of disbelief. "Right."

With a quick goodbye, he turned and jogged back to where he'd parked his truck along the street.

He started the engine and headed for Pleasant Ranch.

His gut told him Emmaline was there.

Emmaline and Hayden both refused to explain their sudden association. It didn't seem accurate to call it a friendship, because he was pretty sure they just met. He doubted they ever had a conversation before that night at the party.

There was something weird happening and he was going to find out what.

He knew Hayden lived near Beau. He'd spotted her walking on the sidewalk before. Freshman year. Before any of them could drive themselves anywhere. He'd noticed her as far back as then, though he tried not to think too deeply about that fact now.

He punched in Beau's number.

Beau answered on the second ring.

"Hey, man," Nolan said. "Where does Hayden Vargas live?"

A beat of silence stretched between them, and then Beau's voice came out slowly, as though he were still processing the question. "Two streets over from me. Tangled Wood. Why?"

"Going to get my sister."

"Emmaline's at Hayden's house?"

"I think so."

Another pause followed and he knew Beau was thinking that over and probably coming up with more questions, but Nolan didn't feel like giving any answers. "Thanks. Gotta go." He hung up before Beau could ask anything else.

Nolan identified her house easily enough. He recognized Hayden's car in the driveway. He parked in the street and sat there a moment. He stared up and down the road before resting his gaze back on that lone car. His sister had taken his mom's car, and he didn't see it anywhere.

It was enough for him to turn around and go. No sense knocking on the door.

His fingers tapped a few times over the steering wheel until he stopped the anxious motion. With a mutter, he climbed down from the truck and started for the front door.

A pair of dogs flung themselves against a neighbor's chainlink fence. The fence looked ready to collapse from the force. Nolan hoped that wouldn't happen now. He could run fast, but he wasn't sure if he could outrun them.

Hayden's house wasn't that different in size or style from Beau's, except this place was a shithole. He felt a twinge of guilt for the mean thought, but it was the truth. A hurricane could take it down.

There was no grass. Just a lawn full of dead weeds. The wind blew an empty egg carton across the front yard, pinning it to the chainlink fence.

Beau did a good job maintaining his yard and worked to take care of their home.

Before stepping up on the concrete porch, he noticed the drooping gutters, overstuffed with leaves and debris. The aluminum bowed, ready to break under their burden.

He couldn't find a doorbell, so he knocked. Two strong raps.

A muffled cry came from within and then the door yanked open.

It was Hayden. Only not a Hayden he had ever observed before.

She was in a loose T-shirt and shorts — shorts that showed a hell of a lot of gold-skinned thighs. No makeup. Dark hair piled into a knot on her head.

She blinked at the sight of him. "You must be lost."

"I was looking for my sister."

The corner of her mouth kicked up. "Of course you are, Sherlock."

When she didn't look ready to comment further, merely continued to look bored, staring at him as though he were some unwanted solicitor on her doorstep, he added, "Is she here?"

He had already deduced she wasn't here, but he had to ask. Even if he looked pathetic standing in front of her door.

She leaned against the threshold. "No. No, she's not here."

He cleared his throat. "Was she here earlier?"

"No." That smile of hers made him feel funny inside. Like an idiot and . . . other things.

"Lost her, huh, big brother? Thought you better come here and rescue her from me."

Heat burned his face at how close to the truth she was. "No —"

"C'mon." She snorted. "That's it exactly. Why else would you risk driving into this part of town?"

"My best friend lives two streets over," he defended.

"Yeah." She nodded. "But I bet you usually go to *your* house to hang out, not his."

He opened his mouth but couldn't argue that.

He wanted to protest that Beau always preferred it that way. Beau came over. He liked being around Nolan's family. It was Beau's choice. Beau's mother could hardly tolerate having Beau around. She definitely didn't want Nolan creeping into her space.

And while all that was true, he didn't know if Hayden wasn't just a little bit right. Did he avoid the neighborhood?

It was an ugly thought to consider.

Suddenly a loud sound carried from the living room and she darted back inside, leaving the door open, leaving him standing there on the small slab of porch, the wind buffeting his legs.

"Oh! I missed it . . ."

He took a step closer, peering inside.

She snatched up the remote control and punched a button, holding it up and aiming it at the screen. "Ah, there we go."

Her gaze met his. "*Train to Busan*," she explained, as though that would mean something to him.

"Excuse me?"

"It's a movie."

He shook his head. "I've never heard of it."

She gave him a look that conveyed a decided lack of surprise.

"What kind of movie is it?" he asked for some reason, interested.

She sank down on her couch, tucking her legs under her, and reached for a bag of popcorn resting on the scarred wood surface of a coffee table.

"Horror . . . and it's brilliant. Truly."

"Horror? You don't seem like —"

"What? The kind of person to watch horror films?" She angled her head sharply, popcorn lifted halfway to her lips. "Is that because I'm a girl or because I'm me?"

Staring at her, he wondered if he'd ever met someone so blunt.

She answered her own question for him. "I think we already established you don't really know me." She tossed the popcorn into her mouth and chewed, her eyes sparking with challenge, ready for battle if he contradicted her or said anything else she could take as criticism or a verbal attack.

"So tell me why it's brilliant."

She blinked, the battle-fire fading from her eyes. After a beat of hesitation, she waved him inside, motioning to the space beside her on the well-worn sofa. "Come on. Let me convert you then."

"Convert me to horror movies?"

"Not just horror movies. You shouldn't get so hung up on labels." Her gaze held his and he felt, in that moment, that she was talking about something more than movies.

He closed the door behind him and entered the house. Right away he noticed how flat and matted the carpet felt under his shoes, like it was centuries old.

"I'm only fifteen minutes in or so." She briefly gave him a recap, extending the bag of popcorn toward him as she talked, all at once relaxed and casual — like having him beside her in her living room was nothing unusual.

He accepted the popcorn, realizing he hadn't eaten and remembering that Mom was holding dinner for him. *Oh, damn.* He hurriedly dug his phone out of his pocket and sent a quick text to his mom, letting her know to eat without him and asking if she had heard from Emmaline yet, as he hadn't found her.

Lowering his phone back down, he watched as a variety of characters boarded onto a train that was presumably heading into disaster.

"So let me guess," he began. "There's a serial killer on the train."

She cast him a disgusted look. "That's not even creative."

"What then?"

She looked at him as though it was obvious. "Zombies."

"Ah. And that's creative?"

At his implication that it wasn't, she looked outraged. "And a guy in a hockey mask is?" She snorted. "The boogeyman in the dark has been around before the written word. There's nothing creative about that fear. Zombies have only been around a generation or so, and only thanks to Romero."

"I can see you've given zombies some thought."

She shrugged. "The subject of zombies always leads to interesting ethical questions . . . dilemmas you're never going to get out of some stupid slasher movie."

She was smart.

Not that he thought her less than intelligent in their recent encounters, but it was exactly as she had said: he didn't really know her.

His phone vibrated and he glanced down at the text from his mom. *Emmaline is here. When are you going to be home?*

He quickly typed back. *Be home soon. Bumped into someone who is helping me with a . . .* He paused and looked at Hayden on the couch next to him.

Project, he finished typing. Yeah, that felt like the right word. He'd claimed it his mission to find out what was going on between his sister and Hayden.

His mom replied back with an okay and he returned his attention to the movie, watching as an obviously wounded/infected person snuck onto a train when no one was looking.

"And so it begins," Hayden announced with some satisfaction as the infected person secured herself in a bathroom on the train.

Despite his general disinterest in horror movies, and his belief that he was here only because of his sister, he found himself getting sucked into the story.

By the time all hell broke loose on the train, he was fully invested.

"Wow," he mused as he watched a human die and turn zombie. "The cracking sound really adds a certain something to it."

"Right?" She nodded. "I mean, it's a little reminiscent of the way zombies turn in *World War Z*, but this is somehow more basic . . . primitive. Less elegant." She nodded once as though in agreement with herself.

"I haven't seen it."

"You haven't seen *World War Z*? That's awful. Truly unforgivable." She stood up and moved into the tiny kitchen. Her gaze remained glued to the screen as she walked. She opened the mustard-colored fridge and took out two cans of Coke.

Returning, she gave him one without comment and resumed watching the movie, tucking her legs under her on the couch.

"Thanks," he murmured, popping the can open and swallowing the sweet burn of soda.

They watched for another few minutes. She interjected, pointing out things for him to notice. "And there's your villain." She waved at a middle-aged man in a suit on the screen.

"Still gotta have a baddie in addition to the zombies, huh?"

"Of course. The zombies aren't evil. They're us ... mindless us. Ourselves without free will. Without conscience. They simply exist. That guy —" She stabbed a finger at the pinched-lipped man in a business suit. "He's the worst because he still has free will and he *chooses* evil. He'd throw a baby to the zombies if it saved himself. He's who we should fear being like more than the zombies."

She looked back at the screen, but Nolan found himself staring at her, wondering if he ever had a conversation with Priscilla — with anyone — like this. Over a movie, no less.

At one point in the film, the lead child actress started crying.

She dropped her fist on the couch cushion between them. "Casting that girl was genius. She's so cute. There's nothing like throwing in an innocent, sweet-faced child to really highlight the ..." She paused, searching for the right word, her gaze still fixed on the screen.

"The hopelessness," he provided, "when the most innocent are in danger and in danger from their own loved ones ... that's the greatest horror. I mean, your father or best friend or spouse could be the one to kill you."

She snapped her fingers. "That's it exactly." She smiled at him then, her lips a wobbly, awkward curve. "You get it." Clearing her throat, she shifted on the couch as though he had impressed her and she didn't quite know how to handle that.

Gaining a little bit of her respect shouldn't have mattered, but it did. A warmth spread through his chest.

They watched the havoc on the screen in silence. She inched closer to share the popcorn. He was aware of her arm brushing with his, but that was so they could share the popcorn. There wasn't anything deeper to it than that.

He glanced at her, then back to the screen for a split second, and then back to at her again. She was fully invested in the movie. She might have seen it before, but that didn't seem to matter. Her whole body was alive, leaning forward like a vine reaching for the sun.

He ate more popcorn. As far as dinner went, he was used to eating more. He had a big appetite. Still, he could not seem to move from his spot on her couch.

After he finished off the bag they were sharing, she got up and popped them another one. She settled back down beside him and Nolan pointed to the screen. "Okay, the rope of zombies hanging off the train —"

"Clever, right?" He nodded as she added, "We have to watch *World War Z* next. It has some really smart zombie scenarios."

He did not let himself think about the fact that they were both in agreement that he would be staying — that he would be watching another movie with her. Somehow, they had already both reached that assumption.

The movie was winding down.

He felt her breathing change beside him as one of the main characters, the father, died in a grand gesture of sacrifice and love.

Her inhalations came deeper. A quick glance revealed her eyes were brighter, glassy.

He fixed his gaze back on the movie. It was a pretty emotional scene. As someone who had lost his own father, his mind went there, thinking how his father would have done anything for him. Dad would have embraced death to save Nolan and the rest of his family.

As the credits rolled, Nolan rubbed his hands up and down his thighs. "I'll have to tell Emmaline about this movie. She'd love it."

"But not your girlfriend?" she asked as she hopped up from the couch to tap on the keyboard of the laptop connected to her TV. Her dark bun bobbed on her head with her movements. "She won't like it?"

He hesitated, thinking about Priscilla and realizing it had been easier to sit here when he had not been thinking about her. "She's not into horror movies —"

She sent him a reproving glance over her shoulder.

"Yeah. I'm labeling," he admitted. "I know zombie movies are more than horror. They beg grand existential questions. You've educated me on that. But Priscilla would consider them horror. She's more into rom-coms."

Hayden said nothing to that, but he felt a certain level of disdain radiating from her. She didn't approve of his girlfriend, which was kind of funny considering his girlfriend didn't approve of Hayden either.

"You're not into rom-coms?" he asked.

"I've liked a few, but mostly they feed into false expectations."

She stood back as the opening credits for *World War Z* appeared on the screen.

"False expectations?"

She returned to the couch beside him. Reaching up, she pulled her hair loose of its constraints and then worked to reknot the mass. He watched the fascinating dance of her fingers in the inky mass of her hair.

"Um, yeah. Happily ever after with another person." She snorted like it was a joke.

"That's a false expectation?"

She crisscrossed her legs and dropped her hands down into her lap. "I haven't seen much proof of happily ever after."

He thought about his father's death and how, at the time, it had seemed the end of everything — how nothing could ever be good or right again after that. His mother had been broken, and even though life was better now, there were still nights when Nolan heard her crying through the walls.

"Yeah, but there's happiness out there." He'd come to believe that again. Priscilla had actually helped him believe in that. "You can have happiness some of the time, which is better than not at all. And rom-coms highlight the existence of it. They give hope."

Never had it occurred to him that he had an opinion on rom-coms, but apparently he did. Hayden Vargas was teaching him things about himself.

Her expression was cool as she looked him over, and he got the sense that she didn't believe a word of it. "Happily ever after with another person *is* a lie. Contentment and happiness comes from yourself. Not other people."

She looked back at the TV and lifted the remote, turning up the volume and effectively ending the conversation.

What made an eighteen-year-old girl such a hard cynic that she didn't believe happiness existed outside of herself?

As Hayden watched Brad Pitt make breakfast for his movie kids, Nolan looked around the cluttered living room, observing her home. An old recliner, the fabric worn so thin the white stuffing peeked out of its arms, sat beside the sofa they occupied.

His mother would have had the chair reupholstered long ago. Or simply bought new furniture. They weren't rich, but they were comfortable. They had nice things. The nicest thing in this room was Hayden's laptop.

Except it wasn't the shabby surroundings that made the place feel . . . *off*. He looked around the space, trying to pinpoint what it was that felt wrong about this house.

And then he figured it out.

It was the lack of family photos. There wasn't a single photograph on a wall or sitting anywhere. No pictures to capture a moment or immortalize an event.

Photos of Nolan with his sisters lined the walls of his house. Last Christmas his mom had forced them into matching sweaters and posed them for a family photo that now loomed in a sixteen-by-twenty-four-inch frame above the fireplace. Because they were still a family. Mom never stopped reminding them of that.

It didn't seem like a family lived here.

"Are your parents home?" he asked.

Her gaze shot to him, her dark eyes suddenly wary. "No."

Nodding, he looked back at the screen, watching Brad Pitt and his family drive through traffic.

"Here it comes," she said.

"What?"

She nodded at the movie, reminding him that he was supposed to be watching it with her and not dissecting her. "All hell is about to break loose."

True to form, it was a zombie rampage. Quick and breath-stealing. Spectacular effects.

It wasn't until things slowed down in the movie that she spoke into the humming quiet between them, revealing that she was still thinking about his question. "I don't have a dad. It's just my mom, and she isn't here right now."

"Oh."

"My dad died, too," he volunteered. "Three years ago."

"Oh, my dad isn't dead. At least not that I'm aware." She gave a single-shoulder shrug as though her lack of knowing was no big deal. "Not dead. Just a deadbeat. He and my mother split before I was even born. I've never seen him. He's never seen me." Nolan watched as she helped herself to more popcorn. "Sorry though. About your dad.

Emmaline mentioned your father died. That must suck . . . losing a dad that way. Was he a good dad?"

"Yeah. The best."

Chewing, she nodded, watching the movie. "Then maybe I got off easier. Never had to deal with the pain of losing a good dad."

"Maybe," he answered, glancing around at her naked walls, staring at the absence of good memories, and thinking she was wrong, but not wanting to contradict her. He wasn't about to explain to her how her situation was worse than his. That he would never trade in the time he had with his father just to escape the pain of losing him.

Instead he settled deeper on the couch beside her, wondering if this was the kind of thing that she talked about with his sister. Existential rhetoric and zombie movie commentary?

"Have you watched this movie with Emmaline?"

She smirked. "You're fishing."

"Just wondering."

"We haven't hung out that much. No movie nights."

Nothing like this then. Nothing like what they were doing right now.

"Yet," she added, still smirking.

He frowned. "You're planning on movie nights with my sister?"

"I don't plan these things." She motioned between them with a shrug. "Definitely didn't plan for you to be sitting on my couch."

"Me neither." He glanced down at the now empty bag of popcorn and gave it a few shakes, rattling the handfuls of kernels. "You want to order a pizza?"

"You buying?"

"Absolutely."

LESSON #11

ATTRACTION MIGHT EXIST, BUT THAT DOESN'T MEAN YOU SHOULD ACT ON IT.

x   Hayden   x

She woke with her neck at an awkward angle. Wincing, she moved her head, forcing the stretch, fighting through the pain shooting up the side of her throat.

Stifling a moan, she reached for her pillow, hoping to adjust it more comfortably under her head.

She couldn't find her pillow. Her fingers searched, but nothing. It must have fallen on the floor.

Frowning, she opened her eyes and studied the old popcorn ceiling with its stains and cracks. For a moment her gaze fixed on the stain in the shape of Michigan. She knew it well. Her frown deepened.

That stain wasn't in her bedroom. It was in the living room.

Huh. She'd fallen asleep in the living room on the less-than-comfortable couch. That wasn't like her. With all the strays her mom brought home, she liked to be locked up in her room safe and sound every night in her own bed.

The air was a shade between purple and gray, soft and swollen like a bruise on skin.

She knew about bruises, knew all their many shapes and sizes and colors. Mom was frequently peppered in them. Hard living did that to a person — cast you in a rainbow of shades.

Hayden had suffered her share, too. The times when Mom lost her shit over something and Hayden took the brunt of it with a slap or an object that flew and caught her before she could dodge it. Those were the early days, though.

Now she was older. Wiser. She knew how to avoid. How to duck. How to be gone before the fight even broke out.

Of course, there were the bruises you couldn't see. They were the worst. They never fully healed.

She glanced at the time on the analog clock on the distant kitchen oven. It was a little after five in the morning. She didn't need to be up for another hour and a half, but she didn't think there would be any going back to sleep.

She swung her legs off the creaky couch to the floor, still working her neck, pushing down on the couch with one hand, preparing to stand.

Except the surface under her hand didn't feel like the sagging couch cushion. It felt too firm for that. Solid, but with a little give.

Turning her head, she looked down. That definitely wasn't the couch under her hand.

She was touching Nolan Martin. He was sprawled asleep on her couch. They'd slept on the couch together. Side by side.

Like a couple.

Except not. Not like that at all.

She wrenched her hand off Nolan as though burned — as though she were touching a hot stove.

Because. Yeah. *Hot.*

He slept on, his features serene, unaware. She screwed her eyes shut tight in a pained blink and tried to rid herself of the sight of him. It did no good. Opening her eyes, he was still there.

He'd spent the night with her. Here. On her crappy couch. Nolan Martin had spent the night *with her.*

She didn't spend the night with guys. Not at her house. Not at theirs. Never.

This was not a scenario she could have ever imagined. Not with him. Not with anyone. She wasn't one of those girls who envisioned meeting her prince someday. She didn't see a future with anyone. Her dream was for a place of her own. Independence. Money in her bank account. Not a person.

She shook him. "Nolan."

He jerked, startled awake, and she felt a flash of guilt over her less-than-gentle handling.

He blinked several times, his eyes focusing on her. "Hayden?"

"Yep. Me." She waved a hand around her. "What? You didn't feel like going home last night?"

He looked a little shocked as he glanced around. "Um . . . wow. I'm sorry." He sat up and dragged both hands through his hair, sending the dark locks flying in every direction.

He looked good. He'd spent the night crammed bedside her on her creaky old couch and he looked good. It was vastly unfair.

She knew what she looked like in the mornings — probably *this* morning — and she wouldn't call it anything close to good. Why should he get to close his eyes, sleep, and wake up looking cover-shoot ready?

"I can't believe . . ." His voice faded away as he lifted his head and met her gaze directly. "Did your mom come home?"

He glanced around as though he might spot her, an angry parent he would have to justify his presence to, lurking somewhere in the room. That image of her mom was ridiculous.

Nolan rubbed his palms over his thighs as though the prospect of coming face to face with her mother made him nervous.

And it should.

But not for the reasons he thought.

"My mom isn't home. Trust me." She expelled a breath, imagining that scene. "We would have known."

Mom would have made a grand spectacle. Sober, drunk, or high, she would have reacted to a boy sleeping on the couch with her daughter.

Nolan nodded as though he understood that. As though he assumed her mom was like other moms — like his — who would react with outrage.

Except . . . no. Her mother would have been thrilled to see Hayden with a boy. Delighted. She complained that Hayden never brought her friends around.

Hayden never commented on that. Never spoke the truth. Never reminded Mom of the bitter past. She knew better.

Mom didn't want to hear criticisms. There was no changing her. No getting through to her. No point trying at all.

Which is why Hayden couldn't understand what happened last night. Why did she let Nolan stay? Why had she even invited him inside? What had she been thinking? She never did that.

He blew out a breath. "Well, that's a relief."

Again with the assumption that her mom — had she found them asleep together on the couch — would have reacted in a way *normal* for *normal* moms.

"Yep. No parent here. You can be relieved." Relieved that her family life was so dysfunctional her mother didn't even come home half the time. Relieved that so many of her nights were spent alone.

His face looked suddenly apprehensive. "Er, I should probably go before she does come home though."

She stifled a snort. It was cute that he was worried about *that.*

He slipped on his shoes, and she wondered when he had removed them in the first place. She'd never noticed. Of course, she had failed to notice a lot of things last night, including the moment either one of them drifted off to sleep.

"Sorry," he murmured. Again.

She shrugged, wondering what he was apologizing for. His voice, his face, the way he moved, all smacked of regret.

Regret for being here. Regret over last night.

Even though it had felt so natural. So easy. She had enjoyed herself with him. It had felt like they were friends, which was a strange thing, as she had so few of those.

Sitting on the couch beside him, she had actually started to feel guilty keeping the truth of her relationship with Emmaline from him. Not that it was any of his business, but he cared about his sister and Emmaline was going through something. Maybe he should know about that.

Hayden had almost told him. Now, in the murky air of dawn, she was glad she had kept it to herself. The idea of telling him that his sister wanted to *hire* Hayden to teach her to be . . . She didn't even know the proper word. *Sexy? Seductive? A girl with game.*

Yeah, he would not approve. In fact, he would think it was the worst thing ever — that Hayden was the worst thing ever.

"It's okay," she said, even though she didn't know what she was reassuring him for. Maybe she was reassuring herself.

He glanced at his phone, his thumb swiping over the screen. He muttered something low under his breath.

"Everything okay?" she asked, assuming his phone was riddled with messages and unanswered calls from his mom. "Your mom looking for you?"

"No. She must've gone to bed. Hopefully I can get home before she wakes up." He stood and moved toward the door, and then stopped to turn back and face her. "You're not going to . . . um, tell anyone, are you?"

She scooted to the edge of the couch. "Tell anyone . . ." She arched an eyebrow, prompting him to spit it out.

"Yeah. That I spent the night here?"

"Ohhh," she said slowly, sounding deliberately dim. "You're worried what people will think."

He nodded once in acknowledgment. "Yeah. I have a girlfriend. I wouldn't want her to . . ."

"You wouldn't want her to know you spent the night shacked up with me, right?" she finished for him.

He released a brief laugh. "You're blunt as usual, but yeah."

"We didn't do anything," she reminded him. Even as she said the words, they rang false to her ears.

Sure. They hadn't kissed. They hadn't even touched each other in that kind of way. Just harmless arm brushing. There had been absolutely no shenanigans. And yet last night felt like the very definition of intimacy. She imagined it was the kind of night BFFs had all the time. Movies and popcorn and junk food and conversation that ranged from silly to profound. Only he was a guy who happened to smell *really* good.

He rubbed at the back of his neck. "Yeah, I know that. But it just won't look very good."

She shrugged. Of course he cared about the way things *looked*. That was the way it was for people like him. Guys like him who had girlfriends would care about appearances. Sure. She understood that, but it still stung. "Whatever. It's not like I talk to anyone in your circle anyway."

It's not like she talked to much of anyone at school.

"You talk to my sister," he reminded.

"Actually *she* talks to me," she corrected. There was that distinction. It kind of mattered. It was the reason he came over here, after all.

"Well, I would appreciate it if you didn't mention that I stayed over to her or anyone."

"You want me to lie?"

He winced.

She shook her head and spoke so she didn't have to hear another word from him. "No worries. It's not a big deal. I'll probably forget all about it anyway."

Just like she would forget that she had thought he was a decent guy.

Just like she would forget that she had thought they could be friends.

Temporary madness.

Shrugging, she snatched her phone off the coffee table. It gave her eyes and hands something to do while she grappled with her sudden disappointment. *No.* Annoyance. She was annoyed with him and annoyed with herself.

She immediately spotted a text from the night before on the screen. It must've come in after she fell asleep. It was from Emmaline.

Having a sleepover this weekend. You in? I'll pay you for your time.

It was all the reminder she needed. She wasn't friends with these people. Not with Emmaline. Not with Nolan.

She was someone to be used. Bought. Someone Nolan couldn't own up to being friends with. A dirty secret.

Lifting her face, she donned a smile. "You better head home. Don't want your mom to wake up with you gone. She might put out an Amber alert."

He nodded, staring at her intently in the murky space of her living room. She sensed he was trying to read her, trying to peer past her snarky tone and pasted smile.

On she smiled, holding his steady gaze, determined that he see nothing.

"Okay. Yeah." Another nod and he picked up his keys from the coffee table.

She watched as he opened her front door. Limned in the smoky light of dawn, he faced her again. "Thanks. It was fun."

"Yeah," she agreed, still wearing her fake smile.

It had been fun, and it could never happen again.

LESSON #12

IF YOU'RE DOING SOMETHING YOU SHOULDN'T BE, DON'T GET CAUGHT.

x Nolan x

Nolan was home before anyone woke.

Mom worked long hours. Since Dad passed away, she had no choice. He knew it was pure luck that her bedroom door was still shut as he crept up the stairs to his room.

Grateful that he didn't have to explain where he spent the night — or with whom — he showered and got ready for school. He was brushing his teeth in front of the mirror with a towel wrapped around his waist when he heard Mom tromp down the stairs. He paused, listening. He knew the routine, knew the sounds of her making coffee and toast. A few minutes later, he heard her exit out the side door, so he left the bathroom and finished getting ready in his room.

Nolan didn't know how he would have explained his whereabouts to Mom, considering he didn't know how to explain it to himself.

He still had to face Priscilla, though. She'd sent him several messages last night. He'd sent her a quick one before getting in the shower, telling her he had fallen asleep while watching a movie.

Not a lie, but not the full truth either.

Hayden was right. Nothing had happened between them. Nothing physical anyway, but he knew Priscilla wouldn't see it that way.

You don't see it that way.

Because it felt more than that. It felt *more* than a good time between friends.

He'd never even spent a night with Priscilla, but he had just spent the night wrapped up in Hayden Vargas.

He knew how that information would affect Priscilla. She'd view it as a betrayal, even though he hadn't technically cheated on her.

There were degrees of cheating. Not that it was ever anything he had considered before, but last night had him thinking about that now. Last night had him thinking about it very hard.

He had always thought cheating was black and white. Couples either remained true and faithful or they didn't. Now he knew there was more to it than that. He may not have laid a finger on Hayden, but his mind had gone there. His emotions had crossed lines.

He'd had a good time with Hayden, but he was also attracted to her. He *liked* her. He couldn't deny that to himself. Not any longer.

He also couldn't deny he was overreacting about Emmaline hanging out with Hayden.

Sure, she wasn't like any of Emmaline's usual friends, and she had a reputation. But was that Hayden's fault? Should he hold it against her that guys looked at her and immediately thought about how they could get in her pants? That seemed like a *them* problem.

When he emerged from his room, his sisters were already downstairs finishing their cereal. He grabbed a protein bar. "Ready to go?" he asked.

"Where were you last night?" Emmaline asked as she set her bowl in the sink. "Mom said you were looking for me."

Avoiding her question, he asked Savannah, "You have a game after school today?"

It served to distract.

"Yeah." She nodded. "It's an away game at Campion. Five o'clock."

"I'll be there." Mom couldn't always make it to her soccer games, so he made a point to be there when he could.

"Me too," Emmaline said.

They all piled into his truck. His sisters sat in the back seat, leaving the front passenger seat open for Priscilla as was customary. It was habit. For all of them.

Heading for Pris's subdivision, he felt a twinge of something. He flexed his hands on the steering wheel and stared straight ahead, trying to ignore the discomfort pinching at the center of his chest as he wondered what would happen if picking up Priscilla every day wasn't his normal anymore. The world wouldn't end. It would just be different. Isn't that the way life worked? Nothing ever stayed the same.

He pulled up to the curb of her house. In seconds, Priscilla was hurrying down the walkway. She hopped in beside him. "Hey there."

The girls murmured a greeting from the back seat.

"Study for the math test?" she asked.

He'd forgotten all about the test they had today. Last night he had forgotten about everything the moment he walked inside Hayden's house.

"Yeah," he said, wondering when had it become so easy to lie to his girlfriend.

A FULL STOMACH MAKES EVERYTHING BETTER.

x Hayden x

Hayden splurged on pizza in the cafeteria.

It cost two dollars and seventy-five cents a slice, but she couldn't resist. The large gooey squares were laden with nitrates and deliciousness.

They served pizza every other week, and she sacrificed hanging out in Ms. Mendez's room during her lunch period, enduring the cafeteria so she could enjoy it. It was an indulgence, and she felt like indulging today. Nolan's request earlier this morning that she not mention their time together still rang in her ears, a bitter reminder that she might have been good enough for him last night, but in the bright light of day she was just a dirty, shameful thing to be kept buried and secret.

Who would she even tell?

Holding her tray, she wove through the crowded lunchroom and picked a spot in the far corner, near the doors. Quick entry and exit. She sat at the end of the table, alone, scrolling Instagram, happily sinking her teeth into saucy, cheesy, greasy goodness.

Her thumb swiped over the screen. She followed several of the country's leading tattoo shops and they regularly updated their portfolios on social media. She liked to keep up with current trends.

A tray clattered in front of her. "Hey there."

She looked up, startled as Emmaline sank down across from her.

"Hey," Hayden said slowly, glancing around as though Emmaline had maybe picked the wrong table and meant to sit somewhere else — at another table full of perky, chirpy girls like her. There seemed to be plenty of those tables around.

More trays slammed down. Suddenly perky, chirpy girls were on each side. She was surrounded. Emmaline Martin and her friends circled her, invading her space.

"I can't believe you're all eating that slop." A girl with disapproving lips critically eyed Hayden's and everyone else's pizza as she opened her lunch bag and took out her turkey on wheat.

Hayden glanced around. "Um. Are you sure you're at the right table?"

"Oh. Were you saving these seats?" Emmaline motioned to the chairs she and her friends now occupied.

"Um, no." Clearly they didn't get it. They didn't understand that she *preferred* to eat alone. She didn't want bubbly girls around her. She wanted pizza and solitude.

"You get my text?" Emmaline asked as her friends broke into overlapping conversations. She picked up one of her pizza squares. She'd bought two.

"About the slumber party?" Hayden hadn't replied to the message. She had assumed her silence would be taken for a decline.

"Oh, fun! Are you coming?" One of Emmaline's friends piped in like Hayden was just one of the girls — one of them.

"No. I don't think —"

"Of course she is." Emmaline looked at Hayden in rebuke.

Hayden opened her mouth to set the record straight. She was not going to any slumber party.

Suddenly, the cafeteria fell quiet. Hundreds of voices ceased talking.

"What the—" Emmaline twisted around in her seat as a guy walked down the middle aisle. He was hard to miss. He carried a sign and at least a dozen pink balloons.

"Oh God," the girl with a sandwich groaned. "Spare me."

People stood up from their seats, craning their necks to get a better view.

"What is it?" Hayden leaned forward in her chair, trying to peer through the obstructing crowd.

"It's started." Sandwich Girl shook her head.

The balloons the boy held bobbed in the air as he walked. There was something drawn on them in black sharpie.

"They're pigs! The balloons have pig faces drawn on them. How cute," Emmaline exclaimed, clapping in approval.

Ah. Hayden could see the faces now. Bubble eyes and piggy noses were boldly outlined against the pink latex.

"What's the sign say?" Emmaline asked, straining to read.

It all clicked then. The balloons. The sign. The guy with the purposeful stride. He was asking someone to the winter formal.

It was that time of year. Dance proposal season.

It actually happened a few times a year. Homecoming in the fall. The winter formal in February. Then prom in the spring. Three times per school year Hayden witnessed this teenage of rite of passage. In the halls, in classrooms, in the parking lot. *Vomit*.

She couldn't think of anything stupider than getting worked up over a dance. Not when there more important things to worry about. Things like food and clothes and clean sheets.

Emmaline hopped in place. "It says: I'd love to go to the dance with you . . . when pigs fly!"

The boy must have reached the girl he was targeting. The cluster of balloons stopped their advance.

"Clever," Sandwich Girl announced blandly, delving into a bag of carrot sticks and biting into one loudly. She looked as unimpressed as Hayden felt.

Suddenly, the balloons were released and lifted up into the air.

Girls squealed in delight. The cafeteria erupted into applause.

"So cute! The pigs are flying!" Emmaline stared up at the pink balloons as they bumped into the ceiling. Hayden stared at her, marveling at the joy all over her face and knowing she had never felt that. Well, maybe she felt that kind of joy when Ms. Mendez oohed and aahed over one of her designs or when she stumbled onto a new zombie movie. She definitely didn't feel joy over balloons and a boy with a cheesy sign or a dumb dance.

Unlike everyone else, Hayden stayed in her seat and finished her pizza. Swallowing the last bite, she sipped her chocolate milk and stared down at her empty tray unhappily. Emmaline was still totally wrapped up in the proposal. So wrapped up she hadn't even touched her pizza.

Not about to let it go to waste, Hayden reached over and plucked one of the squares off her tray.

She sank her teeth into the fresh slice with a delighted moan. Hayden was halfway through the pizza when the girls all settled back in their seats, immediately chattering about the proposal.

"I want someone to ask me to the dance." The girl with the beautiful dark hair and eyes pouted, picking at her pizza as though it were to blame.

Sandwich Girl bit into another carrot and rolled her eyes. "Big shock."

"Be nice, Monica," Emmaline chided.

Hayden nodded at the last slice of Emmaline's pizza. "You gonna eat that?"

Emmaline shoved her remaining pizza toward Hayden and continued talking. "I want someone to ask me, too. I mean, it's my junior year and I've never been asked to the winter formal. Or homecoming. Or prom."

"It's just a dance," Hayden muttered around a mouthful of pizza.

"This is why I need your help." Emmaline leaned across the table, tapping the surface.

"So I can get you promposals?" Hayden snorted. She didn't have guys lining her up to ask her to dances either. Thank God. "That's not my department."

"But attracting guys is," Emmaline insisted, waving her hands for emphasis. "I mean, look around right now. Notice how many guys are checking you out?"

Hayden shook her head, not bothering to look around. She didn't care if guys were checking her out. She did not measure her worth on whether or not guys found her attractive.

"They could just be watching her eat like a wolf. What is that? Your fourth piece?" Monica bit down on another carrot.

"Third," Hayden corrected. "And I'm actually getting full." She polished off the last square and wiped her mouth with a napkin. "Well, it's been fun, girls," she lied, pushing up to her feet.

"So we'll see you later?" Emmaline looked at her hopefully.

Hayden hated to crush the girl's hopes. She really was nice. Too nice. Hayden wouldn't be doing her any favors if she showed up for her slumber party. She couldn't help her — she could barely help herself.

The bell chimed, signaling the end of lunch.

Hayden said nothing and nodded noncommittally at Emmaline. "Gotta go. I'll see you around."

She hurried through the double doors, her breath falling a little easier once she was free of the cafeteria, free of Emmaline and her friends.

She started down the hall toward her fifth period class, stopping when she heard her name.

She turned and watched Emmaline jog to catch up with her, a bulging backpack bouncing on her shoulders. "Hey," she said breathlessly. "You never answered my question."

"Uhh —"

"Seventy dollars," Emmaline blurted.

Hayden forgot whatever she had been about to say. "Seventy dollars? For one sleepover?"

"And lessons. I'd like you to answer all our questions." Emmaline's eyes fixed on her. "But yeah, seventy dollars. Easy money."

She couldn't make that much money in a ten-hour shift at the Tasty Freeze. Not after taxes. Plus, she'd be asleep for the majority of the sleepover. Hayden sighed. She couldn't afford to say no to money like that.

"Okay."

Emmaline squealed and jumped up and down, her backpack thrashing almost violently behind her.

Hayden reached out and clasped her arm, giving it a calming squeeze. "Take it easy there before you hurt yourself."

Emmaline nodded and started to back away. "Yeah, okay. I gotta run. My class is on the other side of the building. Bring your swimsuit, and I'll text you anything else I can think of." She curled her fingers and flapped a quick wave. "See you soon!"

Hayden watched her hurry down the hall, wondering what she had just agreed to do.

LESSON #14

DON'T LET ANYONE
MAKE YOU FEEL NOT GOOD ENOUGH.

x   Nolan   x

Nolan watched as Hayden hurried out of the cafeteria.

Priscilla was still critiquing the dance proposal with her friends as though they were judges evaluating a complicated Olympic-level floor sequence. They had a lot to say on the matter. The general consensus seemed to be that the guy should have had at least twice as many balloons and he should have gotten someone else to do the poster. Apparently the writing was not legible enough and there should have been glitter. Lots of glitter.

His sister waved goodbye to her friends and hurried after Hayden.

He felt the urge to chase after them. God knew their conversation, whatever it was, would be better than this one. At the very least it would be informative. It might possibly even shed light on his sister's sudden fascination with Hayden Vargas.

After spending the night with Hayden, he might share that fascination, but he suspected Emmaline had different motives.

His sister didn't have anything in common with Hayden. Emmaline wasn't into horror films. She was into rom-coms and training for her academic decathlon team with all her friends.

His chair screeched against the tile as he stood up.

"Where you going?" Priscilla looked up at him. He was guessing she wanted him to stick around to hear her thoughts on proper dance proposals. The dance was a month away. She would be expecting him to ask her soon, and in grand style, of course. He had to admit, after two years with her, he was running short on creativity.

"I need to get to class early. I want to go over a homework question with Mr. Akwasi."

Frowning, she nodded.

He hurried from the cafeteria. In the hall, he noticed his sister at the end of the corridor, hopping excitedly in front of Hayden. Emmaline's face was bright with happiness. Okay, that wasn't normal. He headed their way with purposeful strides, determined to find out what was going on.

Before he reached them, Emmaline hurried off.

Hayden turned and caught sight of him.

She shook her head ruefully. "Come to investigate?"

He stopped in front of her. "Emmaline looked . . . happy."

"Your sister is a happy person." She crossed her arms over her chest.

"Yeah, she's always been that way."

"Then why so suspicious?"

"I'm not suspicious."

"Yeah, you are." She gave him a disgusted look. "We both know you think I'm a bad influence." She waved a hand around them. "You sure you want people to see you talking to me? You have a reputation to maintain."

He winced. "Hayden, come on. I didn't —"

She shook her head. "I don't have time for this." She started to turn away but stepped into a path of girls running down the hall. Hayden's notebook clattered to the ground, papers flying loose.

"Sorry!" one girl called out, but they didn't stop.

Muttering, Hayden squatted to gather up her papers. Nolan joined her, helping her gather everything.

"I got it," she bit out.

He ignored her, reaching for a paper close to him. Once it was in his hand, he stopped and studied it. It was a very detailed tree, growing from the side of a craggy mountain. Tiny colorful flowers sprouted from the branches. It was mesmerizing. "Did you . . . do this?"

She looked up abruptly, her gaze flicking from him to the paper he held. She snatched it from his hand. "Give that here."

"You did that?"

She shrugged one shoulder as she stuffed it inside her notebook with her other papers. He strained for a better glimpse. He could see that they were all brightly colored.

"That's amazing," he said. "I didn't know you were an artist."

She straightened to her full height and leveled him with a glare. "Yeah, well, you don't know me. Do you? I thought we covered that already."

He buried his hands in his front pockets, unable to argue with her assessment. What could he say? He felt like he got to know her better last night and then he blew it this morning. He'd offended her and now she was pissed at him.

"No," he said. "I guess not."

"Right," she snapped. Hayden glared at him a moment longer and then turned away. Without a word of farewell, she marched down the hall, her steps quick in her eagerness to be away from him.

LESSON #15

SOMETIMES YOU HAVE TO FAKE IT TO MAKE IT.

x   Hayden   x

Heated pool or not, it was freeze-your-butt cold.

Hayden watched Emmaline and the others hop like fools from one end of the pool to the other, screaming at how freezing it was. Not that it stopped them or had them rushing back into the warmth of the house.

"Get back in the pool, you idiots," Hayden laughed, slapping the water with her hand. The water was seventy-five degrees, and it felt a lot better *inside* the pool than outside of it.

Shrieking, they all jumped back in.

They were idiots, but they made her laugh. She couldn't deny it. She had to keep reminding herself that this was business. They'd hired her for her "expertise." Nothing else. This wasn't really friendship.

She was here for the money.

Hayden treaded in place and asked Emmaline, "Is this what happens at your slumber parties? You swim when it's forty degrees and catch pneumonia?"

"We usually swim when it's warmer," Emmaline admitted. "What do *you* do at slumber parties?" Emmaline's hands swished through the water in front of her and Hayden felt the undercurrents against her bare stomach.

"I don't know." She lifted one shoulder. "Never been to one."

Emmaline's hands stilled. "You've never been to a slumber party?"

Great. Now she was feeling sorry for Hayden.

With that tidbit of information, Hayden felt the gulf widen between them. They might be two girls in the same town, going to the same school . . . but they had nothing else in common.

Hayden shrugged as though it was no big thing. Instead of answering Emmaline, she said, "It's getting late. Did you want to start on those lessons?"

That's why she was here, after all. Not because she was really friends with these girls. Hayden needed to remember that.

"Yeah. We should."

"Hey, guys, let's go in," Emmaline called out to everyone.

"That's right. There's work to be done," Sanjana called cheerfully as she swam to the steps. "I've been waiting for this all night. The legendary Hayden Vargas is going to teach us all her dirty tricks."

Hayden stifled her wince. *Dirty tricks.* Well, that put it in perspective. Clearly they thought Hayden was here to teach them all her depravities. At least they weren't thinking she was going to get them promposals anymore. That was somehow worse in her mind.

Emmaline shot a quick glance to Hayden, as though worried they had offended her. Hayden schooled her expression to reveal nothing. She was good at that, after all.

More screams ensued as they all emerged from the pool into the icy bite of air.

"Cold is bad enough," Hayden said through clacking teeth as she moved toward the towels. "Cold *and* wet, though, is . . ." Her trembling voice faded away as she noticed the two figures standing on the other side of the glass door.

"Ugh, my brother," Emmaline muttered. "And he's all scowly. As usual."

Nolan was scowly, but he wasn't scowling at Emmaline. He was looking directly at Hayden. He was probably worried she was telling his sister that he spent the night on her couch. *Good.* Let him worry.

He didn't want her here. She could feel his disapproval radiating off him in waves. Heat flashed under her shivering-cold skin as his gaze crawled over her in her bikini. Cheeks burning, she reached for a towel to cover up. It was dark, and he was several yards away, but she detected a ruddiness to his cheeks — as though he were red-faced with anger. That seemed a more likely reason.

Hayden averted her gaze and shook out her wet hair, telling herself to ignore him entirely. That would annoy him.

With a sniff, she turned her attention on the other figure looking out through the glass door. *Of course.* It was Beau. Who else would it be? He was looking directly at Emmaline, his gaze roaming over her in quick appraisal. There was nothing brotherly in his look. *Interesting.*

"We better get inside before we catch a cold," Emmaline announced.

"You know that's a myth." Monica shook her head as though Emmaline were the silliest thing to make such a suggestion.

"I don't know that at all," Emmaline snapped. "And neither do you."

"Yes, I do," Monica insisted in a level voice as she twisted her wet hair, wringing out the water. "A cold is a virus. You don't catch it from being cold or wet."

"You're such a hypochondriac, Emmaline." Sanjana laughed.

Emmaline grabbed a towel and vigorously rubbed it over her chilled skin. "I am not," she grumbled.

"Yes, you are," Monica started. "Totally understandable though."

Emmaline frowned and looked up. "What's that supposed to mean?"

"Well, you lost your dad, so it's natural to have a fear of death, to see the threat of it everywhere, when death has touched you so closely and so intimately."

Everyone fell silent.

Hayden shook her head. She might not have a lot of friends, but she was more socially adept than Monica.

Emmaline's face turned splotchy red.

"Um, wow, Monica." Lia shifted uncomfortably, her gaze swinging between Emmaline and Monica. "Rude, much?"

"What?" Monica blinked several times, clearly unaware she had crossed a boundary.

Suddenly feeling sorry for the girl, Hayden announced, "Well, my dad isn't dead, but he might as well be. I've never met him. Last I heard, he was in prison, but that was three years ago." Hayden tossed in a shrug to underline the casualness of this confession.

Everyone gawked at her.

Clearly none of them knew quite how to react to that, even Monica, who always seemed to have something to say.

Hayden had everyone's full attention. Just as Hayden intended. Everyone forgot about Emmaline and her dad and her issues.

It was the kind of thing a *friend* would do, even though they weren't remotely friends. But while Hayden may not be Emmaline's friend, she was the one paying her. And Hayden didn't really care what Emmaline's friends thought of her. They weren't her people. None of them were. Even if they invaded her lunch table and might make her laugh.

She didn't have people. She only had herself.

She glanced around the backyard, with its pool and patio furniture and a wooden sign hanging on the back brick wall that read **Family** in bold letters, and under those letters, in smaller lowercase text:

A LITTLE BIT OF CRAZY

A LITTLE BIT OF LOUD

& A WHOLE LOT OF LOVE

It was like she had stepped into an alien world. The very strangeness of it made her feel like there was a neon arrow above her head pointing at her and flashing the word *misfit*.

This was not her life. At no time had this ever been her life. This place was for family and friends and love.

She didn't have a place like that. But right now, she was going to fake it.

LESSON #16

IF YOU ALWAYS PLAY IT SAFE...
YOU MAY NEVER ACTUALLY GET TO PLAY.

x Nolan x

Hayden Vargas shouldn't be here.

It was Nolan's only thought as the girls rushed inside the house to get out of the cold. Trembling in their towels, they chatted excitedly as they filled the kitchen, leaving wet puddles everywhere that would send his mother into fits.

Several greeted Nolan and Beau. He could only nod hello because he was busy looking at *her*.

She met his gaze head-on and grinned, clearly aware that he wasn't happy to see her here. Any makeup she'd worn had washed off and she looked younger. Not at all like the hard-edged girl she usually presented to the world. Her honey complexion was marred with faint smudges under her eyes, giving her a hint of vulnerability. She looked human. Approachable. More like the zombie movie aficionado who had shared popcorn with him.

He realized he was staring and forced himself to turn away.

Emmaline and Sanjana were busy pulling food and drinks out of the fridge. Apparently, the pizza they had finished earlier wasn't satisfying enough.

"You like — what is this?" Sanjana pulled a lid off a pitcher and sniffed. "Kool-Aid? You want Kool-Aid, Hayden? I think it's cherry."

"I can't have red dye," Monica interjected, as though the question has been posed to her. "Hayden, do you have any allergies?"

"I found the dip!" Emmaline proclaimed, brandishing the container in the air. "Hey, Lia, get the chips from the pantry, would you?"

Lia did as commanded and dived into the pantry, emerging with several bags of chips. "I love these jalapeño potato chips! My mom never buys them. Says they give her heartburn. Hayden, do you like jalapeño chips?"

Was it just his imagination or were all the girls fawning over Hayden like she was a new toy in their midst?

"What's happening?" he murmured to Beau, who was also watching the scene in apparent fascination.

Beau shrugged. "I think your sister is having a slumber party . . ."

"Yeah," he replied in a voice only Beau could hear. "With Hayden Vargas."

Hayden Vargas was spending the night at his house. Hayden would be under the same roof with him all night. *Again*. Yeah. Okay. He'd spent the night with her at her house, but that had been an accident.

Hayden asleep in *his* house, just a few rooms down from him . . .

It was a fact that didn't compute. With the exception of Hayden, the girls in his kitchen had been sleeping over since elementary school. Hayden was the piece that didn't fit.

His gaze fixed on her again. She was laughing at something Sanjana was saying — a full-bodied throw-back-your-head laugh that hit him right in the gut.

He muttered a curse and felt Beau staring at him again, like he didn't know what to make of him, and that was fair, because Nolan didn't know what to make of himself either. Usually he was the calm one. Composed and collected.

How many times had he dragged Beau out of a fight or some scrape? Or stepped in when some guy was being rude to a girl? Or wrestled the keys from some inebriated friend determined to drive home?

He wasn't the one to lose his cool or get overly affected by anything.

But right now he felt . . . unsettled, and he didn't like it.

Beau leaned in. "Man, you're totally staring at her."

He knew that. He couldn't stop it though.

What was she doing here?

What did she have in common with a bunch of girls on the academic decathlon team?

Nolan knew he was probably a douche thinking that . . . but there was something going on here, and no one was talking about the new addition to his sister's friend group. Illogical or not, after their night together he felt as though Hayden could trust him enough to explain what was going on.

Except she wasn't here for him, and it's not like he could just pull her aside and demand an explanation. Again. She was at his house for Emmaline and that annoyed him. He knew it was messed up to feel like he had some sort of bond with Hayden, but that didn't make the feeling go away.

Even as he looked across the kitchen at her, he couldn't stop seeing her as he had seen her outside, *not* wrapped in a towel. Now he knew where her tattoo was.

She'd mentioned having a tattoo that night at the party, and every now and then, the random thought of it would pop in his mind and he would wonder where it was . . . what it looked like.

Now he knew.

He kept seeing it low on her hip, that green twisting vine crawling over her skin and opening up into a bright flower in varying shades of pink. The artwork was stunning, practically leaping off her golden skin. It couldn't be very old. The color was so vibrant.

He gave himself a mental slap. He shouldn't be thinking about her tattoo or her skin. He swallowed against the sudden lump in his throat.

The girls all chattered, oblivious to him and Beau as they continued to eat and raid the fridge. Now they were pulling ice cream from the freezer. He watched mutely as they made bowls of mint chocolate chip.

"Hey, Nolan." Hayden looked at him, daring to speak to him with the memory of their night together throbbing on the air between them. He could read the knowledge of it in the deep brown of her eyes. She was taking smug pleasure in the secret of that night, in the power she held over him.

He stared, waiting for whatever she was going to say.

Her bold eyes sparked as she lifted her spoon from her bowl and licked the ice cream clean off it in a long, savoring swipe of her tongue. "Want some ice cream?"

All around her the girls froze.

Conversation ground to a halt. It was deliberate. A provocative little display meant to rattle him. He knew that much about her. Knew she was enjoying herself. Enjoying his discomfort.

Everyone picked up on it and watched him, waiting for his reaction.

He knew it was meant to embarrass him. It worked.

It also infuriated him, but he wouldn't satisfy her by losing his composure.

"No, thanks," he said tightly. "I'm fine."

Although he didn't feel fine.

He wasn't fine.

The girls grabbed their ice cream and skipped off to Emmaline's room, leaving the kitchen a disaster behind them. Mom was going to love that when she woke up in the morning.

Beau released a heavy breath beside him. "What the hell was that?"

Nolan shook his head. He didn't know, but before this night was over, he would.

He was going to find out.

LESSON #17

SOMETIMES BEING BAD IS VERY GOOD.

x Hayden x

Hayden really should grab her stuff and go home.

Everything about this felt wrong. She'd gone and done what she did in the kitchen with the spoon. She couldn't help herself. Nolan Martin made her angry and she wanted to rattle him.

He'd spent the night with her, but no one could know that. He'd made it clear that no one could find out. He made it clear that no one could know they were becoming friends and that stung.

She'd liked him. Crazy as it seemed, she thought they had a connection. She could talk to him and he was willing to watch her favorite movies and listen to all her theories. She had a good time with a guy and it hadn't involved making out. When he asked her to keep it quiet, he'd cheapened it. She hadn't even kissed him, but she felt dirty.

His dirty little secret.

If that's what she was to him, then she might as well act the part. So she had licked that ice cream off the spoon in the naughtiest way possible.

Yeah, that had been wrong, and as much as she wanted to chalk it up as a lesson for Emmaline, she knew hanging out with these girls was wrong, too.

It was the kind of thing other people did. It was the kind of thing normal girls did. Not Hayden. Hayden had never been a normal girl. She wasn't one of them.

Not since . . . well, not since ever.

Girlhood was reserved for those who didn't feel compelled to hide a bug-out bag in their closet. For girls who hadn't had to fend for themselves since the age of four. For girls who didn't know the phone numbers to all the local dive bars.

Sometimes Hayden would have to hunt down her mom if she was desperate enough. If the fridge was empty. If the power went out. If some angry guy was pounding at the door and windows, yelling threats for her mother.

Once one of Mom's boyfriends forced his way into the house and tore the place apart, searching for her mother's stash. She'd tried to stay out of his way. She'd tucked herself into a corner and cried when he ransacked her room. He'd used a knife to slash through her bedding. For a moment he had looked at her with such crazed eyes, she'd feared he would turn that knife on her. When he couldn't find what he wanted, he'd destroyed the place even more out of retaliation.

Hayden was nothing like these girls. She had nothing in common with them. She never would. Even once she secured a comfortable life for herself in Austin, she would never be like them. They'd be in college, living their lives of privilege, sharing stupid memes on social media and buying six-dollar coffees between classes. That would never be her.

But she couldn't bail on tonight. As much as she'd like to, as out of place as she felt in here, she had agreed to come. She had agreed to this night, crazy as it was. She'd made a deal, and she was here now.

She'd come to this sleepover to give a "tutorial on seduction" — Emmaline's words, not hers. The girl was a nerd, without a doubt, but delightful. She was also an expert at persuasion — and she promised Hayden seventy bucks.

Money like that was nothing to sneeze at. If Mom forgot to get groceries this week, which was not uncommon, that kind of money would keep Hayden fed and still help with gas. There might even be a little left over to stash in her honeypot. She couldn't walk away from an offer like that.

To be honest, she was even having a little fun. But that was before she came face-to-face with Nolan Martin glowering at her in his kitchen.

He was so damn *pretty*, with his dark hair and mesmerizing eyes and athletic build. She shouldn't have done the thing with the ice cream and spoon, but he kept looking at her like she was some bad seed come to taint his precious home and corrupt his family. She couldn't stop herself from teasing him just a little.

Now she was sitting in a circle with Emmaline and her friends, talking about boys and kissing and other intimate stuff like she was a normal teenage girl who did things like this all the time.

She forced a smile and wondered if they knew.

Did they know they had a fraud in their midst and were just too polite to reveal it? She tried to hide her discomfort and tune back into the conversation going on around her. Or conversations, rather. They had multiple going on at once.

It was difficult to focus, however, knowing Nolan was right down the hall while they were talking about kissing.

This jitteriness wasn't like her. She wasn't someone given to awkwardness or embarrassment. She'd have to care about what others thought. Her skin was too thick for that.

"So, I don't understand what to do with my tongue," Sanjana was saying loudly, motioning to her mouth with Cheetos-dusted fingers. "The one time I got kissed, it was like the guy was pushing a slug in my mouth. I had to fight not to gag."

"Wasn't that in ninth grade? With that guy from band who had the giant Adam's apple?" Lia clutched her knees and laughed at the memory. "I forgot about that."

"Maybe I should hook up with him again?" Sanjana mused. "Maybe he's better at it now?"

"Doubtful," Monica replied. "I think he's been as celibate as you since then. You idiots would be just as lost as you were in ninth grade."

"Yeah," Sanjana agreed. "Plus, he told everyone we made out . . . and that I played with his you-know-what."

Hayden resisted rolling her eyes. She had her work cut out for her if they couldn't even say the word.

"High school guys lying about how much action they actually get? You're joking," Hayden drolly intoned. She'd been the subject of more than one fictional account.

Everyone laughed at her sarcasm.

Except Emmaline. She watched solemnly and scribbled notes on her pad like there would be a test later.

Hayden searched for a way to explain how to execute a good kiss, knowing that's what she was here for. Despite the vibe of camaraderie, she was here to provide a service for them. "Kissing is like dancing. There's a rhythm — a give-and-take between partners . . . at least when you're good at it. But if your partner sucks, well, you're doomed. There's no hope."

"Alex definitely sucked." Sanjana shook her head.

"How do you get good at it?" Monica asked. If Hayden didn't already know the girl was a science geek, she would have figured it out by the way she was studying her. Monica looked at everything like it was an equation to be solved. "Especially if, as you say, your partner is equally inexperienced. Something tells me the average adolescent boy doesn't know what to do with his tongue." She sniffed. "I'm thinking I'll save my first kiss for college."

"Ha! You think some freshman at Stanford is going to come in with a wealth of kissing experience? I'm guessing you're only going to spend time with other bioengineering geeks, and I bet they've spent the last four years of high school studying and not making out," Sanjana scoffed. "If you were *smart*, you'd get some experience in now, and then when you get to college you'll know what you're doing and then you can teach those other geeks a thing or two."

"She's right. It does takes practice to get good at it . . . as with anything. Sports, art," Hayden agreed. "My first kiss —" She stopped and considered it. She hadn't thought about that in years. Her first kiss wasn't actually that bad. She had to be a rare case, though. She didn't want to share that story with them and give them false hope.

The quality of that first kiss probably had something to do with her partner.

There were worse boys to share a first kiss with than Beau Sanders.

To make matters even more remarkable, that kiss had been his first, too. Neither one had known what they were doing, but they had gotten good at it quickly. They'd learned together. It took about five minutes and then they were pretty decent at it. She chuckled at the memory. It had been a typical scorching Texas summer. She'd found enough change under the couch cushions to meet up with Beau and head to the corner store for a hot dog and soda. Neither one of them were eager to go home to their houses, so they went to the local park and clambered up into the playground set. No little kids were around.

It was too hot. One minute she had been sucking down her Dr. Pepper and the next thing she knew, their lips were attached.

"And how do we get practice?" Monica asked reasonably. "It's not like we have guys lined up on standby to kiss us."

"Yeah," Lia murmured. "We don't have boyfriends."

Hayden shook off the memory and smiled at their naiveté. "You don't need to have a boyfriend to get kissed . . . or give a kiss. You don't need the shackles of a relationship for that." She scanned each of their faces. Something told her they would be appalled at the number of kisses she'd shared outside of a relationship. *Um, all her kisses,* in fact, since she didn't do relationships.

They all stared at Hayden with blank looks and then looked at each other, equally stupefied.

Hayden sighed. "You're supposed to be the smartest girls in school." At their bewildered expressions, she motioned to the door. "You've got Beau Sanders in the house. He's one of the biggest players in school. The boy knows how to kiss, and I'm sure he'd oblige and showcase his skill."

They erupted into various reactions, but Monica was the most vocal. "I will not kiss Beau! Who knows where his mouth has been!"

"Well, for starters, it's been on me," Hayden admitted to the group. "His mouth." She felt compelled to clarify.

Everyone gasped.

"You kissed Beau?" Emmaline demanded.

"Yeah. It was in eighth grade. And he was a good kisser back then, so it stands to reason he's only improved his craft."

Lia shook her head almost violently. "I couldn't. Not Beau! He's too . . . too . . ."

Monica crossed her arms over her chest. "You can count me out."

Sanjana, on the other hand, looked tempted. She glanced toward the door. "So . . . I just, what? Walk up to him and plant one on him?"

"No one is kissing Beau," Emmaline cut in. Her face burned bright red. "He's my brother's best friend . . . and like a brother to me. We're not going there with him. That's just too weird."

"Fine." Hayden shrugged indifferently.

"So what do we do for practice then?" Sanjana asked.

The group fell silent and exchanged uncertain glances with each other.

Hayden looked steadily at each of them, wondering why they were being so dense. Did she really have to spell it out? Had no one thought of it already?

"Isn't it obvious?" Hayden glanced around the circle.

They all stared back at her, blinking, clearly not arriving at the conclusion she had reached.

Hayden exhaled. "We practice on each other."

Silence met her announcement. The sound from Emmaline's TV seemed really loud against it. Hayden wasn't sure why it was even on. No one was paying attention to the rerun of *Supernatural*. Especially now, when everyone was gawking at her as if she just proposed they do something criminal. As if it wasn't a totally reasonable proposition.

She let out an exasperated sigh. They really needed to lighten up, and not just when it came to kissing. Although for this group that would be a start. A good start. The claws of their puritanical roots dug deep.

"C'mon, guys. I'm not suggesting we knock off a bank."

"That would be just as extreme," Monica sputtered.

Lia's lips fluttered, searching, unsuccessfully it seemed, for words.

Emmaline found her voice. "Is that . . . *done?* I mean —" She glanced around at her friends.

Hayden rolled her eyes. "I'm not suggesting an orgy. It's fine. Don't look so appalled. You're all friends. What's safer than a little experimenting among those you trust?"

"Huh. That kind of makes sense . . . 'cause it's not as though I've met a guy I can trust," Sanjana mused, clearly referencing Alex of ninth grade band. She glanced at all of them with a shrug. "I'm in."

"I'm in too," Emmaline added.

Lia nodded, her eyes so large they looked ready to bug out of her head.

"Fine," Monica agreed. "But if I say stop —"

"No one is forcing or pressuring anyone into anything here," Hayden quickly assured her. "If you don't want to, then don't." She shrugged. "You asked for my help. That's what I'm trying to do. Help."

"And we're glad for it." Emmaline nodded, looking encouragingly to each girl. "Let's get started."

LESSON #18

PRACTICE MAKES PERFECT.

x   Emmaline   x

They all brushed their teeth before settling down on the floor in a circle. There were lots of giggles as Hayden started explaining the fundamentals.

Emmaline didn't know why she hadn't thought of this before.

What was more nonthreatening than practicing kissing on your best friends? No judgment. No grossness. No worries that gossip of their practice session would be all over the school on Monday. Just safety among friends.

"Sanjana? You want to go first?" Hayden asked.

Sanjana adopted a serious expression and scooted to sit in front of Hayden.

"Now we'll begin with a basic kiss," Hayden announced, looking at each of them. "Because if you can't perform a simple kiss skillfully, you can forget about French-kissing with any finesse."

With her notepad clutched tightly in her hands, Emmaline leaned in close to observe.

"What do I do with my hands?" Sanjana asked, lifting them up from her knees as though she wasn't certain what to do with the appendages.

"You have a lot of options. You can touch the other person on the shoulders or arms . . ." Hayden demonstrated, resting her hands first on Sanjana's shoulders and then her forearms. "Or not touch at all." She dropped them to her sides. "For a kiss this simple it's too intimate and aggressive to reach up and touch or hold the other person's face. You're starting out here. Don't get ahead of yourself."

They all nodded in mute agreement. It was sound logic, and Emmaline scribbled that into her notebook. *Save face-holding for serious intimacy. Not for a casual make-out.*

"All right." Hayden settled her gaze on Sanjana. "Ready?"

Sanjana nodded, actually looking nervous.

Lia let out a panicky giggle and Hayden sent her a reproving glare. Lia pressed her fingers to her lips, punishing them to stillness.

Hayden readjusted her position, scooting closer in front of Sanjana. Sanjana also nudged forward . . . until their knees were touching.

Simultaneously, they leaned in and pressed lips. It lasted maybe three seconds.

"Okay. Very good," Hayden said as she leaned back, sounding like an encouraging grade school teacher. "Now let's still keep it simple, but try moving and shifting our lips a little this time."

Emmaline looked on with interest.

Sanjana and Hayden came together again, not touching anywhere except for their mouths. Hayden nibbled on Sanjana's top lip and then slanted her lips to deepen the kiss a little.

They all watched, riveted to the lesson.

Hayden pulled back "Everyone get that? Take it slow . . . don't dive in like it's a race. Ready to try now?"

Lia and Monica squared off in front of each other as Hayden turned to Emmaline. "Want to try?"

Her heart started to pound faster. "Er. Yes."

Hayden peered closely at her face. "You don't have to do this." She paused and gave her an encouraging smile. "No one should ever feel pressured into doing anything they don't want."

Emmaline nodded. "Sure."

She knew that. She knew no one here was forcing her into doing anything she didn't want. These were her friends. Even Hayden, though she hadn't known her for a long time. This was a safe group.

But she was hovering on the brink . . . about to hit a milestone — her first kiss. That's what had prompted all these lessons, and yet she wanted her first kiss to matter. She didn't want it to be an empty encounter, something to toss away for the sake of practice.

She wanted her first kiss to be with someone who gave her butterflies.

As much as she cared for the girls in this room . . . none of them made her stomach somersault.

She wanted that.

She needed that.

Hayden stared at her in such a knowing way. "Maybe you can just observe and take notes tonight."

Emmaline released a relieved breath but still felt conflicted. Actual hands-on experience was obviously best.

Monica and Lia were oblivious to her internal struggle. They'd already started practicing. In fact, they were practicing quite enthusiastically. Lia lifted a hand to brush the hair back from Monica's shoulder, and then her fingers stayed there, lingering in Monica's hair, caressing the brown curls between her fingertips in a way that seemed almost sensual . . . as though she was really into it.

They kissed for several more moments without appearing inclined to stop.

Hayden glanced at Emmaline's bedside clock, obviously noting the time they were dedicating to this kiss.

Sanjana cleared her throat, as though that might part the two of them, but they didn't look ready to stop.

Emmaline shifted where she sat, starting to feel like a voyeur witnessing something personal and intimate.

Sanjana leaned sideways and whispered with a hand over her mouth, "Maybe they need their own room?"

Suddenly a knock sounded. Emmaline's gaze shot to her bedroom door and then back to the two girls kissing, lost to each other and oblivious to the potential intrusion on their practice session. Maybe the music was too loud. Or maybe they just didn't care.

There was one more knock and then the door opened, swinging wide to reveal Nolan and Beau in the threshold.

"Hey, we're going for another pizza. Can Hayden move her car so we can back —"

The rest of Nolan's words died and then he and Beau just stood there, gaping at Lia and Monica in a full make-out sesh.

The girls must have finally sensed their audience. They eased apart, faces still very close, almost cheek-to-cheek, as they turned to find everyone staring at them.

"Hey," Monica greeted, her eyes a little bright, her voice a little breathless.

"What's going on?" Nolan demanded, looking thoroughly perplexed.

"Nothing, Nolan," Emmaline snapped. "Did I tell you that you could come in?"

"Emma!" He looked again at Lia and Monica. "They're kissing and you're sitting around watching."

Sanjana started laughing.

Lia and Monica joined in, their laughter much quieter, almost nervous as they exchanged shy glances with each other.

"Oh, just tell him, Emmaline," Sanjana managed to get out amid her laughter. She pointed at Nolan and Beau. "If you could see your faces. Priceless. If you had come in earlier, you would have seen me and Hayden kissing."

Nolan's eyes widened. *Great.* Now he was convinced they were having some kind of orgy in here. "Sanjana," Emmaline snapped.

"Oh, just tell him," Monica agreed, pushing her glasses up her nose. "It's healthy experimentation. Nothing to worry about."

Nolan pressed his fingers to his temple. "What. Is. Happening."

Emmaline looked to Beau, hoping he might help her. He'd been silent this whole time. For him, a couple girls making out was probably just another Saturday night.

Sanjana chose that moment to answer Nolan's maybe rhetorical question. "Emmaline hired Hayden to give us lessons."

Oh no no no no no.

She did not just tell her brother that. In front of Beau no less.

Emmaline punched Sanjana in the arm. Even Hayden's usually passive expression cracked. She looked suddenly wary, watching Nolan like she didn't know how he would react to that news.

"Lessons? On what?" He glanced around like he expected to see textbooks and laptops open or something.

Goodness. He wanted them to spell it out.

Sanjana was still rubbing her arms. "Lessons on seduction. Tonight, we were specifically working on kissing."

Nolan closed his eyes in one long, weary blink. He looked a lot older than eighteen in that moment. It really was like getting busted by a father.

For a moment she wondered what her dad would have done in this situation. He would probably have backed out of the room with a stammering apology, too embarrassed to stick around and interrogate a bunch of girls.

Not Nolan. He looked ready to lose it . . . and he never got mad. Never raised his voice or lost his temper.

When he opened his eyes again, he was staring at Hayden with enough contempt to blast the wrapper off a lollipop. "You're teaching my sister how to seduce a guy? So. In other words . . . you're teaching her how to be like you?" The implication was clear.

To be like Hayden was unacceptable.

Everyone fell silent then. The only sound was the music from her laptop.

"Nolan," she reprimanded in a hushed voice, fearful he'd crossed a line and hurt Hayden's feelings.

Hayden might be tough, but words could wound, and the way Nolan was acting was not okay.

A muscle ticked near Hayden's eye, the only sign of emotion she gave. She didn't react, but Emmaline knew something was simmering very close to the surface. This whole situation could get ugly if she didn't do something to diffuse it right now.

"It wasn't her idea," Emmaline blurted, deliberately not looking Beau's way. If she was making this admission, she was not looking at him. She'd been crushing on him too long to have to endure his expression right now.

It was mortifying enough that he now knew she had to *hire* someone to help her attract a guy. More mortifying than her brother finding out. Because it all boiled down to one thing.

Beau was *not* her brother.

He was a guy. A guy she'd always had feelings for. An attractive guy who always smelled good and had no problem walking around without his shirt, showcasing his washboard abs. He didn't need to know the level of her desperation. If he looked at her with pity, she might have to move schools, change her name, and don a permanent disguise.

Nolan turned on Emmaline now, which had been the plan, she guessed: get him to stop being so rude to Hayden. Except now she felt a little nervous to have his full attention. "Why would you come up with a scheme like this?"

Why? *Why?*

Wasn't it obvious?

The nervousness turned to outrage at his question. "Because, look at me!" She threw her arms wide, forgetting everyone else in the room at that moment. "I need something to happen . . . I want to have a life in high school. A life you seriously keep stopping me from having. I'm home every Saturday night because I don't have anything else to do. I've never been asked out on a date, much less been kissed by a guy."

His expression softened and he reached for her arm. "Emma —"

"No!" She yanked her arm away. Had she just been thinking that Hayden's emotions simmered near the surface? Well, now Emmaline's emotions were overflowing. "Don't act like you care. If I ever try to do anything fun, you're always there shutting me down, while you get to go off and have fun whenever you want. If I just want to be a girl and go to parties and fool around and kiss a random guy, I can't! Because you're my brother and you scare everyone away."

"Good!" he snapped.

"No! No, not good!" She shoved him in the chest, but he didn't budge. Her hands were like flies battering at the wall of him. "I want you to butt out of my life! I can't wait for you to go to college."

He stared at her in shock.

The words just popped out. She didn't mean them. Not really, but they were out there now.

She looked around, her heart beating a wild drum in her ears. Everyone stared at her like she had lost her mind. And she felt like she had. A little. She'd just gone off in front of her friends. In front of Hayden, a girl she was starting to admire. In front of Beau, a guy she worked so hard not to crush on. In front of her brother, who actually meant a lot to her, despite her outburst. But it'd all become too much.

With a choked little sound, she fled.

LESSON #19

BE CAREFUL FLIRTING. IT'S ALL FUN AND GAMES UNTIL YOU CATCH FEELINGS FOR SOMEONE.

x Beau x

Beau should have stayed home tonight. If he had he wouldn't be standing in the middle of this mess, feeling a little shell-shocked and wondering what was happening.

The Martin family wasn't dysfunctional. He knew dysfunction. He lived it every day. Sure, they'd lost their dad, but that had only bonded them. It had only made them stronger. Nolan and Emmaline did not fight. They weren't those kind of siblings. They had their shit together.

So the fact that they were at odds now didn't make a whole lot of sense to him, but he felt an overriding desperation to fix it, to help set everything back to rights.

Emmaline rushed out of her room.

Nolan started to go after her, but Beau put a hand on his chest, stopping him. "I'll go. Let me talk to her."

It seemed the better idea. If one was to believe Emmaline's own words, she wasn't exactly a fan of Nolan right now, and Nolan wasn't being his usual calm self either. They needed a time-out.

Nolan must have recognized that fact. He nodded stiffly. "Okay."

Beau left everyone behind in the bedroom. There was no sign of Emmaline on the second floor hallway, so he took the stairs down to the first. She wasn't in the kitchen or living room. He even checked the dining room and the rarely used home office. He called her name, mindful not to be too loud. He didn't want to disturb Mrs. Martin. No answer.

She wasn't downstairs, and he doubted that she'd taken refuge in her mom's room.

Remembering that Savannah was gone, sleeping over at a friend's for the night, he went back upstairs to check the youngest Martin's room. He knocked lightly before pushing open the door. Sure enough, there she was, cuddled amid an army of pillows and stuffed animals covering every inch of Savannah's bed.

"Hey," he said softly, closing the door behind him.

Emmaline sat up swiftly, looking at him warily, but without tears. At least there was that. She wasn't crying. He hated tears. He'd rather deal with fury. Angry words and punches he knew how to cope with. Chalk it up to experience.

"I'm so embarrassed," she said quickly.

He breathed easier. Embarrassment he could handle too. "Aw, Pigeon. Don't be." He sank down beside her on the bed.

She was hugging one of the ugliest stuffed animals he'd ever seen. It was purple . . . and maybe a dragon. Possibly a bear. There was no telling what the thing was. It had glittery horns and snake eyes.

"Who's your friend?" He tapped one of its possible-bear ears.

She looked down at it and shrugged. "Nolan won it for Savannah at a carnival."

Of course he did. Nolan was that type of big brother. The sort who took his sisters to carnivals and won them stuffed animals. Family mattered. It was everything to Nolan, and for a moment Beau felt a pang of longing.

It wasn't the first time. The feeling struck him whenever he was with the Martin family. Whenever he witnessed their camaraderie, their loyalty and love for one another. It was evident in all their interactions.

He'd never had that connection with anyone. There was just his mom, and there was definitely no closeness there, despite the times he had tried to bridge the gap between them. She was too bitter and jaded and resentful of all the things in her life that had gone wrong — and in her eyes Beau was one of those things.

Sometimes people were so broken, there was no mending them. It was a lesson he had learned at an early age.

As much as the Martins included him, he was only ever on the fringes, watching, looking in. He'd never be one of them.

He was all alone.

"I kind of made an ass out of myself," she confessed in a small voice.

"That's okay. I do that all the time." He bumped her shoulder with his own.

"Great." She grimaced. "I'm like you now. Should I go out and get suspended from school? Arrested?"

"*Hey!* I was suspended a long time ago, as a freshman, and I've never been arrested," he said in mock indignation, but really he was just glad to see her cracking a joke.

She smiled for a moment and then it faded from her face. "I don't want him to go away." It was a change of subject, but Beau immediately knew what she meant.

"He knows that." He looped an arm around her.

"I'm not sure he does. I mean, why would he after my little word vomit in there?" She waved in the direction of her room.

"Just tell him you didn't mean it. I promise, by tomorrow, neither one of you will remember any of it."

"Maybe." She dropped her head to rest on his shoulder, and he inhaled a thin layer of mint toothpaste over the chemical aroma of chlorine.

And then the image came, unbidden, of her in that bikini. The one she was *still* wearing.

The strap of her bathing suit was unmistakable through her shirt. He could feel the heavy knot of strings she had tied at the back, branding his arm where it touched him. It would be tricky to undo. At least for her. He'd have no problem with it though. Or she could just remove her bikini top by pulling it over her head and squeezing out of it.

Yes, he went there.

He swallowed as a vision of Emmaline stripping off her bathing suit filled his mind, singed his eyeballs — and it wasn't even real. Just a fantasy. He blinked, fighting to get rid of it.

Help. Me.

She exhaled and her moist breath warmed his neck. He froze, his lungs seizing, no air going in or out of him. Every muscle in his body locked tight from the horror of what was happening.

He was lusting after his best friend's sister. A girl he had always thought he loved like a sister of his own. He didn't want these unbrotherly ideas in his head.

Especially not when he was alone with her in a dark room and on a bed.

He inhaled thinly through his nose, telling himself it was okay. As long as he didn't act. As long as no one knew what he was feeling. As long as his gutter thoughts remained buried deep. This was normal, he reminded himself; he was a guy, after all. The night had just been weird.

He swallowed hard and fought to regain his breath.

She started talking again. "I'm not wrong though. Nolan casts a long shadow."

He tried to process her words, but his thoughts were muddled from the nearness of her. It was like she was speaking another language.

Her head shifted on his shoulder and he had the sense she was looking up at him.

He looked down and then quickly away, realizing that brought their mouths much too close. Her words finally penetrated, finally making sense. "Someday you'll be glad you have a brother looking out for you," he said diplomatically.

A brother who would kick Beau's ass if he knew what he was thinking about Emmaline.

She sighed. "I know. I'm glad now, truly. I just don't need him to be so protective. It's suffocating." She straightened abruptly, lifting her head from his shoulder and grabbing hold of his hands. "You can talk to him."

"What?" He tried tugging his hands free. "No —"

"At least get him to lay off me about Hayden. You know her. Tell him she's a decent person and not a bad influence." She frowned. "I don't need him getting it into his head to tell Mom that Hayden is —"

"He wouldn't do that." Beau was sure of that. It seemed gossipy and the height of judgmental. Besides, Nolan didn't like to burden his mother. She worked hard as a surgical nurse for a hospital in town, and Nolan would take on the weight of the world rather than bother her.

"Come on." She gave his hands a beseeching shake, her entire body bouncing in front of him, quivering with eagerness. He fought to keep his eyes on her face and not look down. "Nolan trusts you."

Yeah, he trusts you not to check out his sister's rack.

She continued, "Just tell him Hayden is cool. You knew each other when y'all were kids, right? She told me that." Her expression turned sly. "She even told me you were her first kiss."

His face went hot, which was a surprise. He was not easily embarrassed, but the idea of Emmaline talking about his first kiss felt too personal. "She told you that? You were talking about me?"

"Yeah," she replied slowly, uncertainly, as though picking up on his discomfort. "It was all in the name of research. We were discussing good kissing, *good* kissers —"

"And I came up?" he snapped, before managing to even out his tone. "Well, then. Where did I rank?" He said it like a joke but inside he wasn't amused.

Her hands softened on his, her thumbs stroking in small reassuring circles. "Good," she replied in a quiet voice, as though he needed that assurance from her. "Not that I expected any less, but Hayden vouched that you're a good kisser, Beau."

His name on her lips felt like a caress. God help him, but her eyes moved to his mouth . . . and then *he* looked at *her* mouth.

How had he never noticed the perfect shape of it before?

Not that I expected any less.

So, she thought about him and kissing? That was . . . interesting. And dangerous, because he shouldn't find it so very interesting.

They sat close. The aroma of chlorine swirled around him, a strangely heady and intoxicating scent — who knew? Maybe it just morphed into something else when it came into contact with her skin.

The air crackled between them. One spark and they could both go up in flames. He was sure of it. It would be so easy to ignite that fire. He just needed to dip his head.

And that would be a colossal mistake. Still, he felt his head inching down.

Alarms bells went off in his ears.

Abort! Abort! Abort!

He slid his hands free from hers and stood. He rubbed his suddenly perspiring palms over his thighs.

Emmaline blinked up at him, adjusting her position on the bed, and he wondered how all her movements had suddenly become so sinuous and so seductive to him. What was going on? Best to retreat.

He backed away. "You and Nolan will be fine."

She angled her head, worry lines knitting her smooth forehead. "So you won't talk to him?"

"Ah. Sure." He nodded. It was easier just to agree. "Yeah, I will."

She smiled. "Great. He listens to you. That will really help . . . because I'm not going to stop hanging out with Hayden."

Translation? She wasn't going to stop hanging out with Hayden and learning all her tricks on how to attract guys, which he was starting to think would only translate to misery for him.

As far as he was concerned, she didn't need any lessons.

Beau already found her attractive.

Shit. This was bad. *Really* bad for him. The last thing he needed was for her to become *more* enticing.

Then he reminded himself that what he wanted didn't matter here. In fact, what he wanted was totally off the table. This wasn't about him. He didn't control Emmaline. She was her own person. She could share her lips with whomever she liked. It was none of his business, and he needed to stop thinking about her lips — stop thinking that he'd like her to share her lips with him.

Nolan Martin was his best friend. Emmaline Martin was like a sister to him.

He winced. Maybe if he said that enough times he would start to believe it.

APPEARANCES CAN BE DECEIVING . . .
JUST LIKE REPUTATIONS.

x   Nolan   x

After Emmaline stormed from the room and Beau went after her, Nolan was left to deal with the aftermath: four girls staring up at him who
he had just interrupted in the middle of kissing lessons. They had been
practicing on each other. At the behest of Hayden Vargas, who fancied
herself some kind of guru on the matter, apparently.

He winced. Actually, he guessed a lot of people would attest that
she was an authority on the matter — if her reputation was to be believed. Not that he believed half of what people said. Or even the majority, especially now that he had spent some time with her.

Everyone always thought he was some perfect guy, but here he was,
thinking about Hayden when he had a "perfect" girlfriend. Not all rep-
utations, good or bad, were to be believed.

Still, when it came to his sister, he didn't like to take chances. And
he shouldn't. The promise he'd made to his father left no room for
chances.

Of all the things he imagined taking place after dark in his house, and all the reasons he suspected Emmaline had struck up a friendship with Hayden, *this* had *never* entered his mind. Sure, he and Priscilla had been pretty intimate, but never when anyone was home. Never would he risk his sisters or mother walking in on them. It would be an embarrassing situation all around. He would spare them that.

Never had he worried Emmaline might be the one to step out of bounds. Naively, he had thought the most illicit thing to take place in his sister's bedroom was a game of Ouija.

Nolan was a caretaker. That's who he was ... what he did. He had a duty to protect his mom, Savannah, and especially right now, Emmaline — even if that meant protecting her from herself and her bad decisions.

His chest pinched with discomfort because Hayden was also starting to bring forth that protective urge in him. He felt this misplaced longing to look after Hayden, too — even if she wasn't family and she seemed the complete opposite of vulnerable. Even if she didn't want or need his help.

She didn't want or need his help. That's what he needed to remember. Emmaline was his priority and she was obviously going through something.

He cleared his throat awkwardly and turned his attention to the girl at the center of it all — Hayden Vargas.

This is all her fault. The thought flew through his mind even as he knew it was unfair. He wanted to blame someone.

When had Hayden agreed to tutor his sister? Had she agreed after he'd spent the night with her and then asked her to keep quiet about it? He knew he'd insulted her. If he could take back the words, he would, but it was done. Had Hayden leaped at the opportunity to tutor his sister knowing it would get under his skin?

He knew he was being irrational, but Emmaline had *hired* her. His little sister thought she was somehow *lacking* and needed to engage the services of Hayden Vargas to help her be more . . . *more*. He didn't even know what. Enticing? Sexy?

This was his sister. He didn't want people talking about her the same way they did Hayden.

If it were left at just this — Emmaline kissing her friends in the safety of her bedroom — he wouldn't care. He wouldn't worry.

But he did worry.

Evidently this was some kind of practice run. Emmaline wanted to take her newfound kissing skills and try them out there in the world.

Well, that scared the hell out of him. He knew how the minds of teenage guys worked. Hell, a lot of grown men weren't any better.

He'd heard things come out of his coaches' mouths that would scandalize his gray-haired grandmother. His own mother would probably reconsider letting him play sports if she knew.

He spent plenty of time in the locker room. He knew how boys could be. He knew what "boys will be boys" really meant. It was just an excuse for bad behavior, for guys to be predators, and he wanted to protect his sister from that and offer her advice and guidance, just like their dad would want.

Not all guys were like that, of course. He knew this reaction was more to do with his own fears. Yeah, he was being overprotective, but he wanted his sister to be safe.

"Can I speak to you? Alone?" he asked Hayden.

She eyed him warily but nodded.

He turned and led her from Emmaline's room into his bedroom across the hall. Once they were in his room, he shut the door and faced her.

"How much?" he asked calmly, keeping a careful distance between them.

She looked confused. "How much what?"

"How much is my sister paying you?"

"Oh. That." She squared her shoulders and took her time answering, as though weighing whether or not she was about to reveal something she shouldn't. Did she view herself as some kind of a professional? Did kissing gurus operate under a code of confidentiality? "Seventy dollars. For tonight."

He nodded. "Okay then. I'll pay you a hundred dollars to walk away."

"Excuse me?" She uncrossed her arms.

"Hundred dollars to forget about my sister and these lessons."

She shook her head. "You're that scared of your sister coming into her own?"

"She's not coming into *her* own . . . you're teaching her to be —"

"To be what?" she challenged, her voice hard, angry.

"You're teaching her to be like you." That was fair to say. They'd all admitted as much as that to him.

She laughed harshly. "So you're afraid I'm going to turn your sister into a slut."

It wasn't the first time she flung that word at him, but it was still jarring. It was an ugly word and he'd never explicitly applied it to any girl. He lived among females. He had more respect for women than that, but he heard the word all the time. At school. In the locker room. At parties. He heard it and just carried on as though it didn't matter. He was starting to realize passivity could still be part of the problem. "I didn't say that."

"You didn't have to."

"I didn't say it. I didn't think it."

She crossed her arms again and looked at him in distrust. "I know guys like you, either from school or the neighborhood or creeping around my mom . . . 'nice guys' — they act like they're so different, but I know what's in their heads. And I know what's in *your* head."

"You don't know my mind. Maybe you're used to that . . . to guys that think that way, but I'm not one of them."

She stared at him blandly, looking unimpressed.

Sighing, he reminded himself that this wasn't about him. He wasn't trying to persuade Hayden Vargas to like him — and the quickest way of making her put her guard up was by insisting he "wasn't like other guys." Words weren't much if actions didn't back them up.

Again, this wasn't about him. This was about what was going on with Emmaline.

He continued, "These guys you know? The ones who think some girls are sluts? Is that who you're getting my sister ready for?" She flinched and he knew he had hit a truth even she hadn't considered until he said the words. "Has it occurred to you that my sister flying under the radar in high school might not be a bad thing?"

"Has it occurred to you that you should let her make her own choices, her own mistakes?"

He scoffed. "Don't act like you're looking out for her interests when you're doing this for money. Your reasons are totally selfish."

"And you're not being selfish?" she charged, stabbing a finger in his direction.

"Not in this, I'm not. I'm thinking of Emmaline."

"Really?" she mocked. "You haven't considered yourself at all? You're not embarrassed for your sister to hang out with a *skank* like me? That potential shame hasn't crossed your mind? Isn't that the same embarrassment you felt waking up at my house? Isn't that why you asked me to keep it quiet?"

Nolan inhaled a breath for patience. "It's not like that. And would you stop calling yourself names and then laying them at my feet like I've said them?"

She stepped closer, her voice dropping. "Do I make you uncomfortable, Nolan?"

Yes. Yes, she did.

"Of course not."

"Admit it. What bothers you so much is my reputation . . . and that I might taint your sister, and, thereby, taint *you*."

"No," he said calmly, holding his ground as she eased up to him, her body brushing his.

He jerked back a step.

She angled her head sharply, her expression equal parts curious and cunning, with a face free of makeup. This close, he could see a faint smudge of mascara edging her top and bottom lashes, the only remnant after her time spent in the pool. It made her look human. Vulnerable. Somewhat at odds with the tough energy she exuded. She inched much too close to him.

He took another step back.

Hayden smiled widely. "Are you afraid of me, Nolan Martin?"

He scoffed. "Of course not." His voice was firm, but alarm bells started going off in his brain. He was afraid of something. Maybe himself?

Why was she standing so close to him?

"You don't like my influence on your sister . . ." She flattened a hand on his chest and he felt her touch like a brand. "What about my influence on you?"

He backed up another step and collided with his desk.

He must look a coward, backpedaling from someone he outweighed by fifty pounds at least.

She followed with one more step, closing in, her hand still on his chest, directly over his heart. Her gaze dropped to where they were connected, and then back up to his face. "Your heart is racing. Why is that?"

"What are you doing?" he rasped.

"Just wondering if this is even about your sister and me at all. Wondering if it's about you and me?"

You and me.

No such combination existed. There was only Nolan and Priscilla. Ask anyone.

He inhaled and tasted that indefinable *other* that was quintessentially Hayden. Until that moment he didn't realize he knew her scent. He didn't realize he had marked it and cataloged it in his head as Hayden Vargas.

Her upturned face was so close, and he had to face the truth.

It wasn't that he couldn't move away.

He just didn't want to.

LESSON #21

SAVE FACE-HOLDING FOR SERIOUS INTIMACY. NOT FOR A CASUAL MAKE-OUT.

x   Hayden   x

What am I doing? Hayden inched her face a little higher. A little closer. Nolan was tall, but she wasn't a short girl. She used to bemoan that fact. Not a year of school went by that a basketball coach didn't sniff around all five feet nine inches of her hopefully. Laughable, really. Even if she wanted to play sports, being involved in extracurricular activities required a level of support from parents that she just didn't have. Plus, she needed to work, which didn't leave much time for sports.

It was almost as if Hayden were floating outside of her body. She'd wanted to prove a point, teach him a lesson of his own. But without conscious thought, she had closed the last bit of distance separating her from Nolan and brushed her mouth over his, testing him, soft as a brushstroke. Testing herself, too, she supposed.

He held himself still, and that was different. She usually didn't need to coax a guy into kissing her. His lips quivered under hers, but otherwise they didn't move. He didn't kiss her back. He didn't grab her or crush his mouth to hers or jump on her like some overeager puppy.

She pulled back, staring at him in awe. And perhaps a little bit of confusion, but whether it was at him or herself, she couldn't decide.

His liquid-dark eyes glittered in the shadows of the room as she assessed him. He really had the deepest, most beautiful eyes. She wondered what was going on behind them. What was he thinking?

She shifted her fingers on his solid chest. His heartbeat was still going mad against her palm. He was affected, and that gave her a small thrill . . . made her feel powerful—as seductive as his sister thought her to be.

Despite Hayden's bold words, she always thought he failed to see her, or he looked through her blindly. Or around her. Or over her. Never really *her*. Never Hayden. Just the myth of her. What people said about her.

Nolan wasn't moving away though. Of course, she had backed him into his desk, but a big guy like him could stop her or pull away.

She knew it was madness, but she moved her face closer again, stopping just shy of kissing him. "Is this okay?" she whispered. She'd been around a lot of people in her life who were takers. They took and never asked. She would not be one of them.

A ragged breath escaped him. "Yeah."

She pressed her mouth to his almost tentatively.

She had started all this as a way to rattle him, to push him just a little for judging her, but now it felt like something else. Something bigger. Something she was doing to herself—her own torment. Because if he rejected her . . . spurned her, well, it wouldn't feel great.

Nolan's previous restraint cracked, just a fissure, as he bent his head a fraction, making it so she didn't have to stretch up on her toes to reach him.

His lips were warm and dry and perfectly soft. Who knew a guy's mouth could be this soft? This gentle?

Hayden deepened the kiss, unconsciously adding her other hand to his chest. He brought up his own to cover hers to anchor them, his palms completely swallowing her hands as he kissed her back, slowly at first but then with increasing pressure.

Ah, hell. He was into it. Into *her* . . . and she reveled in it, feeling as though she had won something.

His lips, the warm clasp of his palms on the back of her hands, the strength and solidity of him against her — it all went straight to her head in a way that she never experienced before. And she was used to kissing guys.

But this felt different.

Despite the rumors of her wild ways, she had only ever been drunk once. When she was fourteen, her mother had a bunch of her questionable friends over for a New Year's party. They had all enjoyed pumping Hayden with alcohol and sitting back to watch her antics. Like she was some little circus monkey performing tricks for them. They'd laughed and encouraged her, applauding.

She remembered their laughter when she fell down the front porch steps and bloodied her nose on the concrete. They had thought that was uproariously funny.

She'd hurt all over the next day. Her entire body felt like it had been through hell.

That was the last time she'd consumed alcohol, but she recalled the pleasant fuzzy-headed sensation leading up to the moment when she crashed and burned. The feeling of invincibility, of flying and not quite belonging to her own body. It had been euphoric.

She felt that way now kissing Nolan. Euphoric. Like she was flying.

Her hands slid up his chest and around his neck while his hands went to her face with a groan she took for approval.

His warm palms cupped her cheeks, his thumbs dragging in small circles over her skin. He held her face as though touching her was as necessary as breathing.

Save face-holding for serious intimacy. Not for a casual make-out.

Her lips stilled. *All* of her stilled as her own advice from earlier replayed in her head.

Oh no. This wasn't supposed to happen.

Nolan sensed her withdrawal and lifted his mouth from hers.

His dark eyes flickered over her face just as some distant cries of excitement rose up from somewhere in the house.

She gave herself a mental shake and backed away, letting his hands drop from her face.

Feet stomped on the stairs, accompanied by excited voices.

"Hayden," he whispered.

She shook her head. She didn't know what he wanted to say — what that simple utterance of her name even meant. She didn't want to know.

The shouts carrying through the house provided a welcome distraction. "Snow! Snow!"

She looked over his shoulder to the window beyond his desk and saw what all the commotion was about. Snow flurries.

She had been in elementary school the last time it snowed. She remembered it because she and her mom had made snow angels in the yard. It was a good day. A good memory. Rare.

"It's snowing." She nodded to the window, stating the somewhat obvious.

He turned to look and she took it as her cue to whirl around, determined to be gone before he faced forward again.

She hurried downstairs and joined everyone else outside, shifting her bare feet on the cold sidewalk as she raised her face to the falling snow.

No one paid her any attention, thankfully. The focus was on the snow.

The icy flakes felt good on her overheated face.

Nolan arrived next to her. "Here." He dropped a pair of shoes beside her feet.

"Those aren't mine."

"I know. They're mine. Slip them on before your feet freeze."

She crossed her arms tightly against the cold, refusing to accept his shoes.

He laughed low. "You really are stubborn. They're just shoes."

She locked her jaw, watching as Sanjana rushed into the yard and started trying to scrape snow off the leaves of a bush to form a meager snowball.

Emmaline laughed at her and shook her head. "There's not enough snow yet, you fool!"

Hayden's feet were starting to actually burn from the cold. She really should put the shoes on, but she couldn't do it.

She turned to go back inside the house.

She should go home. If it wasn't so late, it wouldn't even be a question. However, in her mind, going home would be admitting that Nolan got under her skin. And what would Emmaline think if she bailed on her? She'd agreed to tutor her.

Hayden moved to the living room window and watched everyone through the open shutters.

Well, not everyone. Beau stepped up beside her, watching the others alongside her.

Sanjana jumped on Emmaline's back and rode her like a horse.

The two girls galloped through the falling snow, laughing and shouting loudly, indifferent to the neighbors they were probably waking. Even Lia and Monica were getting into it.

"How long until someone calls the cops?" Hayden asked Beau.

He chuckled. "It won't happen. Everyone on this street loves the Martins. They have barbecues and block parties. Whenever a kid falls and scrapes a knee, they run them over here so that Mrs. Martin can patch them up."

"For real? Block parties?" She shook her head with a snort. "Definitely isn't like our neighborhood, is it?"

"No, it's not," he agreed.

A few more moments passed as they observed the antics of Emmaline and her friends in silence. Then Beau asked, "What are you doing here, Hayden? Is it really the money?"

"You say that with such skepticism. Like money is so *not* important. But we come from the same world, Beau." A world where lack of money only added to the misery. She didn't need to explain such things to him, but she did it anyway. Maybe his closeness with the Martins had blinded him. "You know it matters."

"This is causing a lot of trouble. Is it worth it?"

She resisted asking, *Trouble for who?*

She stared through the shutters at Emmaline. She was a nice girl, and she thought Hayden could help her. She wanted some pointers from Hayden so that she could come out of her shell. That wasn't asking a lot. Wasn't she entitled to that? Couldn't Emmaline make that simple decision regarding her own life?

Her gaze drifted to Nolan Martin.

The boy could kiss — and that had absolutely *nothing* to do with what she was doing here. She had to keep telling herself that. He had a girlfriend. She had to keep telling herself that, too. She'd never fooled around with someone else's boyfriend before. At least not knowingly. She wasn't looking for more drama in her life. She didn't love that she had done it . . . didn't love that while she was kissing him, his lips belonged to someone else.

"There won't be any trouble," she said as Nolan turned his head to look at the house, directly at the window. Her breath caught even as she told herself it was too dark for him to see her standing there.

Yet she felt certain that he did know she was right there on the other side of the glass — that he could see her.

And she felt certain he knew she was staring back at him.

She turned and took herself to Emmaline's room and waited for them to join her.

She would be good. She would focus on why she was here in the first place. Under no circumstances would she think about what she just did with Nolan. It would not affect her. Instead, she would play the part of a "normal" girl spending the night at a slumber party — as though she did these things all the time and didn't just watch them on TV.

They piled back into the room, still excited over the snow, and Hayden faked it. She pretended to be like the rest of them, staying up and answering their hypothetical questions and going to bed later than she ever would. With school and her job, she valued her sleep, but tonight she acted as carefree as these girls and stayed up way too late.

She woke with a foot in her face — another reason why sleepovers weren't her thing. Why be crammed into a double bed when she could have a bed to herself? She pushed the offending foot away with a grunt, thankful at least that it didn't stink.

Hayden lifted her head and scanned the room, locating Emmaline on the floor, curled under a SpongeBob blanket. Sanjana and Monica were nowhere in sight.

Lia's foot drifted back into her face and she shoved at it. "Gah! Enough with the foot already."

Emmaline stirred on the floor. Lifting her head, she rubbed at her eyes and looked around. She took in Hayden and Lia on the bed. "Sanjana?" she called out, twisting her head toward her bathroom door. "Monica?"

"They left," Lia muttered. "Parents picked them up hours ago."

Hayden didn't know exactly what time they all fell asleep. It had been well after three in the morning. They'd watched a movie and gone over a few more kissing techniques. It was why she was here, after all. That hadn't changed.

Groaning, Hayden pushed herself up. "I have to get to work."

"Aw, do you have to? I thought we could run to get some dough-nuts." Emmaline propped herself up on her elbows. "My treat."

Of course, it had to be her treat. Spending money on doughnuts wasn't an option for Hayden.

Hayden stood up and started folding her bedding. "It's been . . . fun, but I really need to go." She didn't know if fun was the word, and she knew she didn't sound convincing.

"Can we hang out tomorrow?" Emmaline asked hopefully.

Hayden hated to crush her, but this wasn't good for her. Money withstanding, she felt the need to put distance between herself and the Martin family. "I'm pretty busy."

"What about my lessons? We've only just started. I've got a lot left to learn."

"I don't know, Emmaline," Hayden hedged. Now that Nolan knew about it, she didn't feel right coaching his sister. "This is . . ."

"Is it because of last night? My brother?" She blew out a quick breath. "Don't let him intimidate you."

Hayden met her gaze directly. "He doesn't." Yes, he made her feel things, but he didn't intimidate her.

"Wow. It's like a winter wonderland out there," Lia announced from where she stood peering out of the blinds.

Right then Hayden's phone dinged. She frowned as she read the text from her manager.

"What is it?"

"Work. They're closed for the day because of the snow."

"Yep," Lia declared, still looking out the window. "Nothing will shut down a Texas town quicker than snow or a hurricane."

"So, you don't have to go to work now," Emmaline said brightly. "You can stay."

Now that her excuse was gone, Hayden took her time answering. "I guess." It was that or come clean about not wanting to do the lessons anymore — and why. Plus, she figured the roads needed to melt a little before she drove all the way home in her less-than-reliable wheels.

"C'mon. I bet there's a doughnut shop open." Emmaline flung back her blanket and hurried to get dressed.

"Hopefully Sunrise Doughnuts — I'll call ahead and make sure." Lia started scrolling through her phone.

Hayden drifted to the window to look out at the world as Emmaline changed inside her closet like a sixth grader uncomfortable stripping off her clothes in front of other girls. Hayden had no such modesty, fumbling for her clothes in her backpack and getting dressed in the middle of the room. Grabbing her makeup bag, she moved into the bathroom and took a moment to stare at her reflection before finally deciding to pile her dark hair atop her head and secure it with sticks.

She applied her makeup: eyeliner, eye shadow, mascara. She swiped a deep red over her lips and then nodded at her reflection, feeling better. Ready to face the world.

"Doughnut shop is open," Lia announced in triumph, hanging up her phone as Emmaline emerged in a T-shirt and leggings.

They left her bedroom and bumped into Mrs. Martin coming up the stairs with a basket of laundry. "There's our sleepyheads." She looked them over with a slight frown, clearly observing they were all dressed to go out. "Where are you all going?"

"Hayden is taking us to get doughnuts. You want one, Mom? Or two?"

Mom's frown deepened. "The roads are pretty nasty out there, Emmaline. I'm not sure I want you to leave the house today."

"Mom," she said.

Emmaline's mother turned her attention to Hayden. "Do you have tire chains, Hayden?"

Tire chains? They lived in Texas. It hadn't snowed here in years, and when it did, it hardly required chains.

"*Mom.*" Emmaline dragged out the single syllable.

"No, ma'am," Hayden replied, trying to act normal in the face of parental interrogation.

"I'll drive them, Mom. My truck has good tires."

They all swung around, looking down at Nolan standing at the base of the stairs, one of his hands gripping the balustrade.

"Great." Emmaline looked to her mother, evidently willing to forget she was mad at her brother in this moment. "Okay, Mom?"

Mrs. Martin bit her lip. Her dark eyes, so like Nolan's, flitted back and forth between Emmaline and her brother, considering them both. She shifted her basket to her hip so she could hold it with one hand.

With her free hand, she pointed a finger at Nolan. "Precious cargo, No-lan. Yourself included. You got me?"

"Yes, ma'am." He nodded.

They all grabbed their coats near the door and traipsed out of the house together.

Hayden carefully trained her gaze to steer clear of Nolan, wondering at this awkwardness. When was the last time she felt this uncomfortable around a guy? Or anyone? She didn't like it. She didn't want it.

"Where's Beau?" Emmaline asked as they rounded to the front of the house and walked down the icy driveway.

They all picked their steps carefully. Unlike Nolan. He strode purposefully ahead, his long legs eating up the distance to his truck with no fear of slipping, reminding Hayden that this guy was a superior athlete.

"Went home," he replied.

Emmaline nodded and slid into the back seat. Lia joined her, leaving the front seat for Hayden. *Great.*

"You two should get to know each other. I bet you have more in common than you think," Emmaline chirped from the back seat.

Earth. Open. Swallow.

Heat flushed through Hayden. She knew what Emmaline was trying to do. She was hoping Nolan would decide Hayden wasn't a terrible influence. It wouldn't work, of course. They'd already had a night together where they got to know each other better. Hayden had stupidly thought they could be friends then. She'd been wrong.

Nolan didn't say anything.

Hayden sat rigidly, looking straight ahead, glad that she'd applied her makeup. She had that armor at least.

She felt Nolan turn to look at her when they stopped at a red light. She held her breath, willing him to look away.

He was probably wondering what she was doing in his front seat and how to get rid of her. The light turned green and the stare ended.

The doughnut shop was only a few miles from the house, and, true to his word, Nolan drove carefully. The parking lot was packed though, and they had to park on the street. The Tasty Freeze might be closed, but plenty of people were comfortable driving on the nasty roads, venturing out to the few businesses bold enough to open their doors. Hayden fell in beside Emmaline as they walked, leaving Nolan to walk ahead of them.

"Man," Lia whispered with a giggle. "Your brother's ass in those jeans —"

"Ew. Just stop before I throw up, okay?"

Lia laughed.

Emmaline gave her friend a disgusted a look. "I'd expect that from Sanjana, but you're usually better behaved than that."

Lia grinned and shrugged. "Must be Hayden's lessons. They're helping me express myself."

Hayden dropped her eyes to Nolan's backside, and that annoyed her. The whole conversation annoyed her. Lia annoyed her. She didn't like her talking about Nolan in a weirdly possessive way, and that was messed up. *Get it together, Hayden.*

"Oh, look, Nolan," Lia called out and pointed to the striped Fiat in the parking lot. "Even Priscilla is here."

"Yeah," Nolan commented, his voice bland. He must have already noticed. Of course he had. They were a couple. They probably had a built-in radar for each other.

They hurried in from the cold and got in line at the counter, except for Nolan, who left them to join Priscilla's table.

"Your mom didn't say what she wanted," Lia said as she peered around the bodies at the doughnuts on the display in the glass case.

"I'll just pick out a variety for her." Emmaline turned to Hayden. "What kind do you want?"

Hayden wasn't looking at the doughnuts. She was looking to where Nolan had squeezed into the booth with Priscilla and her friends. *God.* She was so transparent. She needed to stop this. She didn't obsess over guys.

Just at that moment, Priscilla looked up at her and their eyes met — her expression clearly disapproving.

"Ugh. Don't stare at her," Emmaline advised.

Hayden faced forward and said evenly, "She doesn't like me." Her mouth twisted wryly. "Don't get me wrong. I could care less."

Emmaline chuckled. "Obviously. Why should you? You're way cooler than she is."

The words pleased Hayden and she smiled genuinely at Emmaline. "Thanks."

As they inched up in line closer to the counter, Hayden couldn't help sliding another look behind her to the booth where Nolan sat with Priscilla. She meant what she said. She didn't care what Priscilla thought about her. However, she was starting to care what Nolan thought.

They got their doughnuts, delighting over the fact that they were still warm, and found a booth just as a family of four vacated it. Unfortunately, the booth sat diagonal to Nolan's booth, so they could watch each other as they ate. Hayden and Emmaline sat side by side with a direct view of Nolan and Priscilla. *Great.*

Nolan wasn't looking at them, but Priscilla was. She daintily popped a doughnut hole in her mouth and turned her head to say something to Nolan.

He lifted his gaze to observe them, his eyes settling on Hayden. Nolan gave a swift shake of his head at whatever she asked him.

"Think they're going to cancel school tomorrow?" Lia asked, oblivious to the stares from the other table.

"The snow isn't melting," Emmaline remarked, staring out the window.

"If it's still like this tomorrow, we won't have school," Hayden offered.

"That's not a bad thing. I could use more time to study for my physics test."

Around ten minutes passed and Nolan left Priscilla and her friends to head over to their table. "You guys ready?"

"Sure." Emmaline wiped off her sticky fingers and stood up.

Nolan held the door open for them.

As they all walked over the mixture of ice, snow, and mud, Emmaline announced to her brother, "Look. This has to be said. I need you to cut me some slack. I like Hayden. She's my friend, and I'm going to hang out with her. Not that I need your permission, but I want you to be cool with it."

Heat stung her cheeks. Did Emmaline really have to start this conversation in front of Hayden? Couldn't she do it later when Hayden wasn't around to witness it? If they were actual friends, she would realize how much she was embarrassing Hayden. It was a reminder. Hayden had no one. No friends who understood her.

"Fine," Nolan said quickly, staring intently at Hayden.

He might be answering Emmaline, but his gaze was fixed on Hayden, his deep brown eyes full of something that looked like an apology and that gave Hayden pause.

He knew. He understood her embarrassment and he was sorry for it.

Emmaline blinked. "Fine? Just like that?"

"Yeah." He shrugged and the gesture seemed as uncomfortable

as Hayden felt. Incredibly, *her* discomfort actually made *him* uncomfortable. She slid her gaze away, not sure what to do with that realization.

"Em, you're seventeen," he said in a level voice. "I'm not going to be here next year, as you've pointed out."

"That's true." Emmaline smiled brightly. "You know I love your stupid face, right?"

He released a little laugh that sent flutters over Hayden's skin.

Nolan pressed a hand over his heart. "Your love overwhelms me, Em."

Emmaline punched him in the arm. "Cut it out."

"I might as well let you start living your own life now without me butting into it. Gotta get you ready for when I'm not around every day."

Lia slurped loudly from her straw. "You guys are so cute. For real, you're like a Hallmark movie."

Emmaline rolled her eyes. "Shut up, Lia,"

She wasn't wrong. They were what family should be. Functional.

Lia rushed ahead to Nolan's truck. "Guys! C'mon! All my bits are freezing."

Emmaline hurried to join her. "You're such an idiot," she teased.

For a moment, Nolan and Hayden stood alone.

"That was nice of you," Hayden murmured. Embarrassing for her, but nice for them.

He shrugged. "It was nothing. The right thing to do."

And that summed up Nolan Martin. He was a nice guy who ultimately did the right thing.

I'm not the right thing.

His eyes softened as he looked at her and that did funny things to her.

Stomach churning, she turned away and joined the girls waiting outside the truck. Nolan unlocked the doors and then they were headed back to the Martins' house.

Hayden spoke up as a CVS appeared in the near distance. "Hey, can you pull over real quick?"

Nolan obliged, parking near the front doors.

Hayden swung around and beckoned Emmaline with a crook of her finger. "C'mon, you."

With a wary smile, Emmaline hopped out of the truck and followed her into the store. "What are you getting?" she asked.

"I'm not getting anything. You are."

"*I* am?"

Hayden walked with purposeful strides, turning down an aisle and stopping. With her hands on her hips, she faced rows and rows of boxes.

Emmaline followed the direction of her gaze.

"Um. What . . ."

Hayden bent and plucked a box up off the shelf. "Again. *I* am not doing anything, but you are." Holding on to the box, she resumed her search, selecting a second one from the shelf and then assessing them side by side with squinting eyes. Apparently satisfied, she handed both of them to Emmaline. "Here you go."

Emmaline glanced down at one of the boxes. "Brazen Bombshell," she read. Then she read the other one. "This one is a bleach!"

Hayden nodded and buried her hands in her pockets. "We've got to lighten your hair first. Don't worry. I know what I'm doing, and Brazen Bombshell sounds about right for what you want."

"You want me to color my hair?"

She arched an eyebrow at the younger girl. "You want to signal to the world that you've changed . . . that you're ready for a change? This can be that signal."

Emmaline looked back down at the box uncertainly while fingering a lock of her hair. "It's . . . extreme."

"I thought extreme was what you wanted. Look, this isn't some teen movie. I'm not talking about a full makeover that's going to change your world, but you want to get noticed? Spice things up a little? Brazen Bombshell will achieve that. Plus, that shade of red will look hot on you."

Emmaline stared down at the boxes again, clearly imagining the vibrant hue on herself. "You're right." She nodded. "Let's do it."

They walked to the waiting cashier.

As Emmaline paid, Hayden's gaze drifted out the glass door to where Nolan was parked, his hands draped casually over the steering wheel, his gaze fixed straight ahead. Directly on Hayden. Prickles of heat cascaded over her face and she forced her attention on the cashier ringing them up.

It was scary how good those eyes felt on her.

IF YOU'RE NOT HAVING FUN ANYMORE, WHY BOTHER?

x Nolan x

Nolan couldn't hide from Priscilla forever.

It was time to own up to his feelings.

His encounter with Pris at the doughnut shop had been strained. She'd been with friends, sparing them both from a serious conversation, but she'd made her displeasure abundantly clear at seeing Hayden with him, and her judgment didn't sit right with him. She had no reason to dislike or disapprove of Hayden other than allowing rumors to influence her. Other than buying into what other people said. What other people thought.

The opinions of others prejudiced her, and even though he knew he had been guilty of the same bias, he wasn't anymore.

Since the night he sat on Hayden's couch and watched movies with her and listened to her theories on surviving a zombie apocalypse, she'd become a real person to him. Not just a rumor.

Things were different now. He was different too.

He'd lost it during Emmaline's slumber party and acted like a jerk, but he was over that. He was done being like everyone else who was quick to condemn, say terrible things, and then go about life blithely ignorant or indifferent to their prejudice. He didn't even know what was worse: Ignorance or indifference?

Whatever the case, his eyes had been opened.

He could not go back now.

Hayden lived a hard life. She had her armor, but she was interesting and real and different from all his other friends.

Since the night she spent at his house, he couldn't stop thinking about her. He couldn't stop wanting to see her again. Be with her again like they'd been together then.

Nolan didn't regret that kiss. Maybe that made him a bad person, but he couldn't regret it. It didn't matter who initiated it because he'd kissed her back. He'd wanted it to happen.

He had kissed her like his life depended on it. As though it was his last act on earth, he had kissed her back. It only confirmed what he had felt for a while now. Or at least how he felt toward Priscilla. He expelled a breath. Apathy.

Okay, so apathy was a decided *lack* of feeling, but that's how he felt when he was with Priscilla. That's how he had felt *about* Priscilla for quite some time. A lack . . . of *everything*.

He'd been trying to deny it. He'd fought it because two years was a long time to be with someone. Priscilla had been there for him in what was probably the darkest time in his life — at least as of yet.

Even before his interaction with Hayden, he had actually used the excuse that he needed to give his dog a bath rather than hang out with Priscilla. It wasn't a lie. He did bathe his dog then, but that only took forty minutes. The rest of the time he had played basketball at the nearby park and watched TV.

It was time to face the truth. He didn't want to be with Priscilla anymore. He felt awful about how this played out — that it took kissing another girl for him to acknowledge that, but the sentiment had been there for a while now.

He *had* loved Priscilla. Truly. At least in the beginning. And in the middle. She'd made him feel good when he had felt so bad following Dad's death.

At home, Nolan had been the rock his mom and sisters needed. He had been there for them while Priscilla was there for him. At first as a friend, and then more. Since freshman year, Priscilla had been a constant in his life.

It was hard letting go of that. He felt disloyal for even considering it. So, he had never allowed himself to consider it.

Until now.

He couldn't lie to himself anymore.

He wasn't sure when he had stopped loving her, but now he knew he had, because if he loved Pris, he would not have kissed Hayden Vargas back. He was not the type of guy to love someone and be okay with kissing another girl.

He knew what needed to be done. He just wasn't sure how to do it.

He dodged Priscilla at lunch, texting her that he needed to go over some college stuff with the counselor. Not true. He hid like a coward in the library, but there was no evading her after school.

"Nolan!"

He stopped at the sound of his name, recognizing the voice instantly. His palms grew clammy with sweat even though his breath fogged in the cold air.

Don't be a coward. Get it over with.

Tightening his grip on the straps of his backpack, he turned to face her.

"Hey, babe!" She stood on her tiptoes to give him a kiss. He turned his face slightly so that it landed half on his cheek and not on his mouth. It didn't feel right to accept a kiss from her. Not now. Not with what was coming. "I haven't seen you all day."

"Yeah, it's been busy." He'd had to be at school early, so she drove herself this morning. There was that small relief.

They walked together through the parking lot, side by side.

"What are you doing tonight? Do you want to study at my house?"

A normal request. He'd studied at her house countless times.

He sucked in a breath. He'd never done this before. Priscilla had been his first serious girlfriend. Breaking up with a girl wasn't in his repertoire of skills.

He didn't know how to do it. Maybe there wasn't any right way. Maybe ugliness was unavoidable.

A year ago, he'd thought they would never break up. He thought they would last, that they would be one of those rare couples to make it — high school sweethearts who went on to marry. It happened. Those couples existed.

At her car, he stopped and faced her. A quick glance around revealed no one nearby. *Good.* They didn't need an audience.

"We need to talk, Priscilla."

She stilled, almost like an animal in the wild. As though she had caught the scent of something . . . blood in the water. She cocked her head to the side, her sleek auburn hair sliding over her shoulder from the motion. "That sounds ominous."

"I don't mean for it to be."

Her gaze locked steadily on his face. "You don't *mean* for it to be . . . but you're not saying anything to reassure me."

He winced. Reassuring her would just be a lie. "Yeah." He lifted a hand and rubbed at the back of his neck.

173

Her expression twisted with emotion. Just a flash of it, and then she composed herself. "Just spit it out, would you?"

He released another gust of breath. "I'm sorry, Priscilla. So sorry. I didn't want this to ever happen."

A long beat of silence fell.

A breeze lifted the hair from her shoulders. After a moment, the air stilled and the strands settled back into place.

She nodded stiffly, understanding dulling her eyes. "You didn't want this to happen," she said slowly. "But it's happening. That's what you're saying, isn't it?" Another beat of silence as she considered him. "It's happening. You don't want me anymore."

"Priscilla, what we had —"

"*Had?* Already speaking in past tense, Nolan? Is it that easy for you?"

"Nothing about this is easy," he quickly returned. He swallowed against the lump in his throat. "I've thought about the best way to do —"

"You've *thought* about this?" She studied him intently, starkly, emotion entering her gaze. "For a while now, it seems. How long have you wanted to break up with me, Nolan?"

He shook his head. No way was he answering that. Even if he could pinpoint the precise moment, he was definitely not going to tell her their relationship had been broken for some time.

"You will always mean a great deal to me. You got me through some really shitty times —"

"Tell me," she demanded. "How long has our relationship been dead to you?"

He stifled a cringe and wondered what he could say to make this any less awful. "Oh, come on, Pris. Can you honestly say you've been happy with me lately? It hasn't been *good* between us in a while. It's nothing like it was in the beginning."

"Oh, Nolan. Don't be an idiot. So we're out of the honeymoon phase. That happens. Relationships are hard work. They're about compromise. It can't be all butterflies and rainbows forever."

He shook his head. That seemed reasonable. Except . . .

"We're still young, Pris. Not a middle-aged married couple that should have to work at it and compromise," he countered. "We don't *need* to do that. Shouldn't it still be fun? Exciting? Don't you want that? You deserve it. We both do."

She fell quiet.

He hoped she was turning that over in her mind . . . seeing that this was right for both of them.

She nodded once, the motion as stiff as a robot. "This is it then. We're done."

"It's just not the same anymore. Haven't you felt it too?" he pressed, hoping to get her to at least admit that. Maybe it was just to make himself feel better, but he needed her to say it.

"You mean have I felt *you* pulling away? *You* rejecting my every effort to pull us back together? Your impatience with me? Yeah, I felt that. I felt all of that."

Okay, so maybe it really was all on him. Maybe he didn't get to feel better about this and that was simply his burden to bear.

"That's fair." He nodded. He'd take the hit. He'd be truthful. "I guess it's me. I just don't feel the same way anymore, Priscilla."

"Well, isn't that great for you?" She released a bitter laugh. "You want to know how I feel? I feel like I just wasted two years of my life on you."

He shook his head, genuinely sad she felt that way. "I don't feel like that. Not at all. I don't regret us. We were good when we were good, Priscilla."

Her laugh twisted even more. "Are you kidding me?"

He blew out a frustrated breath.

It made sense to him. But then this breakup made sense to him and not to Pris. There was no easy way through this.

She continued, "*We were good when we were good?* What the hell is that supposed to even mean? Is that from a fortune cookie or something?"

Maybe it would never make sense to her. Maybe anything that came out of his mouth right now would only succeed to hurt and anger her and he just had to accept that.

She looked away from him, across the parking lot, her nostrils flaring as she inhaled. "Who have you told?"

He blinked. "What do you . . . mean?" he said haltingly. "I haven't told anyone. I'm telling you. I'm telling you now. Only you."

She looked back at him with sharp annoyance, her eyes bloodshot. "Your sister? Beau? Who knows? You need to tell me."

He shook his head, confused by her train of thought. "I haven't told anyone, Priscilla. I'm telling you. Now. Why would I tell anyone before you?"

She gave him a disgusted look. "You're breaking up with me. Dumping me. And you seem pretty determined about it. When things end, it's never pretty."

"I thought we could be better than that. We can keep it civil, maybe be friends in time."

"And I thought we were going to be together forever. I guess we were both wrong."

"I guess so," he agreed slowly.

She sighed and blinked her eyes as though fighting off tears.

Ah, damn. He didn't enjoy making her cry, but he didn't know how to make this any easier. Was there any way to make her feel better? He took an uncertain step toward her, and she stopped him with a swift swipe of her hand through the air. "Stop. Don't even think it. Do not touch me."

He jerked to a halt, holding himself apart from her.

She dropped her hand to her side and lifted her chin defiantly. "Is there someone else?" Her gaze pinned him to the spot with such laser-beam precision that he feared she could see beneath his skin and bones to the truth of him.

Seconds ticked and he didn't answer right away. "No. Of course not." By the time he got the words out, it was too late. He took too long to respond.

"There *is* someone else," she accused with a hard nod, full of conviction.

"Priscilla, no. There isn't. Things have been *off* for some time now and that isn't because of anyone."

Her eyes narrowed to slits. "Maybe. But maybe there's someone you're thinking about. You might have been thinking about dumping me, but what compelled you to finally act? *Who?*"

He fought to school his expression into impassivity. Was she right?

Since the night at her house, Hayden was there in his mind every time he closed his eyes. Was she the reason he was finally standing here? Doing this?

"Fine," she bit out into the stretch of silence. "Deny it. The truth will come out eventually, I'm sure." She looked him up and down in scathing contempt, heaved a breath, and swung around on her heels, yanking the door to her car open.

Nolan stood back a few feet as she started the car, well aware that in her present mood, she could run him down.

She rolled down the window. "Don't call me out of some noble sense of obligation. You ended this. Just let it be over. I might have to see you around school, but I don't want to hear from you."

Then she was gone.

He watched as she tore out of the parking lot and then he glanced around, noting that a few people were staring at him.

He and Priscilla hadn't been completely audience-free, after all.

Despite the ugly last few minutes — a lightness filled his chest, spreading and eclipsing any lingering regret.

He turned and walked back to his car alone for the first time without Priscilla or his sister. Alone for the first time in a long time. And that felt okay.

LESSON #23

EVERYONE TALKS.

x   Hayden   x

It was all over school by the next day.

Hayden may not travel in the highest social circles of Travis High School, but the news trickled down to even her lowly outcast earholes.

She was sitting in third period when she heard two girls talking behind her. Hayden stilled, listening, absorbing the words, and feeling more things than she should. A maelstrom of feelings. Too many to recognize.

Nolan broke up with her.

Right there in the parking lot yesterday.

Hannah saw them and then Priscilla hauled ass out of the there. She looked pissed.

Hayden's fingers tightened around her pencil as she replayed the gossip over and over in her head. He broke up with his girlfriend. She let that sink in.

Nolan broke up with his girlfriend.

After Hayden kissed him. It was coincidental. It had to be. *Right?*

She didn't want the responsibility of that. She — their kiss — could not have anything to do with them breaking up.

She wasn't responsible for anyone except herself. It had always been that way. Almost from the beginning — right out of the womb.

She knew the kiss was wrong. She'd known it was wrong the moment she did it. Not only did Nolan have a girlfriend (she never knowingly messed around with guys in relationships before), he was totally not her type. For starters, he was the kind of guy who did relationships. He was a commitment guy, and she was not a commitment girl.

Did Nolan tell his girlfriend about the kiss? Correction. Ex-girlfriend. She grimaced at that possibility. Was this the result of a guilty conscience? He seemed like that kind of guy. A guy with a conscience. A good guy.

She had known so few of those, but she recognized that in him. She hoped he hadn't confessed the kiss to Priscilla. She didn't need some cheerleader with a vendetta after her. And it wouldn't be just one cheerleader. They moved in a pack. She'd have a group of them after her. God, she'd prefer a zombie horde to a pack of cheerleaders, at least she would be prepared for zombies.

Hayden moved through the day in a fog, but perked up on the way to sixth period.

She hadn't heard her name whispered once in all the hot gossip. Maybe she was actually spared being associated with the drama. Additionally, she'd made it to her favorite class. She had some new sketches to show Ms. Mendez and thought they might be good enough to add to her growing portfolio. She was running a little late, but that concern flew out of her head when she rounded a corner and came face-to-face with Nolan.

He stopped when he caught sight of her.

She stopped too, digging her thumb deeply into the strap of her backpack.

They stared at each other.

Students passed through the halls, blurred figures in her peripheral vision, bodies hurrying to their classes, oblivious to them.

The final tardy bell chimed on the air.

She was officially late to her favorite class, but still, she could not move. It was like her feet were planted to the floor.

Silently, without a word, Nolan stepped forward, his strides slow and even. Hayden held herself motionless, mesmerized by his movements.

He stopped in front of her.

Her chest lifted on a breath.

He stretched an arm between them, his hand seeking, finding, grabbing hold of her hand hanging at her side.

She should pull away.

His fingers squeezed hers. His gaze left her and scanned along the hallway.

"C'mon," he murmured, giving her hand a tug.

"What?"

"This way." He nodded to a door down the hall.

It wasn't like her to go along with what some guy wanted.

She came first. She put herself first . . . and that hadn't changed.

But she wanted to go with him. Wherever he was taking her, she was wholeheartedly okay with it. Even if it did make her late for the only class that she enjoyed in school.

She nodded once and it seemed to be the answer he was waiting for.

He pulled her down the hall after him, his strides swift. It took two of hers to match one of his. His hand felt warm and strong wrapped around hers. *Nice.* It felt nice, and she hated herself for noticing. Not that she was a hand-holder, but most guys had sweaty, clammy hands. Except him.

"This is an interesting turn of events," she mused.

"What do you mean?"

"Here you are getting me to skip class. Who's the bad influence now?"

He shot a grin at her over his shoulder and she grinned back at him, a frisson of pleasure skipping down her spine. If she wasn't careful, he would weave some spell over her. She'd be little better than her mother then. Her smile faded. *That* wasn't happening. No way in hell.

"Nolan? Where are we going? I'm going to be really late for class —"

"So am I." He opened the door to the empty science lab and tugged her inside the room after him.

"Yeah, but I actually like this class."

He dropped his hand from hers and closed the door behind them.

So that was good, at least. They weren't touching anymore. Her hormones could settle down a little — hopefully.

She crossed her arms over her chest and continued, "I didn't think you were the kind of guy to break the rules. I mean, have you ever been tardy in your life?"

"I've broken a few rules." His voice held a touch of defensiveness.

"Is that a fact?" She laughed once, but the sound came out nervous and uneasy — not at all what she intended. Immediately she thought of their kiss . . . again. Okay, it was never far from her mind.

She remembered it distinctly. Felt it. Still tasted it. He broke a rule then. He had a girlfriend and he'd kissed her.

"I just wanted to apologize to you for the other night. And before that, actually," he said.

She flinched. Oh, he was going there.

They were going to hash this all out right now. This should be interesting. She didn't have a lot of experience with people willing to talk about their feelings and examine their actions. She especially didn't have anyone in her life who ever *apologized*.

"Why are you apologizing?" She shrugged. "You shouldn't. I was the one who crossed the line." *The one who kissed you.*

"What are you talking about?" He looked genuinely confused.

"What are *you* talking about?" she countered.

"I've been a real jerk about you and my sister. You can hang out, be her friend, give lessons . . . whatever. I know I said that to her, but I didn't say it to you. Not directly. I won't stand in the way of you two being friends. I never should have tried. And I'm sorry about calling you a bad influence and judging you."

"Oh." She processed that. So this wasn't about what happened between them Saturday night. She felt like such an idiot. He probably wasn't even thinking about their kiss.

He canted his head to the side. "What did you think I was apologizing for?

"Um."

Understanding lit his eyes, followed by a slow grin. That grin was lethal. "Oh. You're talking about the kiss. You thought I was apologizing for that?"

"No!" she shot out, indignation rushing through her.

God.

The kiss.

They were really, really going to talk about it, and all because of her big mouth.

Heat swamped her face.

"We're not talking about this." She started for the door, her hand closing around the knob. She needed to get to class. She wanted to show her new sketches to Ms. Mendez. That's what she cared about. Not him.

She needed to get away from him.

His voice stopped her, as deep and dark as his eyes. "I wasn't apologizing for the kiss. Because I don't regret it."

Her hand shook as it closed around the knob. "Well, I hope you didn't break up with your girlfriend because of that. It was a mistake."

"I wouldn't call it that."

She looked over her shoulder. "I kiss boys all the time. So I kissed you." She shrugged. "It doesn't mean anything. Don't make what happened into something more." She flung the words at him like arrows, hoping they would strike and kill any idea he had that there was something romantic between them.

She knew what she was doing. Pushing him away was for the best. There was no future in them. Maybe they'd fool around, but nothing would come of it. It would complicate his life, thereby complicating hers. He wasn't the kind of guy who did casual hookups.

"Sure. Okay." He sounded almost bored and unimpressed with her mini speech.

"You broke up with your girlfriend," she accused.

"Yes," he admitted.

"That wasn't because of me, was it?" She held her breath, dreading that he would tell her breaking up with his girlfriend had *everything* to do with kissing her.

He took his time replying. "Do *you* think it's because of you?"

She didn't know. She didn't want it to have anything to do with her. "It *shouldn't* be because of me. I hope it's not. I don't want to be in the middle of you and your girlfriend's —"

"Ex-girlfriend. I don't have a girlfriend anymore, remember?"

Oh. God. "I just want you to say your dumb breakup wasn't because of me."

He cracked a smile. "Well, you can be relieved. It's not because of you. Priscilla and I weren't working out long before you and —"

"Don't say it. There is no 'you and me.'"

He smiled tightly, as though it hurt his face. "You just said it though."

She blew out an exasperated breath.

He went on, "I decided to put an end to my relationship. It was overdue and the best thing for both of us."

"Good. Glad to hear that." She heard how that sounded, but it didn't stop her babbling. "I mean, I'm not glad you broke up, but I'm glad it had nothing to do with me."

He was grinning again at her. "I'm glad you're glad."

Now she felt certain he was laughing at her. Mocking her. She pulled the door open, startled to come face-to-face with Lia. "Oh. Hey there." Just behind Lia stood Monica.

"Hey there yourself," Lia returned. "I didn't think anyone was in this room." Her gaze landed behind Hayden . . . on Nolan. Her expression turned speculative. "What are you two doing here?"

"Nothing," Hayden said defensively. "What are you two doing?"

Lia blinked and shrugged. "Well, we were planning to do in here what everybody else does in the empty science lab. You sure that isn't the same thing you two were doing?" She arched an eyebrow smugly.

Monica let out a noise that sounded suspiciously like a giggle.

Heat swamped Hayden's face for the second time. "We were only talking."

"Oh, really? Is that what we're calling it these days?" She and Monica shared a long glance. "Well, to be honest, that's not what *we* were planning on doing in here."

It took Hayden a moment to find her voice. "Oh." And then: "*Oh. Wow. Okay. Yeah.*"

Apparently, the other night's kissing lessons had started something between Lia and Monica. Maybe something real. At the very least it was something they were into exploring. Good for them.

"Yeah, so it's our free period and we came here to make out. Are you done 'talking' then?" Monica asked, her tone direct. "If so, can we have the room?"

"By all means." Hayden passed through the door, holding it open for the girls as she did so. "Enjoy yourselves."

"Hayden," Nolan called after her. "Hayden, wait up."

She didn't stop. Waiting for Nolan felt like a bad idea. She didn't like how he made her feel — like maybe something more from him, *with him*, was okay. Something other than a casual hookup, and that was *not* Hayden. It violated her own rule: never get attached. Keep it casual. You couldn't get hurt that way. That was a lesson she had learned herself the hard way.

She hurried down the hall, making sure not to look behind her. She knew better than to do that.

You never regret and you never look back.

LESSON #24

THERE'S FREEDOM WHERE NO ONE KNOWS YOU.

x   Emmaline   x

"Are you sure we can just go in there? We don't know anyone." Emmaline hated that she sounded so nervous, but she kept visualizing being turned away at the door.

"There's no one checking invites at the entrance, if that's what worries you," Hayden called over her shoulder. It was like she could read Emmaline's mind. "Oh, and don't forget what I said." She stopped and looked back at Emmaline and Sanjana. "Never leave your drink unattended and don't accept a drink from anyone you don't know well."

"Sounds like the warnings they announce at the airport," Sanjana remarked.

Hayden frowned. "It's no joke. There are all kinds of threats out there. Always look out for yourself and your friends."

Turning back around, Hayden led the way toward the big house that was lit up like a Christmas tree. A giant pond sat beside the house, wrapping around to the back. From her vantage, Emmaline could see a dock stretching out over the water, a boat and several Jet Skis parked alongside it.

"This place is pretty fancy." Sanjana whistled in awe. "You know who lives here?"

"Nope," Hayden replied.

"How did you get invited then?"

Hayden looked at them like the answer was obvious. "Snapchat."

"So you've never met the person throwing this party —"

"He's a Snapchat friend," she answered.

Emmaline knew that Hayden had a lot of followers, which was kind of ironic considering Hayden didn't have a tight circle of friends and mostly kept to herself. But that was Snapchat for you. Connecting beautiful strangers to beautiful strangers.

Emmaline watched her in admiration.

Hayden walked with expertise, clearly accustomed to her two-inch boot heels that put her close to six feet. Emmaline's own attempt to walk in heels was woefully inadequate by comparison. Relief swept over her when she finally entered the house. It was so crowded that movement was at a minimum. She only had to suffer a few steps at a time.

Navigating this party wasn't as hard as she thought it would be. Guys talked to them, offering drinks and stupid come-ons. She didn't even have to say much. Quality conversation didn't seem to matter.

"It's the hair," Sanjana told her over the loud pump of music, nodding knowingly. "Guys love redheads. You know what they say. Redheads have more fun."

Emmaline considered that for a moment. "I think that the saying is 'blondes have more fun.'"

Sanjana reached for a chip from a bowl on a nearby table. "No way is that true." Munching on her chip, she nodded at Hayden. Hayden still attracted the biggest crowd. The girl didn't know her own power.

Or maybe she did. Maybe that's where her power originated — in her awareness and her absolute indifference to it.

Sanjana continued, "I've known too many miserable blondes. And look at her. She's *not* a blonde." She picked up another chip and waved it at Hayden.

But was Hayden having fun?

Staring at Hayden, Emmaline got the sense that she wasn't enjoying the attention. She didn't even seem to be looking at the guys talking to her. No, as the evening wore on, it became clear that Hayden would have preferred to be anywhere else than at this party. But she was doing this for Emmaline. She had become a good friend, lessons aside.

Hayden broke free of her admirers to join them. "Hey, you guys want to leave? Let's go get a pizza or something."

"We've only been here like an hour," Sanjana said. "It's not even nine yet."

"Actually, pizza sounds great," Emmaline agreed, strangely relieved at the prospect of leaving.

"All right." Sanjana shrugged and they headed back through the party. It was slow going considering Emmaline could barely manage in her shoes. She was debating taking them off and going without them altogether when she rolled her ankle. She yelped and went sideways, colliding into some guy holding a full cup of beer. A full cup that went all over the front of her sweater.

He cursed, shot her a glare, tossed his now empty cup aside, and moved on, more than likely to get a refill.

Yeah, her ankle was throbbing and she was soaked in beer. She was definitely over this party scene.

Hayden and Sanjana helped her to her feet.

"That's it," she muttered. "No more shoes." Holding on to Sanjana's arm, she undid the straps.

With her shoes dangling from her fingers, she straightened. "Ick. Now I smell like beer. My mom is going to freak."

"We'll go by my house first and you can change into one of my tops," Hayden offered.

"Thanks." She hobbled outside, sucking in a sharp breath as her body hit the cold air. "Yeah. Wet sweater. Cold air. Not a fan."

"Well, hurry up, then." Sanjana grabbed her hand. Together they rushed to the car. Emmaline hopped into passenger seat, cursing the cold and vowing never to wear uncomfortable shoes again for any reason, no matter how good they looked.

Hayden stuck her key in the ignition. The car sputtered and choked, but nothing happened. She slapped the steering wheel. "It's not starting." She blew out a hard breath and glared straight ahead into the night. "Sorry. It happens sometimes."

"So what do we do now?" Emmaline asked. "Call someone?"

"Who?"

"I guess we could call my brother," Emmaline suggested. Nolan knew she was out with Hayden. She'd told him where she was going tonight. True to his word, he had not said one negative thing against it.

"Let's not bother him," Hayden quickly said.

"Okay. Who then?"

"Call Beau," Sanjana chimed. "He's kinda like your brother."

Emmaline winced. Beau wasn't like her brother at all, at least, she had never seen him that way, but she wasn't going to argue that point. "Okay," she agreed, fishing out her phone.

She pressed Beau's contact and told herself she was calling him because he was a good friend, reliable and convenient. For no other reason than that. It took less than ten seconds for him to answer her call and agree to come.

They moved back inside the house to wait where it was warmer.

Sanjana helped herself to another beer, drinking deeply out of the red Solo cup.

"Hey there! It's my favorite Martin." A hard hand landed on her shoulder and spun her around.

"DeVecchio!" Emmaline greeted her brother's teammate.

He swept her into a hug. "Didn't expect to see you at a party out of your zip code." He pulled back and swept a glance over her. "Looking good, Martin."

"Thanks," she replied, resisting tugging at the collar of her sweater, for some reason feeling the need to cover up the cleavage she exposed.

His gaze drifted from her to Hayden. "Branching out, I see, Emmaline. Hanging out at new places . . . with new friends."

"Yeah, Hayden is great."

"Mmm." He swept his hand over Emmaline's hair in a long stroke. "This color is hot on you."

Hayden lifted both eyebrows. Sanjana's eyes rounded over the rim of her cup.

He was flirting with Emmaline. No doubt about that.

Emmaline fought the urge to pull away. She was here to get her flirt on. She shouldn't shy away when an opportunity presented itself, and DeVecchio was cute.

"So, you're like genius smart, right?" he asked.

"Well—"

"Yes, she is. We both are," Sanjana inserted.

"I need a tutor. You tutor Algebra II?"

Emmaline nodded.

"Awesome. I really need to pass or Coach is going to have my ass. Want to meet up next week?"

"Sure." They took out their phones and were in the process of swapping numbers when Beau found them.

"Hey." Beau watched as they finished exchanging numbers, a slight frown turning down the corner of his mouth.

"Hey!" Emmaline's chest swelled at the sight of him.

Even Hayden looked glad to see him. "That was quick."

DeVecchio held out his fist to Beau in greeting. "Hey, Sanders. Didn't know you were coming, man."

"Yeah, hadn't planned on it." His gaze fixed on Emmaline.

The tightness in her chest only increased, which was silly. She wasn't special. She called and he came because they were friends. He saw her as a sister. Of course he would come. His nose twitched and he leaned in, inhaling her. "Emmaline? Have you been drinking?"

"Not exactly." She peeled her damp sweater away from her chest. "Just bumped into someone who was."

"Ah."

"Don't worry." Hayden smirked. "I've been taking care of her."

Beau looked less than convinced. "I'm sure."

"Come on. Let's go." Hayden turned and disappeared back through the crowded living room. They all followed her, weaving through the bodies until they emerged outside.

The air gusted out from Emmaline's teeth in a visible cloud as she greeted the chilly night again. Beau glanced back at her, eyeing her up and down. "Cold?"

She nodded.

He motioned to the house. "Why don't you wait inside?" His gaze flicked to Sanjana. "I'll come and get both of you once we have the car running."

"Okay, thanks." She hastily stepped back inside the warm house. They stayed in the foyer, Sanjana finishing her beer and Emmaline people-watching.

"How long do you think it will take?" she asked Sanjana.

Her friend shrugged. "I know nothing of cars." She set her cup down on a narrow table lined with framed photos. "I gotta go find a bathroom. Be right back."

She watched as Sanjana slipped away into the crowd. A few moments ticked by and she found herself staring at Sanjana's empty Solo cup on the table. Sanjana didn't normally drink, but she'd had a few beers tonight. Hayden's voice played in her mind. *Always look out for yourself and your friends.*

Yeah. Emmaline should have gone with her to the bathroom. She started in the direction Sanjana took, searching the bottom floor without any sign of her. The second floor yielded no results either. Emmaline knocked on bathroom doors and peered into bedrooms, annoying more than a few people, but she was starting to feel a little desperate as she searched for her friend.

Where did she go? Maybe Emmaline had somehow missed her and she'd returned to the car and was waiting there now?

Hoping that was the case, she ventured back downstairs, finally spotting Sanjana cornered by a guy.

"Sanjana," she called out as she approached.

Sanjana peered over the guy's colossal shoulder, her eyes wide. Not frightened exactly, but she was definitely in a state of astonishment. She was not one to be singled out.

"Hey, we're ready to go." It didn't matter if the car was fixed or not. Emmaline was convinced she needed rescuing.

The guy turned halfway, not enough to let Sanjana pass, but just enough to settle his bleary half-lidded gaze on Emmaline. "She's busy."

His words were slightly slurred, pretty much confirming that he was wasted.

"Um, yeah. Well, I'm her ride, and we're leaving."

"I'll bring her home when we're done."

When we're done? Okay, that sounded ominous. And gross. He was gross.

"Um. That's okay." She reached around him and seized Sanjana's hand. He definitely wasn't driving her friend anywhere.

He still didn't move. His big body was rooted like a tree.

She glanced around as though help might materialize. The party raged with no one paying them any particular attention. Emmaline looked back at him, staring him down with false confidence. "We're going *now*." She pulled on Sanjana's hand, trying to tug her forward.

Sanjana attempted to go around him, but his arm shot up and blocked her. "Get lost, Red." He jerked his head in the direction of the door. "She wants to stay."

Terrific. He was going to be *that* guy. Emmaline sent Sanjana a pointed look, conveying that it was time for her to speak up for herself and help with her own rescue.

"Um, it's been fun, Trevor." Sanjana cleared her throat. "But I should go."

"No, you don't want to do that," he announced with a certain nod.

"Um, yeah. I do." Sanjana's voice wobbled. She looked at Emmaline beseechingly. She was clearly in over her head and needed help extricating herself.

"Let her go." Emmaline inserted an edge to her voice.

The jock turned then, firmly planting his bigger body between Emmaline and Sanjana. "We were having fun before you showed up, buzzkill, so why don't you get lost?" His oversized hand dropped to her shoulder and shoved.

It wasn't a hard push. It surprised her more than anything. She didn't expect him to put a hand on her. Caught off guard, she staggered back, bumping into the opposite wall of the corridor. She rubbed at the back of her head where she'd banged it.

Trevor stared at her in satisfaction. Then suddenly his smug face was out of her line of vision because Beau was there, shoving Trevor against the wall, holding him with one hand at his throat. "You don't ever touch her, Webber."

So, they knew each other apparently, even though this guy definitely didn't attend their school. She would have remembered him.

"Sanders!" Webber laughed, holding both hands up in the air. "I didn't know she was a friend of yours."

"She's more than a friend, meathead."

Pleasure suffused her, a warm bloom in her chest. *More than a friend.*

Beau continued, "That's Nolan Martin's sister."

Webber's eyes widened ever slightly. "How was I supposed to know that?" To Emmaline, he said, "Hey, I didn't know who you are. No hard feelings."

She glared at him. "It shouldn't matter who my brother is, asshole."

Trevor looked confused.

Beau gave him a hard shake as though that might jog some sense into him. "You don't touch any girl like that."

She grabbed her friend's hand. "C'mon, Sanjana." She pulled her through the party. Angry, disgusted . . . and not just at the guy who shoved her.

She was angry at Beau for some reason she couldn't yet articulate.

Why did he have to even mention she was Nolan's sister? As though that was the only value she possessed. As though her worth wasn't even her own.

Right now she just wanted to get away. She hurried outside, ignoring the cold. She was almost to the car where Hayden waited when she heard Beau calling her name.

"Um, Em, Beau's calling you."

"Just keep going," she muttered to Sanjana.

His words rolled through her mind on repeat. *That's Nolan Martin's sister.*

That was always the bottom line with him — all she was to him in a nutshell. Beau Sanders wouldn't speak to her at school, or out of school, if not for Nolan. They wouldn't cross paths. If he saw her in the halls . . . Well. He wouldn't see her. She'd be invisible to him.

She blinked back burning eyes. *No.* She would not let herself get all broken up about this. She was a new girl . . . a new person. Or at least she was trying to be. She had red hair and she was talking to guys (and they were talking to her) and she was very close to finally getting her first kiss. She felt it. The taste of it was almost there on her lips like salt on a sea breeze.

"Emmaline! Wait up!"

She spun around. "What?"

Beau trotted down the walkway. "What's going on? Are you mad?" His gaze roamed her face intently, peering at her like she was one of those tricky optical illusions, a picture with a hidden image inside it.

"Yes . . . no!"

"You sound mad," he pointed out.

She sighed, feeling tired. "I just want to go home." She motioned to the car. "Thanks for the jump."

"You want me to give you a ride home?"

She hesitated, looking down and plucking at her damp sweater. "I'm soaked in beer."

"Here." Sanjana pulled off her oversized sweater, revealing a black crop top underneath. "Put this on."

"Sanjana!" Emmaline cried, her fingers closing around the mustard-colored sweater. "Aren't you cold?"

Sanjana shrugged. "No."

Emmaline watched her friend traipse ahead toward the car and then glanced back at Beau. "I guess I'll ride with you. I'll just put this on."

He nodded and they marched across the lawn to where his and Hayden's vehicles where parked.

Hayden was waiting beside her car. "There you are," she called as they approached. "Ready?"

"Sure, yeah." Emmaline motioned to Beau. "He's going to give me a ride home."

She nodded and glanced at Sanjana as she plopped into the passenger seat. "I guess I'll handle her."

"She's had a few drinks. She might need to sober up a little before you take her home. Her mom is pretty strict."

"Plenty of time." Sanjana slapped the air. "My curfew is eleven thirty."

"I got her," Hayden reassured.

Beau's truck was angled in front of Hayden's car. They climbed up into the cab. Emmaline slammed the door after her and, hesitating only a moment, she quickly pulled her beer-soaked sweater over her head and dropped it to the floorboard. Beau glanced at her and then looked away. She felt the heat climb up her face as she struggled to slide on Sanjana's sweater. Her hands fumbled and she told herself it was just the cold. Not nerves.

Beau started the truck, adjusting the temperature and angling the vents her way. Her heart squeezed a little. He was nice like that.

"God, I'm ready for spring," she muttered, searching for the neck hole.

It was just a bra. No different than a bikini top. Even as she told herself that, it felt different. Sitting next to Beau in her bra felt . . . different.

"Yeah. It's a pretty cold winter."

She finally succeeded in getting the sweater over her head. Leaning back, she clicked her seat belt on and released a satisfied breath. "There. Now let's go."

Beau smiled and pulled out onto the street.

KISSING SOMEONE YOU CARE ABOUT CAN FEEL LIKE A FIRST KISS ALL OVER AGAIN.

x Beau x

Beau felt guilty.

It wasn't logical. He hadn't done anything wrong. He knew that. He knew Nolan would appreciate him looking out for his sister. He doubted, however, that Nolan would appreciate him checking out his sister . . . something he had definitely been doing when she changed sweaters beside him.

At some point recently Beau had stopped looking at her like Nolan's little sister and started looking at her like a girl he wanted to kiss. A girl he wanted to *more* than kiss.

Nolan would *not* be okay with that. He would never be cool with it.

He mentally groaned. Nolan would kill him, and Beau would deserve it.

Beau took a steadying breath and flexed his hands on the steering wheel as he pulled out onto the highway. "Can I ask you something?"

"You can ask me anything. You drove out here to help me tonight. I kind of owe you."

"Why were you at a party like that?"

"What kind of party should I have been at?"

"Not one like that," he quickly replied.

A quick glance revealed a slight tightening of her features. "What do you mean?"

He lifted a hand from the steering wheel and waved vaguely. "You know, a party like that where people are drunk and act like idiots."

"This is starting to sound a little like a lecture."

"Parties like that are full of inebriated jerks who think they can do whatever they want to whoever they want."

"I have the right to go where I want."

"I'm not saying you don't have that right, but —"

"No buts. Shouldn't I live my life? Go places? Should I hide inside all the time while everyone else has fun?"

He let out a breath. "I'm aware it makes me sound like a huge asshole, but I don't think you should go to parties like that. Can I just say that?"

"No." She shook her head slowly. "You don't get to say that. You don't get to *ask* me that."

He bumped the steering wheel with the heel of his palm. "What is going on? This isn't you. It feels like you're putting on some kind of act lately."

He felt her glare without even looking her way. "Maybe you don't know me."

"Oh, I know you, Emmaline." He exited the highway, his old truck rumbling around them as it decreased speed. He braked as he came up on a stoplight. Turning in his seat to face her, he continued, "I know you're smart and love rom-coms and lasagna and romance novels. I know you're allergic to cats but still pet them even though it makes your eyes swell. I know you cried in ninth grade when no one asked you to homecoming and I know you cry over any commercial with an animal in it. I know that scar on your knee is from when you crashed your bike into the mailbox. I know that you had to wear braces an extra year because you never wore your rubber bands even though your mom nagged you to wear them constantly."

"How do you . . ."

"Because I know you." He went still as stone beside her, his eyes fixed on her face. The stoplight tinted her features red and made her newly dyed hair even brighter. He'd said too much, but he couldn't seem to shut up. "And I know . . . that . . . I . . ." His gaze dropped to her mouth. "I want to kiss you, Pigeon." The words released from him in a pained gust of breath.

Her eyes rounded and she went still, too. Marble-still.

The instant the words were out, he wanted to grab them and stuff them back down his throat. He stretched out a hand and then fisted it to stop himself from touching her. The impulse was strong, but he resisted.

"What did you say?" she whispered.

He leaned across the space separating them, jerking back when a horn blew up behind them.

With a curse, he faced forward and drove. He felt sick. He'd just told Emmaline he wanted to kiss her. He probably would have, too, if the light hadn't changed. And if she let him . . .

He shot her a quick glance. She stared straight ahead, her expression unreadable. He couldn't have her thoughts and he couldn't have her.

They drove the rest of the way to her house in silence. He parked in the driveway and stared at the closed garage door, fingers tapping on the steering wheel as he contemplated what to say.

"Thanks for the ride, and you know, the help."

"Of course."

"You want to come inside?"

He glanced at her swiftly. "Uh . . ."

A flicker of panic crossed her face. "My mom is home . . . and Nolan. I'm sure he'd want to see you," she hurriedly added.

"Oh. Yeah. Sure." Nodding, he turned off the ignition. She wasn't inviting him inside for herself, of course. She was just normalizing things between them again. And Beau going inside the house was normal.

She smiled with a brightness that was blinding. "Great."

He forced a smile. "So we're okay?" He waved between them. "Sorry about . . . what I said."

She made a pfft sound and waved a hand. "We're fine. Forget it. It was just a freak moment."

He nodded. "I'm just glad that we're okay. I wouldn't want anything to be weird between us."

"How could there ever be anything weird between us?" She laughed. Giggled actually. The sound was a little manic. "We're friends."

"All right then. Good. Great." He climbed out of the truck.

They walked to the door together, several feet separating them.

LESSON #26

AVOID ONIONS.

x   Nolan   x

Nolan's phone was oddly silent without Priscilla blowing it up every ten minutes. To be fair, if it was a normal Saturday night, she wouldn't have been texting or calling him because they would have been together. Now he was alone, and that still felt okay. It felt right. Better than before. He'd choose solitude over being with the wrong person.

Mom and Savannah were at a movie. Beau had a landscaping gig all weekend that required a five a.m. wake-up, so he was staying in.

There were parties going on and other friends he could be hanging out with, but Nolan wasn't really in the mood for any of that.

Emmaline wasn't home either. She had texted an hour ago to say that she was spending the night at Hayden's. Instantly he had felt a flash of disappointment. He rubbed at the center of his chest as though he could wipe away the uncomfortable feeling.

Why couldn't they spend the night here? Why couldn't Hayden be under the same roof with him? Like before . . . just across the hall.

As soon as the thought entered his mind, he gave himself a hard mental shake. Hayden wasn't *his* friend. Hayden was Emmaline's friend, and he needed to remember that.

After an hour of channel surfing and finding nothing to hold his attention, he decided to go and get some food rather than eat the leftovers in the fridge.

He told himself it would be good to get out of the house for a little while, and that was the reason he left. It wasn't that he was bored or lonely or longing for something else. Someone else. It wasn't that.

And yet after he went through the drive-through window at Whataburger, he found himself heading toward Beau's neighborhood, but it wasn't Beau he was going to see. It wasn't even his sister he was going to see.

Clearly he was out of his mind, but he couldn't stop thinking about the sensation of Hayden's soft lips. That one kiss they had shared was imprinted on his brain. He couldn't forget it.

He parked in front of Hayden's house and got out of the truck, carrying his bag of Whataburger. He must've known, at least subconsciously, that he was coming here, because inside the fast food bag were three orders of french fries, chicken fingers, and two bacon cheeseburgers. More food than even he could eat, and he had a huge appetite. His mom always complained about having to go to the grocery store every other day. It was enough for his sister, Hayden, and one extra friend. Just in case.

He knocked on the front door, imagining Hayden looking back at him from the peephole. The lock on the other side of the door rattled and suddenly he was staring right at her. She looked so sweet his teeth ached. She wore a baggy T-shirt and a pair of spandex shorts that did amazing things for her thighs. How was she so toned without playing any sports?

"Nolan." She glanced beyond him, as though verifying he was alone. "Are you looking for your sister? Beau drove her home."

"Oh." He looked down at the bags in his hand. "I thought y'all might be hungry."

"You brought Whataburger? Wow. I need a brother like you." She stared longingly at the bags.

He smiled uncomfortably. She thought he was here for Emmaline. He *had* tried to convince himself that he was here for Emmaline, too. Except now seeing Hayden, he knew the truth. This had nothing to do with his sister. He was here for Hayden.

She continued. "Well, *I* could eat." She shrugged and then nodded at the warm, grease-stained bag in his hands. "If you're up for sharing with me?" She met his gaze, lifting her chin almost defiantly. Like she dared him to eat with her — to cross the threshold into her house.

Another night on the couch with Hayden?

His chest lightened and expanded, and he felt like a kid on Christmas morning. "Yeah, sure."

She opened the door wider and motioned him inside. Plopping down on the couch, she patted the space next to her and then leaned forward to clear off a spot on the coffee table. He joined her on the couch and started taking out the food, flattening the bags to use as plates.

"Y'all have fun tonight?" he asked.

She shrugged. "I guess. I think Sanjana had a little too much to drink. She's napping on my bed. I have to take her home in an hour."

"How was Em —" He paused and swallowed, choosing his words carefully, trying not to come across as the overprotective brother again. "Did Emmaline have a good time?"

She shrugged again. "I think so. She wore these ridiculous shoes that murdered her feet and some guy spilled beer all over her sweater. Keg parties aren't really her scene, you know."

"I know." He nodded.

"She's pretending to like it though."

"I don't know why she's forcing it. Parties like that aren't ever going to be her thing."

"She'll figure it out. Give her time."

He hoped so. He wanted to leave for college knowing she could take care of herself. His father would want that.

"I mean, isn't that adolescence? Finding yourself?" she added.

"Is it? So, when we're in our twenties we'll have it all figured out?"

"I already have it figured out. I know myself." She smirked and gave him a challenging look that seemed to say: *Can you claim the same?*

"Yeah? Good for you." Somehow he believed her. She seemed like an adult already — more grown up than any of his friends.

Glancing around the shabby surroundings, he wondered if she even had a mother. Of course, everyone *had* a mother, but was her mother actually in the picture? Was she present in her life or was Hayden raising herself? He realized he didn't know as much about Hayden as he wanted to, and he felt a fresh stab of guilt at his earlier misconceptions about her.

"Are parties your thing?" She propped her feet on the coffee table, stretching out her legs. "It's Saturday night and you're sitting here on my crappy couch eating Whataburger with me." She foraged through the bag and stuffed a bunch of fries into her mouth and chewed, watching him.

He shrugged. "I've been to my share of parties."

She nodded and swallowed. "Me too. But do you *like* parties?"

He gave another shrug. "Sometimes it's nice to stay in and hang out with people you like instead of talking to a bunch of strangers at a party."

Silence fell between them, and he replayed what he just said in his mind, what he just admitted. *Sometimes it's nice to stay in and hang out with people you like.*

So he just confessed he liked her. Okay, well, it was the truth. He didn't regret saying it. He had never been one of those guys unable to express emotion. He was well versed in talking out his feelings.

He slid her a glance to see how she took that admission from him.

She was looking at him consideringly, her eyes a little heavy-lidded. Or maybe he was just imagining that — hoping he was seeing something more there.

She leaned back against the couch. "You like hanging out with me?"

"I'm having fun right now." He nodded. "Being with you here. Yeah, I like it."

She smiled slowly, laughing lightly. "Did you come here to kiss me again, Nolan Martin?

"Do you want me to kiss you, Hayden Vargas?"

Still laughing, now almost soundlessly, she shook her head at him. It wasn't a refusal precisely, more like he was too much, in a good way. He loved that he could make her laugh, that she was so easy to be with.

"You're single now," she said, giving his knee a nudge. "You're free. No more relationship worries. No more sleepless nights contemplating how you're going to ask your girlfriend to the dance."

He grunted. "Yeah. That's nice." The dance was a few weeks away now. If they hadn't broken up and he hadn't asked Pris yet, the pressure would be pretty intense right now.

"What? You don't like dances?"

"Dances are okay. I mean, in theory, they're great, right? Slow dancing with someone you're really into? I just never understood why there was so much work leading up to them. I mean, the whole dance proposal thing has gotten way out of hand. Three dances a year! And I've got to think up something unique every time."

She laughed. "God. You're stressing me out just talking about it."

He chuckled. "For real. It stressed me out, too." He waved his hands for emphasis. "Going to a dance shouldn't be so hard."

"I guess not. Too bad your girlfriend never surprised you and did the asking."

"Now that would have been awesome." He couldn't imagine Priscilla ever taking on that burden. She'd loved being on the receiving end of a promposal. He guessed that was fairly normal.

Hayden nodded thoughtfully. "Yeah. I don't think I've ever seen a girl do a dance proposal."

"Neither have I," he seconded. "That would be a nice change."

"Well. You don't have to worry about it now."

"No, I don't," he agreed, feeling intensely satisfied.

"Now you can go to parties and flirt with any girl you want and not have to worry about any of that. In fact, you could be doing that right now."

"I don't want to be at a party flirting with other girls."

"Oh?" She arched one dark eyebrow and pointed at the center of her chest. "You only want to be here flirting with me?" She was joking. He read the glint of humor in her eyes, but it wasn't a joke to him.

"Yes." He hadn't planned to admit that, but it was the truth, and he delivered it solemnly.

She considered him a moment. "You want me to be your rebound?"

"Yes. N-no. That's not what I meant."

Her grin widened.

He hurriedly clarified, "You're not a rebound. You could never be a rebound—"

"Oh, I could be a rebound." She snorted. "I'm pretty sure I have been before."

"Hayden," he whispered. "You—"

"Oh hush." She turned to face him more fully on the couch, criss-crossing her legs as she dusted the salt off her fingertips, all business. "Okay, before we do this, let's get a few things straight. This is only a rebound, nothing serious—"

"Hayden—"

"No," she said sharply, holding a finger aloft. "A fling. Don't go developing feelings for me or anything. Got that, Martin?"

He understood her, but he didn't like it.

He wasn't sure he wanted a fling anymore. This thing with Hayden was so new, and he wanted to explore it. He didn't want to put them in a box and label it anything this soon. It might be easier calling this a fling, but he wasn't looking for easy. He was looking for what felt right.

She reached between them and plucked the half-eaten burger out of his hand. She peered at it. "No onions, I hope?"

"No," he quickly answered, watching her in fascination, forgetting about arguing with her over the definition of what they were. She was so close, so near. He didn't want to say anything that made her pull away from him.

"Good." She tossed his food on the coffee table and resettled her weight on the couch in front of him, her knees overlapping his. "Well? What are you waiting for?"

His heart started pounding in his ears, the blood rushing to his head as he looked at her. "I have never met anyone like you in my entire life." He shook his head and exhaled a ragged breath.

"I know. And you never will. But just remember what I said. No feelings. This is purely physical." She shook a finger at him. "Say it. Say you understand or we're not doing this, Martin."

"I understand."

She studied him questioningly, almost doubtfully.

He nodded once, firmly, hoping to convey that he did understand and that he was okay with her terms . . . even if they gave him pause. They were her requirements, and he would accept them for now, because he wanted any piece of herself she was willing to share with him. He stared at her wordlessly, his gaze roaming her face.

She moistened her lips. "All right then. Very good. So I made the first move last time. It's your turn now. Let's see what you got, Martin."

Nodding, he took a breath and then leaned in to kiss her softly, tenderly. Several times. Light kisses to her eyelids, her chin, her jaw, the corner of her lips. His thumb brushed the line of her jaw and up to her mouth.

Holding her face in his hands, he settled his mouth on hers more firmly and kissed her slowly. He took his time. He wanted to remember it. He wanted to remember and savor every moment with her.

Her hands came up on either side of his head, threading through his hair and holding him as he held her. Her fingers drifted, brushing his cheeks.

He pulled back slightly so that he could look down at her.

"What?" she whispered in a voice that trembled. It was that tremble that got to him, hinting that there was potentially more between them despite what she said. "Why are you staring at me like that?"

"Like how?" he asked, even though he knew.

Her face, her voice, the softness he thought he saw in her eyes, tore something loose inside him and left him feeling raw and vulnerable. It was good and scary. Scary good.

Her mouth worked, but speech eluded her. She dropped her gaze, as though what she saw in his face was too much.

"I'm just memorizing your face, Hayden Vargas."

A breath shuddered out of her, fanning his lips, and he smiled. He'd respect her terms, but he had the feeling there was more than just physical attraction between them, and maybe she was realizing that.

She shook her head and blinked, the softness disappearing from her eyes. "You talk too much. Just kiss me, okay?"

He reached forward and hauled her onto his lap. She came willingly, straddling him, and they kissed like that, long and deep.

He brought a hand into the heavy mass of her bun, tumbling it loose. "Man, I love your hair," he muttered against her mouth, running his hands through it and holding it back to keep kissing her without impediment.

She was breathless and panting when she suddenly broke away, her eyes heavy-lidded and dazed.

He stared back at her, one hand buried in her hair, the other still holding her face as though she were some fragile piece of crystal. His thumb trailed down her cheek. It seemed impossible that he was here with her, feeling the things he was feeling. He'd never felt anything like this . . . never anything this strong.

He heard her voice in his head. *No feelings. Purely physical.*

Yeah, too late for that.

DON'T BE AFRAID TO TAKE CHARGE AND ASK FOR WHAT YOU WANT.

x Hayden x

The way Nolan's eyes slid over her warmed Hayden from the inside out. It wasn't the kind of look she usually got. This was different. It wasn't purely lust-filled, although there was some of that mixed in there, too. He looked at her like he . . . *liked* her. As though he saw more than her looks or her reputation. Damn that hand of his holding her face and damn these pesky *feelings*.

She'd ordered him not to develop any feelings for her, but here she was, all melty inside when he looked at her. It wasn't smart. Clearly she should have been warning herself. Some expert in seduction she was. Maybe she was the one who needed the lessons.

"Why'd you stop?" she asked raggedly.

"I like looking at you." His gaze roamed her face as his gravelly voice rubbed like velvet on her skin. Skin that suddenly felt overly sensitive everywhere he touched her.

He was staring at her mouth now and her face went from warm

to hot. How could he do that with a look? She didn't get it. Butterflies took off in her belly. And that's how she knew she was in trouble. Everything that set him apart from every other boy she had ever known was what drew her to him.

Maybe it was this giddy realization. It emboldened her. She sat up a little higher on her knees so that her chest was level with his face.

He froze.

Holding his gaze, she pulled her sweater over her head and tossed it to the floor, reveling in the way his eyes darkened, traveling over her in admiration. Pleasure rushed through her.

She ran a hand over her black bra, lightly caressing one lacy cup, finally feeling like she had the upper hand. She knew she had invited him to make the first move, but she liked being in control.

"You're so beautiful, Hayden," he whispered.

"I'm just a girl in a bra. I'm sure you've seen plenty." *This was just physical. This was just physical.* She couldn't lose perspective of that, no matter how much he unraveled her and made her feel things she had never felt. "I think you've seen me in less than this, like my bikini the other night. The girls practically pop out of that thing."

She slowly lowered back down onto his lap.

He chuckled. "Yeah, I noticed, but that was different." His gaze ate her up. "A lot different than this."

She smiled, angling her head to the side. "Hm. Not really." She pressed a finger to his lips, enjoying touching him, enjoying the texture of his mouth. She already knew its taste. Already knew that he could kiss her until she was a quivering boneless lump.

She lowered her head and pressed her open mouth to his neck. She licked and sucked at the salty-clean taste of his skin. He sighed beneath her, his breath rustling her hair. Sitting back up, her hands dived for the hem of his shirt. She tugged it up. He leaned forward and lifted his arms, helping her pull it over his head. The sight that greeted her punched the air right out of her chest and made her hate jocks a little less, if this was a factor of their existence.

He was lean and hard. His torso cut and defined. Her gaze lowered to his abs. Screw six-pack. She counted under her breath. Was that *eight*?

Air sawed roughly from his lips, and when she lowered her mouth to his chest, his breathing spiked a notch as she licked him.

His hands came up to circle her waist. She let them drift until they crept toward her breasts, then she stopped him, grabbing his wrists.

"I do the touching. You just relax." She pushed him back on the couch, enjoying her control. Hovering over him, she felt empowered.

She took a savoring glimpse of his face, of his dark, gleaming eyes fastened on her, before lowering her attention to his chest. She kissed the broad expanse — gentle butterfly kisses, and then long, open-mouthed moist ones.

She inched up to his jaw and neck and blew in his ear before biting down on his earlobe. He tensed beneath her with a groan and she knew he liked it. She felt drunk, which was impossible considering she didn't drink. It was Nolan. He muddled her head and made her blood pump like thick syrup in her veins.

He tried to kiss her and she dodged his mouth. She needed to avoid his kisses. They turned her brain to mush.

His eyes burned her up. "I want your lips," he said hoarsely.

"Oh, you're going to get them," she promised.

"On mine," he clarified.

"You'll enjoy wherever I" — she kissed his collarbone and then the pulse point on his neck and then the top of his chest — "kiss you." Her lips trailed down the center of his chest.

His hands drifted back to her waist, his warm palms caressing the exposed skin above her waistband. His touch was more than tempting, but she moved his hands back to his sides.

"Let me touch you," he begged.

She dropped her hands to his jeans, her fingers closing around the snap and tugging the denim open.

"Hayden," he choked, his voice thick and strangled as his hands came over hers, stalling her. She looked into his eyes and felt herself slipping, drowning. "You don't need to do that."

He lifted a hand to circle the back of her neck and bring her closer. She didn't resist as his lips claimed hers and those feelings she feared came rushing to the surface.

Her brain turned to mush. He had a way of kissing that consumed her, that melted her bones and made her pudding in his hands.

Her heart gave a violent thud against her chest.

"Hayden!"

Hayden and Nolan sprang apart. Her gaze shot to the door, and she realized the violent thud hadn't been her heart at all, but her mom flinging the door open and banging it into the wall.

Mom's gaze swept over her. She laughed, cackled really — her mother had an awful drunken laugh Hayden knew all too well.

She pointed at Hayden as she scrambled for her clothes like she was some great circus spectacle. Most moms would be shouting, maybe even crying, tossing out threats of lifelong grounding. Not her mom. Her mom laughed and offered up a high-five that Hayden ignored.

She had a friend with her. Some guy that looked strung out. Mom elbowed him. "Chip off the old block, right?" Mom eyed Nolan up and down appraisingly. "Well, hello there. Nice job, Hayden. Where did you find this tasty snack?"

"Mom," she said sharply, hot embarrassment flaming through her. "What are you doing home so early? I thought you were going to Galveston." Mom liked to gamble on the casino boats with the money they didn't have. Whenever she did that, Hayden didn't see her until late the next day. Sometimes the day after that.

Mom motioned to the guy next to her. "Alan here thought —"

"Alex," the guy supplied, his eyes tracking over Hayden hotly. Her skin crawled as she hastily finished dressing herself.

"I'm sorry, ma'am." Nolan addressed her mother, reaching for his own shirt and slipping it on over his head in one smooth move. Then he actually offered Mom a handshake. "My name is Nolan Martin."

Hayden fought back an eye roll. He was treating her mother like she was some kind of parent that might react in a normal way to her daughter making out half naked with a boy on the couch. It was sweet of him to think she had that kind of upbringing. Sweet and very misguided.

"Hey, don't apologize," Mom said. "I was a teenager once, too." She waggled her eyebrows and looked at the douchebag she brought home. "Still have the hormones of one."

God. Shoot me.

"Oh! Food." Mom's heavily lined eyes alighted on the fast food littering the coffee table. She stepped forward and dropped down on the couch, picking up Nolan's half-eaten burger. "Come on, Alan. You hungry?"

"Yeah. Starving," he said, even as his gaze continued to roam over Hayden like she was the turkey on Thanksgiving Day.

Gross. But then, Hayden was used to the gross guys her mom brought home. It was the only type of guy Mom seemed capable of attracting. That's why Hayden had a padlock on the outside of her bedroom door and a deadbolt on the inside, and she slept with a bat under her bed. She didn't leave anything to chance. Not while living with Mom.

This world was full of victims and survivors . . . and then there were the people fortunate enough to live a life safe and free of fear.

Someday Hayden would have that. Someday she would have her own place. Someday she would sleep in a bedroom without locks on the door. And that bat she owned? It would take its rightful place in the garage with other sports equipment. Until then, she functioned by expecting the worst at all times and being prepared for it.

Nolan moved to stand beside her.

"I'll walk you to your truck. Come on, Nolan."

He lingered as though he would do the whole polite farewell thing to her mother, but Mom was too busy stuffing her face and fishing for the remote control in the couch cushion. The gross guy was more interested in watching Hayden than eating. *What a creep.*

She spun around and exited the house, confident that Nolan would follow. She hurried down the walkway toward his truck, the sound of his footsteps fast after her. When she reached the driver's door, she turned to face him, her hands rubbing up and down her arms as though warding off the chill night.

Immediately, his dark gaze was assessing, peeling back the layers as he looked at her. It made her skin itch.

"What . . ." He paused, clearly gathering his thoughts and words. Undoubtedly, he was wondering about her train wreck of a mother and that douchebag she just brought home.

Sighing, she looked back at her miserable little house, sagging like a hunkered old body in the night. She needed to get back inside. She had left Sanjana asleep in her bedroom, and even though Mom and her friend didn't know there was anyone else in the house, she did not like the idea of leaving anyone unprotected while they were at her house. It wasn't as though her mother was a predator. Her mother was simply indifferent to the predators who buzzed around her ... and followed her home.

Trying to make light of it, she patted his chest. "That was fun. Maybe we can do it again." She motioned to the door of his truck.

He frowned, looked at his truck and then back to her again. "Hayden ... I don't really like the idea of leaving you in there with ..." He motion toward the house, again searching for the words.

"With my *mother?*" she finished, letting that hang between them so maybe the ridiculousness would sink into his head.

Nolan shifted on his feet uncomfortably.

She continued with an edge to her voice. "Why? Are you offering for me to move in with you then? Because I live with my mom. Like *all* the time. This is my life, and I'm quite adept at dealing with it. I don't need you to save me." She had seen how he could be with his sister. She didn't want his pity. She definitely didn't want to be his little project. She didn't need saving. She could save herself. She had been doing it for as long as she could remember.

She sighed, wishing she could go back to before. When they were kissing on the couch and she wasn't thinking at all. There was no Mom with a douche-date. She didn't have to reveal this part of her life.

"Hayden," he said gently. "Did you even notice how dilated his eyes were? Clearly he's on something."

She snorted. "Yeah, and my mother probably is too. This is my life, Nolan. As ugly as it is. Welcome to my world." She held her arms out wide at her sides. "You can't save me from it."

He blinked and expelled a breath. He was out of his element. And that was okay. She didn't want him to do anything for her. She just wanted him to go back to being the boy on the couch with his lips on her neck. Not a boy who cared about her or wanted to help her or saw the realities of her life she tried so hard to keep hidden.

This concern, this level of care . . . it wasn't part of the deal. She didn't want it from him.

Suddenly, she felt colder. "Just go home, Nolan."

He glanced at his truck and then back at her. "Do you want to hang out tomorrow —"

"No!" she snapped, and then took a breath to soften her tone. She had set the parameters earlier tonight. Evidently they were a struggle for him. "Let's just leave it at tonight. It was fun. But let's stop while we're ahead."

His expression hardened. "That's it then? I tell you I'm worried about you and that I care about you and you're ready to kick me to the curb?"

"*Care* about me?" His words felt like a chokehold. "You don't care about me. I'm Hayden Vargas. The girl your sister hired for kissing lessons. Remember that? You know what everyone says about me. You thought the same thing. I'm the school slut, remember? The only reason you're even here tonight is because you're single now and looking to . . .'"

"And looking to what?" he demanded.

She shook her head in disgust, crossed her arms over her chest, and settled into silence. There was nothing else to say.

He continued, "You act so strong and so tough." He inhaled. "But I never took you for a coward."

She dropped her arms to her sides. "I'm a coward? Just because I don't want to be with you? What? Did you think I could be the next Priscilla in your life? We agreed this was just for fun. Nothing serious."

"No! I never expected you to be like Priscilla. I just want you as you are."

She scoffed. "You don't want *me*."

He ignored her. "I want to be with you and I want us to see where this can go . . ."

"Where it can go?" She laughed bitterly. "This is not going anywhere. Sure, you could probably get in my pants. You touch me and I melt like butter, but that's the only place we will ever go. It's just chemistry. It's only physical. There's nothing deeper than that. You're going off to school somewhere where you'll meet another Priscilla and I'll move out of this house and finally get my own life."

He nodded slowly, as though processing. "If you're not careful, when you get that life, you're going to live it all alone."

Did he think that scared her? That's what she had been planning all along. A safe life all by herself that she could control. She looked skyward and then at him again.

His face was flushed. She knew she had upset him. *Good*. He expected too much from her, and he needed to realize that this couldn't be anything more. She needed him to quit. Like everything in her life, she needed him to quit on her.

She had plans that did not include Nolan. She smiled at him and he blinked, clearly not expecting a serene smile from her while they were arguing like this.

"That sounds good to me, Nolan. No. Actually, it sounds perfect."

IT'S ALL ABOUT CONFIDENCE, EVEN IF YOU'RE JUST PRETENDING.

x   Emmaline   x

Emmaline's mom was washing dishes when she walked in the house with Beau behind her.

She'd invited him inside, not sure if he would accept the offer — especially after the awkwardness that was now between them. It just seemed the thing to do. Over the years, he'd spent more time in the Martin household than his own. He'd agreed to come inside for Nolan. *Of course.* It was the reason Beau was in her life in the first place. He didn't want to come inside because of her. He didn't want to come inside *for* her. Whatever happened in the truck was a fluke. *I want to kiss you, Pigeon.* He was Beau Sanders. Maybe for a moment he forgot she wasn't just a random girl.

"Hey, guys," Mom greeted as she dried her hands with a dishtowel. She glanced at the clock. "Party no fun? It's only ten. Didn't expect you until curfew."

Emmaline shrugged. "It was okay."

"Well, there's leftover pizza from Zio's. Savannah and I went there after the movie. It's in the fridge if you want some."

Emmaline glanced around the kitchen. "Where is Savannah?"

"She got invited to spend the night with Maddie. I dropped her off on the way home." Mom looked at Beau. "Nolan is in his room." She tossed the dishtowel on the counter. "I'm heading up to bed." She pressed a kiss to Emmaline's cheek. "See you in the morning, sweetheart."

"Good night," Beau said as Mom headed for the stairs.

"Night, Beau." She waved without looking back behind her.

Beau was just like another one of her kids to her. As commonplace as a piece of furniture. It was almost insulting. She didn't bat an eye over going to bed and leaving Emmaline alone with him.

Standing in the now empty kitchen, they stared at each other, tension swirling all around them.

Beau cleared his throat. A muscle in his cheek twitched, the only outward sign that he was affected. He glanced toward the stairs and then looked back at her. "I'll go catch up with Nolan."

Yeah, in case there was any confusion. He was here for her brother and not her. They established that. "Sure. Okay." She nodded jerkily.

He took the stairs and she waited a moment, not wanting to follow him directly.

Once his steps stopped thudding on the stairs, she hurried into the shelter of her own bedroom. She stripped off the sweater she'd borrowed from Sanjana and squeezed out of her skinny jeans. Unclipping her bra, she slid it off her shoulders and dropped it to the floor.

She stretched her neck and released a breath. Standing in her underwear in her closet, she surveyed her T-shirts.

All these years she had nursed her crush on Beau privately. She had kissed pillows, pretending it was his mouth. It had seemed harmless enough. Foolish, but harmless. It was just a crush. Not real.

Except tonight all of that had come to a head.

I want to kiss you, Pigeon.

She could not get his words out of her head!

For a moment, she had thought he would. He had leaned in and then that car behind them had honked. What if he had kissed her?

Shaking her head, she pulled an oversized T-shirt off a hanger and slipped it on.

A knock sounded at her door. Before she could call out, it opened to reveal Beau. "Hey, Nolan isn't here. Guess your mom didn't realize he . . ." His voice faded as his gaze landed on her.

Nolan wasn't home. She had assumed Nolan's truck was parked in the garage.

Her mom was in bed.

She digested all of that in the space of a second.

Emmaline froze, achingly aware that he stood mere feet away while she wore an oversized T-shirt and her panties. Beau seemed to reach the same conclusion.

His eyes tracked over her slowly. "Sorry, I should have waited for you to say come in."

She swallowed. "Come in." Yes, that throaty husk was her voice.

He shut the door and leaned against it. He didn't come any closer though. His expression was like stone, revealing nothing as he gazed at her.

Her heart was racing, but a steady calm swept over her as she approached him. She didn't touch him. She was careful not to do that. She had other ideas.

Emmaline reached past him and flipped off the light to her bedroom.

Instantly the room was doused in a red glow thanks to the lava lamp on her dresser.

She met his gaze, holding it, conveying, she hoped, everything with a look. Everything like: she was glad he was here, and she couldn't get his words out of her head, and if he really wanted to kiss her she wanted to kiss him, too.

Slowly, she turned and walked toward her bed, praying that some of her time with Hayden had rubbed off on her. She tried to look sexy as she stopped and slid him an inviting look over her shoulder. He stayed motionless, his back pressed against that door as if he was the only thing holding it in place. As though moving away from it might send the whole house crashing down around them.

She didn't care though. Let the house fall down around them. Let the whole thing crash to dust and rubble. It would be worth it. Being with him . . . making her crush a reality, bringing it to life . . .

It would all be worth it.

With her back still to him, she pulled her shirt over her head. It was bold, but somehow she managed it. Confidence. Hayden told her it was all about confidence.

She'd be confident if it killed her.

She peered at him from over her shoulder, hoping she presented an enticing image, hoping it worked. Hoping he didn't open that door and walk out.

There was a soft thud as his head fell back against the door. "Emmaline," he said hoarsely. "You don't know what you're doing."

"I'm not a kid anymore, Beau. I know exactly what I'm doing and exactly what I want."

"No. You don't."

"I've always wanted you." The air rushed from her lungs. There. She'd said it. She'd made a big show about getting lessons from Hayden

224

so that she could attract guys, but the only guy she'd ever really wanted was him.

She was starting to get a crick in her neck from looking at him over her shoulder. She knew she should turn and face him, but her courage only went so far. It was one thing to take off her shirt and let him feast on a view of her back. Until he moved and showed the slightest indication that he was into her — into *this* — she wasn't turning around and flashing him her boobs.

Beau didn't move, didn't speak. Just when she was thinking he would bail on her and leave her rejected, he cursed and shoved off the door, coming at her in a few long strides.

She didn't turn around.

He stopped directly at her back, the cotton of his shirt brushing her bare skin. His hands landed on her; one at her shoulder and the other slightly lower, flat against her shoulder blade. His ragged breath fell beside her ear. "Is this okay?"

She shivered at his hands on her.

"Yes," she agreed. "You're staying." Her voice didn't even sound like her own. It was more like a strangled croak.

"You think I'm strong enough to walk away from you?"

His arm inched around her waist. He flattened his palm just below her breasts, his fingers splaying wide, almost covering her stomach completely, fingertips brushing her ribs. Not because she was so small, but rather his hands were so big.

With his other hand, he stroked her exposed back, tracing her spine, caressing each and every bump of vertebrae.

She felt her skin turn to gooseflesh. Air shuddered out of her. He made her feel feminine, small and delicate and precious.

Suddenly both his hands gripped her waist. She was airborne for the tiniest moment as he launched her onto the bed. She landed with a small yelp. He eased down, leaning over her, propping his elbows on either side of her head.

She refused to think about her almost-nakedness or how she might look bouncing around on her bed. She'd get too self-conscious if she mulled over that fact.

His face was so close. She reached for his jaw, reveling in the bristly scratch. He held himself still and she let herself explore his face, mapping out the arch of his eyebrows and the bridge of his nose. Her fingers caressed his well-carved lips.

They moved against her fingers as he spoke. "The way you look at me . . ." His voice faded.

"Yes?" she prodded.

"No one has ever looked at me like that before."

"Oh." She breathed the word, not sure she understood. "How am I looking at you?"

"Like you're stuck in the desert and I'm the last drink of water you're ever going to get."

She couldn't believe he didn't have a dozen girls looking at him like that. He was Beau Sanders.

He settled himself between her thighs. One of his hands slipped under her, splaying at the center of her back.

His head lowered. She shuddered as he pressed a kiss to the top of her breast. *Oh.* She ran her fingers over his head, through the short silky hair.

His mouth closed over the nipple, taking her fully into the warmth of his mouth.

She gasped and surged against him, her eyes wide, staring blindly. She had no idea it could be like this.

She wasn't foolish enough to think any boy could make her feel this way. This was Beau. It wouldn't be the same with anyone else . . . it wouldn't be so hot or thrilling if she hadn't known the guy forever and had feelings for him that were more substantial than a crush.

She clawed at his shirt, pulling the fabric, wanting to feel him, his skin to her skin.

He sat up, reached behind him, and pulled his shirt over his head. Then he was back. This time they were chest to chest. His hardness to her softness. His mouth met hers. It wasn't sweet or gentle or easy. He kissed her deep and hard. She kissed him back.

Her hands swept over his shoulders, gliding down his back. The flesh rippled and undulated under her hands. He pulled away and stared down at her, his blue eyes so deep and penetrating they glowed almost silver in the red haze of her bedroom. His breath crashed on the air as his gaze roamed over her. Her self-consciousness melted away and a thrill coursed through her, knowing he liked what he saw.

"You trust me?"

She nodded, a lump forming in her throat.

A slow smile spread across his lips and he slid down the length of her, taking his time. His hands went to her hips, playing with the edge of her panties.

She glanced down and grimaced at the sight of her pale gray cotton underwear. Not exactly sex goddess material. He pressed a slow, savoring kiss right below her belly button. Her nerves sparked like they were shot with electricity. His hand drifted lower and she gasped, jumping at the intimate press of his fingers, certain he felt the wild hammering of her pulse.

She was panting now, embarrassing little whimpers she couldn't stop.

"Emmaline, can I touch you?" The rough catch in his voice was the sexiest thing she ever heard.

She nodded and his hand slipped inside her panties. Sensation bombarded her as his fingers slicked through her. He made a strangled sound as he eased a finger inside.

Oh goodness.

She hardly ever heard of this happening. At school, it was usually about the girls *doing* for the boys — about blowjobs in the back seat of cars. All to satisfy some boy, and then the boys were quick to share all the intimate details of those trysts later so that the girl faced plenty of ridicule and scorn.

The boys were never scorned. Only the girls. That never struck her as fair. The injustice of it actually made her mad when she thought about it.

Right now this was all about her. About Beau giving *her* pleasure.

Shudders racked her as his fingers stroked in and out of her. He even used the base of his palm, building a delicious pressure that unraveled her. She arched off the bed with a cry.

He pressed his mouth close to her ear to breath her name, "Emmaline."

She held tightly onto his shoulders, clinging to him as an orgasm eddied over her.

They stayed frozen, moments stretching out between them. His hands slipped out from her panties and he pulled her into a hug, holding her.

She cuddled close to him, glad for this moment. She didn't know if it would be like this tomorrow or ever again, so she simply held on to him.

"Beau?" she whispered, not even sure what she was going to say.

"Hm, Pigeon?" Everything melted inside her at the nickname. Bones, muscle, sinew. She exhaled, relaxed.

A soft creak killed her lethargy. Tension rushed in. She knew the sound of her door opening. The hinges had needed greasing for a long time now.

Her arms tightened around Beau, squeezing. She knew it was probably the opposite reaction she should be having. She *should* be shoving him off her and grabbing some clothes. She should be hiding Beau.

She should be learning how to disappear — or better yet, how to make Beau disappear.

Instead, she peered over Beau's shoulder, hoping it wouldn't be that bad.

Except it was bad. She couldn't breathe. Her airways constricted to the point of pain.

It wasn't Mom. It was Nolan . . . and he was staring right at Emmaline. At Emmaline and Beau. In bed together.

NOT EVERY SURPRISE IS FUN.

x   Nolan   x

Ever since Nolan left Hayden's, his every step felt like it was attached to an anchor, threatening to pull him down.

He assumed his sister was asleep. The lack of light creeping out from beneath her door pointed to that. But just in case she was watching Netflix on her laptop in the dark, as she often did, he decided to pop in and see how her night went. It couldn't be worse than his night. Maybe she could distract him with a good story — or whatever new show she was marathoning.

He shook his head. The night had started out great with Hayden. Even with her ultimatum. Yeah, she had warned him they would only have a physical relationship, but he hadn't really thought that through. It sounded easy when she said they would only have a fling. Most guys would love that. Apparently, he wasn't most guys.

Now he understood that he could not disengage the emotional from the physical. Not when it came to her. There was something about him . . . something about her. Something he couldn't walk away from. He wanted more from her. More than a hookup.

Where had tonight gone all wrong? Even as he asked himself the question, he knew when it fell apart.

It went wrong the moment her mom showed up. Then it went even more downhill when he had opened his mouth and started giving his opinion like he knew what he was talking about. Like he knew what it was like to be in her shoes and live her life.

Nolan knew hardship. He'd lost his dad. He lived with that gaping hole inside him every day. But he never for one moment lived under a roof where he did not feel safe and loved. That was her burden, and who was he to judge how she managed it? She had made it this far without him.

He knew she didn't need him, but he wanted her to want him.

At least Nolan had his family. He could always count on them.

He eased open Emmaline's door slowly, just in case she was asleep.

The room was mostly dark. She had left her lava lamp burning, casting the room in a reddish light. Mom was always on her about turning it off at night so that she didn't burn the house down.

He took a step inside the room, assuming she'd fallen asleep and intending to turn off the lamp for her. They would talk tomorrow. Maybe they could hang out.

That's when a movement on the bed caught his eye. He stopped and frowned. The shapes were all wrong. Too many. Not just one body.

Two bodies.

Two people . . . but that didn't make sense. He didn't think she was having a sleepover. Beau had dropped her home alone. Sanjana was sleeping at Hayden's house.

He squinted, narrowing his eyes through the gloom, focusing on a face.

A face that wasn't Emmaline's.

Beau's face. Staring right back at him.

It didn't compute. What was Beau doing here? On his sister's bed? *In* his sister's bed? With his sister?

He was slow to process what his eyes were seeing. It was too incredible.

Impossible.

"What . . . the . . . ?"

Nolan never saw it coming. Never suspected Beau would do something like this.

His gaze drifted from Beau's face to his sister. She looked horrified. It was that expression . . . it told him everything. One look at her face confirmed it.

Beau was screwing around with his sister and he'd caught them in the act.

That knowledge rolled over and over in his mind. There was no justification for it. No excuse.

Beau stood up, shirtless . . . and the sight of that — with his sister in the background, scrambling for her clothes on her bed — ignited him.

He charged forward. No longer the composed one. Not the cool-headed one. Not anymore. He snapped.

Beau held up a hand. "Nolan, man, let me explain . . . It's not what —"

"It's not what I think?" He waved at his sister. "You're not in bed with my sister right now? 'Cause that's what it looks like."

Beau grimaced. "Okay. I know it looks bad."

Nolan barked a single laugh. "You forget who you're talking to. I know you. I know what you do to girls . . . how you use them."

Beau flinched. "I wouldn't —"

Nolan was in front of Beau in three strides, unable to let the lie even drop on the air. He shoved him hard in the chest. Beau staggered.

"But you did, Beau. You went there. You just couldn't help yourself. You could bang any number of girls out there, but you had to go after my sister."

"Nolan!" Emmaline lifted her voice. "Stop! It's not like that."

Nolan laughed harshly. Ugly anger sizzled through him. "Really, Emmaline? I thought you were smarter than that. You think you're the one for him? Beau has never had a girlfriend. There's a reason for that. The guy doesn't commit. He's all about getting laid."

Emmaline's face burned red. "It's not like that. Beau and I are . . ." Her gaze slid to Beau and the uncertainty surfaced. It was written all over her face. She blinked several times, as though she had something in her eyes.

Seeing her doubt only angered him more. What kind of lies and promises had Beau told her? She shouldn't look that way.

Nolan wanted to think Beau would never use Emmaline like he did other girls, but then five minutes ago he would have sworn Beau would have never climbed into bed with her in the first place.

Nolan didn't know anything anymore.

He was in deep over a girl who didn't want anything to do with him. He didn't know his own best friend. He didn't know his own sister. He didn't even know himself. Not his own heart.

"Get out of my house." He grabbed Beau by the shirt and flung him in the direction of the bedroom door, ready to haul him out if need be. Ready to vent all his anger, all his disappointment, on him.

His sister hopped up from the bed, wearing nothing but an oversized T-shirt, and the sight only added to his foul temper.

"You don't get to do that, Nolan!" She planted her fists on her hips. "This is my home, too. You're not the only one who lives here!"

Beau shook his head. "I'll just go."

"Yeah. Great idea," Nolan said bitterly. "Go. Leave. Don't ever come back. Don't ever think you will be welcome here again."

"Nolan!" That horrified look was back on Emmaline's face.

He shook his head. He wouldn't be swayed by it. It didn't affect him. Everything he felt ran too deep. This was a betrayal he would never forgive.

Beau's face was all grim acceptance. He was smart enough to not even attempt to defend himself. His actions were indefensible.

Beau moved slowly toward the door, stopping for a moment and turning to look back at Emmaline. "I'm sorry —"

"You don't get to speak to her. Not even to apologize." He grabbed Beau and pushed him toward the door again.

"Stop it!" Emmaline cried, latching onto his arm.

Beau's face contorted and he twisted around and knocked Nolan's hands off him, severing the contact.

From there, everything just spun out, happening too quickly to track.

Nolan didn't know who moved next, or who pushed who, but suddenly Emmaline was on the floor and he and Beau were locked together, struggling, grunting, flailing around the room like a pair of gladiators hungry for a kill.

They collided into the dresser, knocking over several of his sister's knickknacks. He managed to land a punch in Beau's side before they twisted around and banged into the wall. One of Emmaline's shelves collapsed, raining books over them.

Beau took advantage of the distraction and sent his fist crashing into Nolan's face.

Nolan returned the favor with a shout, releasing all his anger on his former best friend and plowing his fist into his face with a satisfying whack.

He was dimly aware of Emmaline screaming, and the arrival of his mother, shouting and wedging herself between them.

Then they were apart. He took another swipe for Beau.

"Enough!" his mother shouted.

He stilled, his chest rising and falling with hard breaths. Blood trickled hotly down his face and he wiped the back of his hand against it.

Beau stared back at him, wild-eyed, the skin around his left eye quickly reddening and swelling.

He heard crying. Nolan's gaze shot around the room, taking in his mother's shocked expression.

And there was Emmaline — sobbing, sliding down the wall until she was a crumpled ball on the carpet. She tucked her legs inside her oversized shirt and sat there, rocking back and forth as tears ravaged her face.

"I think you should leave, Beau," Mom commanded. One look at her face told Nolan she had correctly assessed the situation. She had grasped the basic gist of what happened. Once you got an eyeful of Emmaline it wasn't hard to figure out.

Nodding, Beau turned and left.

KNOW WHERE YOU STAND WITH SOMEONE BEFORE YOU HOOK UP. IT WILL SAVE YOU DRAMA LATER.

x Hayden x

Hayden couldn't shake her sense of regret. It felt as dark and bottomless as an abyss, sucking her down inside its unknown depths.

She let it pull her under, escaping through sleep. Regret couldn't follow her there. She knew it was unhealthy. Problems had to be faced. Eventually. She knew she couldn't sleep forever, but for the time being, staying holed up in her room the rest of the weekend was her form of self-care. Curled up on her bed, the door locked, a barrier between her and the world outside, was the height of comfort.

She didn't usually do regret. Regret was for people who didn't know their own minds. Neither one of those things was her.

At least that was what she had always told herself. She'd believed she was too strong for that.

She was not like her mother, who complained incessantly, about how much life had wronged her, how life dumped on her every time something bad happened, which was all the time.

Hayden had always known herself. Known what she wanted in life. Known what she did *not* want. That was her gift: self-awareness. As soon as she graduated from high school, she would be out of her house, out of this town. She would be gone and never look back.

She fumbled for her phone in the gloom of her room and called in sick for work, something she never did. But the last thing she wanted to do was serve frozen yogurt to the after-church crowd. That wouldn't be good for her soul at all. All those happy families dressed in their Sunday best, coming in on a spiritual high, had a way of making her feel . . . *less.* It always succeeded in reminding her of what she wasn't. What she didn't have in her life.

Nolan had that kind of life. Even if he'd lost his father, he had that kind of sit-around-a-pot-roast-and-talk-about-your-day family.

She snorted.

And then she wondered if maybe she wasn't a little bit judgy. She had condemned Nolan for being judgmental of her when she was guilty of the same thing. Ironic, huh?

She had been hard on him, accusing him of forming opinions of her based on gossip and stereotypes, but when he had glimpsed into the reality of her life with Mom, she didn't want him looking inside. She didn't want him seeing.

He had peeked into her world, stood outside her ugly home with his arms outstretched, offering to help her, offering to be there for her like a true friend. She had so few of those.

Friends expected things. They wanted to be allowed inside, and she was not okay with opening the door.

He'd made her uncomfortable. He wanted things from her. Things no one had ever wanted.

He wanted inside.

Life was so much easier when she was dealing with guys who didn't want anything from her — who didn't want anything *real*. Who never knocked on her door. She knew where she stood with them. Where *they* stood. So yeah, she used them, engaging with them only on a superficial level and never for any significant length of time. Random hookups. She called the shots. She stayed in control.

Truthfully, life was easier when she kept *everyone* on the outside. It had never been hard keeping people at arm's length before, but now she suddenly had Emmaline and Sanjana in her face every time she turned around. They'd wiggled their way into her world right alongside Nolan.

She felt her control slipping. She wanted things to go back to before. To life without people, without friends, without guys who wanted more than a quick make-out sesh.

It was safer that way.

Nolan wasn't okay with being used — or using her. Apparently. *Obviously*. And that was reason enough to stay away from him.

On Monday morning Hayden woke up early, well rested from all the sleeping she'd done in the quest of avoidance.

She stepped out of her bedroom and pulled the door shut after her. With her steel lock ready in her hand, she secured it in place and locked her door from the outside. It seemed extreme, but she'd learned the hard way. Three years ago she had come home to find her room totally ransacked by one of her mom's so-called friends. Some of her clothes were gone, as was her makeup and jewelry. Nothing really valuable, but that wasn't the point. It was her stuff. She'd worked for all of it.

She walked past Mom's closed door, hearing her gentle snores from the other side. She walked down the short hallway, her shoes muffled on the carpet, and pulled up short at the sight of Alex standing in the kitchen in a pair of dingy boxers that hung low on his emaciated-looking hips.

He was leaning against the sink eating a bowl of cereal. *Her* cereal. She'd bought the Froot Loops and milk last week after she got paid.

He looked up. "Hey there, Hallie." Milk dribbled down his whiskered chin.

She didn't bother correcting him. Actually she preferred him not knowing her name at all. He wouldn't be around for long, anyway. These men never were. They came and went through her mother's life like viruses. They ran their course, and she waited them out. Endured. Survived.

She dropped her backpack on the table and moved to the pantry. Spotting a box of cereal bars, she took the last one. She also grabbed an empty water bottle, filling it up at the faucet. She had to have something to wash down her breakfast.

Turning around, she gasped and physically jerked. Mom's douche-date had moved in closer now and stood right in front of her.

"Going to school?" he asked.

She nodded, trying not to show her disdain for him. It was a fine line to walk. Don't look too interested, but don't be so rude as to offend them either. Many of these men did not like to be insulted. They had egos and chips on their shoulders. They got angry when they were insulted. They got mean.

"Good for you." He nodded as though his approval mattered to her. "Never finished high school myself, but I do okay." His hand moved to scratch low on his pale concave belly.

"That's great," she said mildly, injecting no emotion whatsoever into her voice. He frowned as she stepped around him and she wondered if he had detected some of her contempt. Or maybe he was just more perceptive than the usual creep her mom brought home.

Hayden circled around him and picked up her backpack from the table. She was heading toward the door when his voice stopped her. "Nice lock for your bedroom."

So he had noticed that, had he? He was that guy. Always casing his surroundings. Never had she been so glad she put the lock on her door.

He continued, "What you got in there? The Holy Grail?" He laughed at his joke.

"Shoes," she replied breezily, moving toward the front door.

"Shoes?" He looked bewildered, his gaze dropping to the very beat-up pair of Vans she wore. Clearly, she was no shoe aficionado.

"Oh yeah, I'm really into shoes." Girls' shoes were the least enticing thing to a man and therefore the only thing she would admit to having in her room.

She didn't bother with a farewell. She escaped her house, eagerly making her way toward her car. Even though she would probably have to see Nolan today, she was glad to get away from her mother's latest loser.

Except thirty seconds later, sitting in the driver's seat, she was faced with her all-too-frequent ugly reality again.

She wasn't going anywhere. Hayden tried to start her car — and then tried it again. No luck. She pounded her fist on the steering wheel. The living room blinds sprang open and she could see Alex staring at her, still eating her cereal.

No way was she going back in that house. She dug her phone out of her backpack and sent a quick message to the only person she figured could help her out in this instance.

Well, except for Nolan. He could help. He *would* help. That's the kind of guy he was. Good. Decent. He'd help her even though she'd been sure to push him away.

But there would be no calling him. No asking him for help. She couldn't let herself do that.

Beau answered on the second ring, still sounding a bit groggy. "Yeah, I'm up."

He was never a morning person. She had teased him for his grumpy ways all those mornings waiting for the bus — back when they had been friends. "Ah, that's right. You're a bear in the mornings."

"Are you calling for any reason, Hayden? Or just to bust my balls?"

She sighed and rubbed at the center of her forehead, hating asking anyone for anything. "My car won't start. Again. I don't think another jump is going to do it. It might actually be dead this time. Would you mind giving me a lift to school? The bus has already come and gone or I would —"

"Sure. It's fine. Give me five minutes. I'm almost ready."

"Thanks." The line went dead.

She glanced back toward the house. Alex was still watching her through the blinds, still eating her damn cereal.

Beau made it in less than five minutes to her house.

She slid into the passenger seat and sent him a quick glance. "Thanks. I'll figure out something for tomorrow —" She stopped abruptly when she caught sight of his face and whistled between her teeth. "Wow. What's the other guy look like?"

He sent her an annoyed look. "You'll see soon enough."

"Will I?"

"Yes. You two have been cozy lately, after all. Don't think I haven't noticed. I've seen the way he looks at you. And vice versa."

She stared at him for a long moment, uncomprehending. She would not characterize her relationship with Nolan as cozy. It was too messy to be cozy, but who else could he mean?

"Nolan?"

He grunted in what could only be taken as affirmation. She assessed his battered face again. The skin around his eye looked like raw meat.

"He's your best friend. What happened?" She held back the rest of what she wanted to ask. *Is Nolan okay? Is he hurt?*

"I think it's safe to say he's not my best friend anymore."

She looked straight ahead through his dirty windshield. "I don't understand. How can you go from best friends . . . to not?"

Her chest tightened and prickled. She had an overwhelming urge to see Nolan, to check in on him. Not just on his physical well-being, but his emotional well-being. She knew that if he and Beau had a falling out, he would take that hard. They were close. Like brothers.

"It's easier than you think." His lips twisted. He flexed his grip on the steering wheel. His knuckles were white, so she knew that this was not easy for him despite his light tone.

And people said girls were dramatic? Guys. Were. Idiots. "Whatever happened, you need to make it right."

He cut her a sharp glare and looked back at the road again. "Sometimes there is no fixing things. Once you cross that line you can't go back."

"Cross the line? What line? What did you —"

"How do you know *I* did anything?"

She gave him a look.

"He caught me with Emmaline," he admitted in a rush of words, as though he was annoyed with her for making him say it. "I'd appreciate it if you kept that to yourself, too. I could do without the gossip . . . and

I'd like to protect Emmaline from it. You know what assholes people can be."

She stared at him in silence for a few long moments. "Wow. I mean, I had a feeling that you were into her, but your best friend's sister? You *actually* went there. I don't know whether to be impressed or horrified."

"Well, everyone else is horrified," he sneered. "Because I'm *that* big of a douche."

"Everyone who?"

"Oh, Nolan. Mrs. Martin . . . they walked in on us."

"Just . . . wow." She whistled and shook her head. "Like I said though. Not surprising."

"And why is that?"

"Because I've seen the way she looks at you."

He stared ahead, silent for several moments, until he sent her a quick glance and grudgingly asked, "And what way is that?"

She laughed lightly. "Idiot. It's the same way you look at her."

He trained his gaze back on the road, his fingers tapping away on the steering wheel. "I guess it must be the same way you and Nolan have been looking at each other."

That silenced her. She pressed her lips into a flat line.

He chuckled beside her. "Who's the idiot now?"

DON'T OVERANALYZE.
NOTHING KILLS THE MOOD FASTER.

x   Nolan   x

Everyone assumed Nolan's bad mood had to do with his breakup with Priscilla, which was weird considering he hadn't thought much of her these last couple days. And yet it was easier to let people think the obvious rather than explain the complicated truth. The fact that both Nolan and Beau had bruised faces added to the speculation. No one came close to guessing the truth, of course. Rumors circulated. Most people believed they got into a fight with some guys from a rival school. No one suspected their fight was with each other.

The truth was no one's business anyway.

Not that there was anyone he could confide in, since the people he felt closest to — Beau, his sister, and, yeah, Hayden — happened to be unavailable.

Emmaline was avoiding him, taking the bus in the mornings. He wasn't sure how she was getting home. When she wasn't at his car at the end of the day on Monday, he'd texted her and gotten back a terse reply that she had a ride home. For all he knew that ride was Beau. He decided to let the matter drop. He wasn't in the mood for that battle and he knew it would be an all-out war if he pushed her on it.

Emmaline wasn't the only one avoiding him.

He didn't see Hayden at the usual times and places. They often intersected between sixth and seventh periods, but not this week. She must have been taking a different route.

Beau couldn't avoid him quite so easily. They had two classes together, as well as athletics. They saw each other, but no words were exchanged.

When had his life turned into such a mess? He had always prided himself on having his shit together. No drama. No fireworks. He was stable and reliable.

Guess he was just as screwed up as everyone else, after all.

With that grim and somewhat sobering realization, he decided to try and mend at least one of his fractured relationships.

He'd start with Hayden. Somehow, he felt like if he had her in his life he might be able to manage all the rest.

He wasn't sure when he would get around to talking to Beau. That pain, that betrayal, was still too fresh. He would make things right with Emmaline, of course. Eventually, but inevitably. She was his sister and he loved her. That would never change.

Nolan tossed his backpack and gym bag in the back seat of his truck and headed for Hayden's neighborhood. He passed Beau's street, but didn't turn. He wasn't ready to look into his best friend's face and think about the things he had done to his sister — *with* her. Undoubtedly, it was the same thing Beau had done to countless girls. And that only pissed him off all over again.

Would any guy be ready to forgive his friend for something like that? He knew how Beau operated. The girls he used. The girls whose numbers he always seemed to lose once he was done with them. There was a reason why people called him a player. It was always a game. Never serious.

Hayden's vehicle was parked in front of her house. *Good.* She was home. He parked behind her car and headed up the front walkway. He knocked on the door and then buried his hands in his front pockets, waiting in the chilly air, feeling suddenly self-conscious.

She did that to him. Twisted him up in knots. Made him feel less than confident. She made him think. Made him think too much. Yes, there was such a thing. She'd made him look deeply at himself. He'd never had that with Priscilla. Priscilla had given him comfort. Hayden challenged him and made him want to be a better person.

Everyone always told him he was a good person, applauding him for stepping up when his dad died. He never understood that. What else was he supposed to do? Fall apart? Be a burden on the rest of his family?

Hayden was the first person in his life who made him question himself and his motives. She held up a mirror to his face and showed him that he wasn't the perfect person everyone always praised him for being. She saw more than the great son, great brother, great student, great athlete, great friend, everyone always told him he was. It was all great . . . *bullshit.*

The guy from the other night opened the door — Alex, he thought, Hayden's mom's friend.

"Hey there, man." The guy held up his fist for Nolan to bump like they were old friends.

He swallowed back his distaste and asked, "Is Hayden home?"

"Ah, yeah. I think she's getting ready for work." He stepped back and shouted through the house, "Hayden! You got company, sweet cheeks!"

Nolan winced. The guy really was a douchebag.

Hayden emerged, looking like she would enjoy hitting her mother's boyfriend. She paused as her gaze turned on Nolan, and that expression on her face didn't even alter one tiny bit. *Great.* He was in the same class as this creep? That did not bode well for him.

Without a word, she strode out onto the front porch. Nolan took it upon himself to close the front door in Alex's face. He followed Hayden to the end of the porch, where she waited for him with her arms across her chest.

"Hi."

She gave him a disgusted look. "You came over here to say hi? I don't have time for hellos. I'm going to be late for work."

"I want to talk to you. About the other night. I'm sorry about the way things went down —"

"What are you doing here, Nolan?"

Frustration crept into his voice. "I'm trying to get things right —"

"Really? You shouldn't be worrying about me. I don't matter."

He flinched. "Why would you say —"

Again, a disgusted look crossed her face. "Why don't you start by trying to fix things a little closer to home?"

His shoulders tensed. "Meaning?"

"Oh, Nolan. You're many things, but not stupid. No one could ever make that accusation."

"Why do I feel as though I should be insulted right now?"

"Fix things at home. Fix things with your sister. Fix things with Beau. Forget about me." She patted the center of her chest for emphasis.

It was his turn to laugh. "Forget about you. That's funny." He shook his head.

"Don't do that." She stabbed a finger in the air. "Don't act like I'm somehow as important to you as they are." She stepped closer so that

247

her fingertip pushed him in the chest. "I said, forget me and concentrate on them. Fix it with them."

"Oh, that's funny. You want me to fix things at home?" He waved toward her house. "*You* can't even do that. You just live your life like an ostrich with your head buried in the sand, like you can't see what's going on around you . . . like nothing can get to you."

"Stop analyzing me!" Her eyes blazed. "Take care of your own shit before you cast stones. Your sister and Beau are so into each other. Are you just blind to that? Why do you have to get in their way? What are you? The grand blocker of love?"

Blocker of love? He mouthed the words at her. He didn't even go into the irony of that. Hayden was as emotionally guarded as they come. She wouldn't even let him *like* her.

"Oh stop," she snapped.

"You mean I should just let Beau go after my sister? Fuck her and then toss her aside? Sorry. No. Not going to do that."

"Stop being so dramatic . . . and gross." She shook her head as though so disappointed in him. "You think so little of them. She's your sister. She's smart. He's your best friend. You know him. He would never disrespect her."

He stared at her mutely, fury vibrating off him. He came here for her, not to defend himself to her. He didn't want to hear this.

She continued, "Will you be able to monitor the guys she dates in the future? You have to let go. Can you guarantee she'll never go out with a douchebag? You won't always be around, you know? What then?"

"They won't be Beau," he said tightly. "I'll know that."

"Yeah, they won't." She rubbed her face. "You don't see it." She dropped her hands. "Let me be blunt."

"Because you haven't been?"

"Why don't you stop being selfish and get out of Emmaline and Beau's way before you lose them both? And while right now you *think* you're fine without Beau, I don't think that's true. And your sister will resent you forever if you take this choice from her. If Beau is a mistake, he's hers to make."

The words resonated with him and he hated that. He wasn't ready to admit she was right and that he might be wrong on this. "For someone who doesn't like me butting into her life, you sure do enjoy butting into mine."

She cocked her head at an angle. "You're the one standing on my front porch. You drove over here and knocked on *my* door."

True — she had a point. He had asked for this. But he didn't have to stay to listen to another word, even if all the words coming from her were making him think that maybe he was wrong and she was right — at least when it came to Beau and Emmaline.

Maybe if she had family that she cared about, who relied on her and she relied on them, she would understand, but he wasn't that big of a dick to point that out to her.

Instead, he did what she wanted.

He turned and hopped off her porch and headed toward his truck. "You're right," he called. "I came over here, but I won't make that mistake again."

LESSON #32

WHEN IT'S TOO RISKY, BAIL.

x Hayden x

When Hayden reentered her house, Mom was in the kitchen with Alex. She was hunched over, her silk robe riding up and showcasing the bottom half of her ass cheeks. Not that Mom minded. There wasn't an ounce of modesty to her.

Hayden knew the only things in that fridge were ketchup, mustard, and packets of soy sauce, but she didn't bother pointing that out.

She walked a hard line to her bedroom. She had to be at work in twenty minutes and she had no intention of being late. Thankfully, she had gotten her car up and running again. Even though it had cost her a couple hundred dollars to get it serviced.

"Hayden! Do you have any peanut butter in your room?" Mom called through the paper-thin walls.

She knew Hayden kept food in her room. She never once complained about the lock on her door. It was one of the few things Mom seemed to respect — Hayden's right to her own space. That said, she was always asking Hayden for stuff like she was the neighborhood corner store.

"Um. I'll see." She hurried into her room and quickly changed into her work clothes. On the way out, she grabbed the jar of peanut butter sitting on top of her tiny fridge.

Peanut butter in hand, she yanked the door open and yelped to find Alex standing there, waiting.

"Oh." She pushed back strands of hair from her face. "You startled me."

"So you keep peanut butter in there? What else you got to eat?" He peered over her shoulder, trying to get a look into her room.

She turned and shut her door, securing the lock in place. "Just peanut butter," she lied.

The guy was pushy. She hoped Mom got tired of him soon, but the sad thing was, she knew it wouldn't happen that way. Mom never tired of them first. When she found a loser, she usually clung to him until she got dumped. That's who she was. That's the kind of abuse to which she was accustomed. She accepted it. Expected it.

Hayden set the peanut butter on the counter beside the stale loaf of bread Mom was unwrapping. "There you go. See you later."

Then she was out the door.

On her way to work, she daydreamed about her own place in Austin. It could be some shoebox, and likely would be, but she didn't care. It would be hers.

Her own space. Blessed solitude. No locks except the normal one on the outside door. No Mom with her losers creeping around her. No guys like Nolan Martin showing up on her doorstep, challenging her idea of herself and what it was she always wanted — what she *thought* she always wanted.

She refused to think the two things were separate. What she *thought* she wanted and what she wanted were the same thing. They were. They had to be.

Hayden welcomed the distraction of work. Weeknights were slow, but she found plenty of things to occupy herself. She washed out tubs and cleaned the stockroom, letting Chaz work the front and deal with people. Chaz was a much better people person. That wasn't her forte, after all.

She was carrying in some supplies from the storeroom when she spotted Emmaline sitting at a table. Alone.

When had she arrived?

Sighing, Hayden dropped her load on the counter and turned to go back inside the stockroom. Only she stalled once she was standing inside the tight space.

Walking away from the sight of Emmaline Martin was physically impossible. The girl had crawled her way inside Hayden's heart, and she couldn't just ignore her.

With a grunt, she pushed back out of the storeroom.

Glancing at Chaz, she said, "Hey, Chaz, I'm going to take my break now."

Hayden rounded the counter and sank down in the chair across from Emmaline. "Any reason you chose to come here? Of all places you could mope in misery, you chose here." Her fingers tapped idly on the surface of the table.

Emmaline stabbed her spoon into her frozen yogurt. "I came here because I knew you would understand."

"I'd understand your misery?" Hayden smiled and tried not to let that bum her out.

Emmaline snorted. "Yeah, I guess so."

"I must put out that vibe." She gestured to herself, her fingers splayed wide. "Hayden Vargas, Girl Who Gets Misery." And she supposed she did understand that. She was well versed in misery.

Emmaline shook her head and laughed. "I don't know . . ." Her laughter faded. She stabbed her spoon harder inside the cup of her yogurt. "I don't know *anything*."

"You know more than you think you do. You know what you want, Emmaline. I think you've known that since you came to me for lessons. You. Know. What. You. Want." She deliberately spaced those words apart, letting them sink in. "So many people can't figure that out for themselves, but you know. You know, Emmaline."

Emmaline stared somewhere over Hayden's shoulder, her expression pensive, considering.

Hayden continued, "If you like Beau and he's into you, then you need to make your brother understand that he can't get in the way of that. Make him understand it's what *you* want."

Emmaline's gaze snapped to her face. "It's not just Nolan. My mom —"

"If you get Nolan on board, that's half the battle. You do one battle at a time. Just like one day at a time." She glanced at the clock on the wall. "I've only got about five minutes, so let's cut to it. Here's my last lesson, and this one is free."

Emmaline sat up a little in her seat, her eyes blinking once and widening. "I'm listening."

"You gotta take a stand, Emmaline. If you want something badly enough, then fight for it."

"Fight for it," Emmaline murmured to herself.

"That's right." She nodded and then looked away, suddenly uncomfortable in the face of her own advice. The only thing she had ever fought for was herself. Since she was a kid toddling around, largely neglected by her mom, she had been fighting for herself.

She'd never fought for someone *else*. She was telling Emmaline to do that, but she had never done that.

She was eighteen years old and alone. She didn't have anyone. True, she'd never wanted anyone, but she didn't allow herself to want anyone — to have anyone — and for the first time that felt sad. That felt sad and lonely.

For the first time in her life she felt *alone*. She felt *lonely*.

LESSON #33

YOU CAN'T CARE ABOUT WHAT OTHERS THINK.
ONLY WHAT YOU THINK.

x   Nolan   x

It was surprising how easy it was to avoid someone who lived under the same roof.

Nolan wouldn't have thought it possible, but his sister showed him just how it could be done. She was quite skilled at avoidance. He didn't think she could manage it for days, but she did.

Emmaline spent most every night in her room. Mom went in to talk to her, but he didn't even try. She didn't want to see him. She'd iced him out ever since he busted in on her and Beau.

When he woke for school in the mornings, Emmaline was always gone. She got up even earlier and took the bus to school. The *bus*. Emmaline opted for that rather than ride to school with him. She was a junior. No one rode the bus if they didn't have to, and she didn't have to.

He drove to school alone. Savannah usually rode with Mom. So he drove himself. Just himself. No girlfriend. No sisters. A definite change from the way things used to be.

Pulling into the crowded parking lot, he spotted Priscilla. She was getting out of Anthony Morales's Jeep and was all smiles as she looked up at the school's star soccer player. Apparently, she had no trouble finding a new ride to school.

That was good. It was a good thing she was out there again. She didn't miss him, and it made things a lot easier because he didn't miss her. At least one thing was easy in his life right now.

And while he may not miss Priscilla, he missed Emmaline. The inside of his truck was depressingly silent as he pulled into his parking spot.

When he emerged from his truck and started toward the building, he got lost in the river of students. A few people greeted him, and he said hello back, but he didn't linger. If he hurried, he might cross paths with Hayden in B hall. Unless she was taking a different route again. He didn't see her doing that forever though. She wasn't the cowardly type.

He picked up his pace, hoping to see her, despite their final words. Despite *his* regrettable last words to her outside her house. He said he'd never bother her again. He said that and yet he was rushing to see if he could spot her. Just one glimpse.

He wanted to see her.

He wanted to hear her voice.

"Nolan, wait up."

He tensed, his shoulders locking up tight. Wrong voice. *That* was not the voice he wanted to hear.

He kept walking, reaching B hall.

Beau called his name again.

"Hey, Nolan. Hold up," Beau called again, louder this time.

A few heads turned, and he knew if he didn't turn around he would be attracting more attention. Beau would only call out louder, maybe say something people shouldn't hear.

Nolan stopped, sucked it up, and turned around. "What do you want?"

Beau stopped before him, his gaze intent. "You going to ignore me forever?"

The five-minute warning bell rang.

"I don't know, man." He didn't know. He only knew he wasn't ready to talk to him yet. He couldn't stare at his face without all kinds of conflicting emotions rushing through him.

"Well, I'm not going away —"

"You need to go away," he shot out. "Because I'm not ready to see your face."

Beau flushed with anger. "When are you going to grow up?"

"Me grow up?" Nolan's voice lifted. "Me? I'm not the one letting my dick lead me around. I'm not forgetting who my friends are."

Beau's face flushed hotter, splotches of red breaking out over his skin. "I haven't forgotten anything. I just want to be with her, man, see where this could lead. I don't want to hurt her."

People were staring. Nolan felt them watching. He noticed the bodies in his periphery who were stopping to gawk.

Someone muttered, "*Her* who?"

They were attracting too much attention.

Still, it couldn't stop him from threatening, "Shut up. Shut the hell up." He stabbed a finger in the center of Beau's chest. "You don't talk about her. Ever."

Dorian appeared beside them. "Everyone okay here?" His gaze flicked back and forth between them.

"Stay out of it," Beau said tightly. "This isn't about you."

"Yeah. Who is it about?" Dorian smirked. "You fighting over a chick? Come on. You guys are best friends. No pussy is so good that you —"

Beau was the first to move. He grabbed Dorian by the front of his shirt and spun around, slamming him against nearby lockers with a deafening rattle. He pulled back his fist to strike him, and then stopped himself. Panting, he held his fist in the air, poised, frozen.

Nolan stepped forward and dropped a hand to Beau's shoulder. "It's okay, man. He's not worth it."

Beau spit out, "You don't talk about people like that. You don't talk about girls like they're nothing."

Dorian shook his head. "It was just a joke. Relax."

The fury was still in Beau's face, but he lowered his fist, "It's really not funny. You should watch your mouth."

Nolan stepped back, assessing Beau and recognizing for the first time how much he cared about his sister.

And then she was suddenly there. His sister. Emmaline pushed through the gathered crowd, dropping her backpack on the floor in her haste to reach Beau. She grabbed his arm and pulled him from Dorian.

Beau looked at her and froze, the last of the fight leaving him, melting away like an ice cube in the sun.

His sister said something then. Nolan couldn't make out the words. They were words only for the two of them. Just for Emmaline and Beau. She let go of Beau's arm and brought her hand up to his face. It was terrible. His sister was caressing Beau's face, comforting him like some kind of . . . some kind of *more* than a friend, and it was terrible.

Nolan couldn't move. She didn't care that he was watching. She didn't care that anyone was watching.

"Emmaline," Nolan said.

She spared him a brief glance. "What?" Clearly, his commanding-big-brother voice had no impact on her. His influence was gone. At least in this.

She turned her attention back on Beau. Nolan watched her eyes go soft as she looked at him, her fingers stroking his cheek, and he had to swallow back his discomfort.

Nolan turned to go, but then his gaze collided with Hayden's.

She was watching, assessing, waiting to see what he would do, if he would flip out and rage at Beau and Emmaline. Everything he'd said and done before indicated he would do exactly that.

Nolan spotted Emmaline's backpack on the floor in front of him. He scooped it up and walked over to her.

She and Beau looked at him. They both visibly tensed, ready for whatever he was going to say. Ready and willing to take it.

"Here you go." He held out the backpack.

She took it from him. "Thanks." She and Beau swapped uncertain looks.

He inhaled deeply through his nose. "No problem."

They still looked uncertain.

He exhaled. "This is going to take a bit for me to get used to." Nolan gestured to them both. "But I'll work on it."

His sister smiled then. A wide, goofy grin that actually made him feel good.

Turning away, he pushed his way free of the gawking onlookers, hesitating when he reached Hayden.

The expression on her face wasn't smug anymore. It was something else.

"What?" he asked self-consciously.

She shook her head, almost too quickly. "N-nothing."

He grunted.

She waved at his sister and Beau. "That was . . . nice."

"Nice?" He shook his head. It didn't feel nice. It was hard. It was damn hard seeing them together and accepting it. It was hard not knowing if it was a mistake or the right thing or if his sister was going to get hurt.

But he was going to have to let it go. Let his sister decide for herself and maybe make a few mistakes along the way.

"I'm not nice," he muttered.

"Get to class! Break it up, everyone, and get to class!" a teacher shouted into the hall.

Students started to disperse as the tardy bell chimed. Bodies moved in every direction, set on their paths.

Looking away from Hayden, he turned and melted into the flow.

WHEN RISK IS UNAVOIDABLE, IT'S ALL ABOUT HOW QUICKLY YOU RECOVER.

x   Hayden   x

Hayden immediately noticed Alex's truck was parked in her driveway. *Fabulous.* Her mom hadn't managed to lose him yet. Surprising. And disappointing. Or maybe not. Maybe the asshole you know is better than the one you don't. Because Alex wouldn't be the last asshole in her mother's life.

She just wanted to go to work. Was that too much to ask?

She wanted to get in and out without talking to anyone. She wanted to go to work and forget about Nolan and that scene she'd witnessed in the hall this morning.

She'd watched Nolan put aside his feelings about his sister's choices. He'd done it for her happiness and maybe for Beau's happiness, too. It moved Hayden. More than she wanted to admit. She'd watched him and knew it was a struggle. She'd seen it all over his face and in the tension lining his shoulders. He still didn't like the idea of Emmaline and Beau, but he'd put aside his hang-ups.

Maybe she could learn a little from him and start to do the same.

She opened the front door and came to a hard stop.

The first thing she noticed was that Alex had all his clothes on. Usually, he crept around the house in his boxers, so she wouldn't look this particular gift horse in the mouth.

He was not alone. There was a big burly guy with him, and they were carrying the living room TV between them. She did a quick sweep of the living room. Mom was nowhere around.

"What are you doing?" she demanded.

Alex froze. "Hayden. Sweet cheeks. What are you doing here?"

She cringed at the horrible nickname. "I live here. What are you doing here?"

Alex shot his friend a cagey look. "Uh. We're just taking this in for repairs."

The TV was one of the only decent things they owned in this house. Her mother had priorities, after all, and she didn't want to miss her shows.

Her heart started racing. They were robbing the place. Not so surprising, she supposed. She knew what to expect from the kind of company Mom kept.

"Nothing is wrong with the TV."

The big guy spoke up, his voice like gravel. "Mind your business, girl, and there won't be any trouble."

She looked around and noticed other things. A small pile of electronics sat on the kitchen table, including her laptop. *Her laptop.* Which she kept in her bedroom.

Her gaze skipped down the hallway toward her door. It was ajar, the lock broken into bits along with splinters of wood on the floor. No. *No no no no no no no.*

She looked back at the table and her heart surged in her throat.

There, on top of it, was her shoebox. The shoebox that held every dollar she had ever earned. A shoebox full of the cash. The cash that was supposed to give her a fresh start in Austin.

They'd found it.

She reached for her cellphone in her pocket. "You need to put that down and go. I'm calling the police."

She had barely punched in her passcode when she felt a wind of movement.

Hayden looked up just as the big guy charged toward her. He wrenched the phone out of her hand and flung it against the wall, the case shattering to pieces. She knew the phone it once protected was destroyed.

"Like. I. Said." He enunciated each word carefully. "Mind your own business and there won't be any trouble."

Her stomach twisted and heaved. The man was capable of hurting her. She read that in his eyes. In his crazy eyes. He towered over her and he was huge. She couldn't beat him in a physical contest. He could break her just like he broke her phone. If she challenged him, that was precisely what he would do. She knew enough about life, about men like him, to know that.

She nodded jerkily and choked out, "Yeah. Okay." She waved toward the door, inviting him to leave. To take her stuff and go.

"Good." He huffed out a breath, but stayed where he was, glaring down at her like she somehow might go against her word and give him trouble.

Alex appeared in her line of vision, struggling to hold up the TV by himself. "C'mon, man," he snapped at his friend. "Let's go. We got everything."

With a grunt, the guy turned away from her.

Hayden backed up a few steps until she bumped into the wall.

From there she slid down to the floor, landing on her bottom, her legs kicked out in front of her.

She gulped back sobs and hugged herself, watching as Alex's friend moved to the table and gathered everything up in his giant arms. She watched mutely as he took her laptop and shoebox into his hands.

Easy come, easy go.

Except none of it was easy. Earning money wasn't easy, and watching him take it from her was even harder. None of it was fair, but she knew better than to mourn the unfairness of life.

She was so close to graduating. So close to getting out on her own, and now this happened. Hayden gulped back another sob.

She watched as he took her future into his hands and walked out the door, leaving her broken and alone against the wall.

LESSON #35

IF YOU NEED A DISTRACTION, THERE'S ALWAYS EXERCISE.

x   Nolan   x

No one was home when Nolan entered his house. He assumed Savannah had a game. Junior high games were during the week, freeing up the weekends for all the high school games. Mom would have left work and gone straight there.

He didn't have to guess at where Emmaline was. He knew she'd probably be with Beau.

He dropped his backpack on the kitchen table and stopped in front of the fridge, browsing Savannah's game schedule pinned to the door. Suspicions confirmed. She had a game across town. If he didn't have an obligation, he usually went to her games.

Usually. Today wasn't usual though. He didn't feel like sitting in noisy bleachers.

He took his phone from his pocket and set it on the counter, leaving it there as he marched up to his bedroom. He was content to leave it there for the rest of the night. He didn't feel like talking to anyone right now.

Nolan quickly shed his clothes and changed into a pair of athletic shorts and a T-shirt. He needed to let loose some energy. He grabbed a hoodie off the hook near the front door, his only acknowledgment that it was still a little cold out. They were nearing the end of January now, which meant it could be thirty degrees . . . or seventy.

He grabbed his basketball from the garage and jogged down the street toward the neighborhood park, the slap of his shoes on the sidewalk satisfying.

This was a good plan. Just to have something to do, somewhere to go, when he didn't quite know what to do with himself.

Everything had changed. Some of it from his own hand, true, but the rest . . .

The rest had just sort of happened to him.

Like a car crash. Unexpected and just as irreversible.

Like waking up one day and finding out your father had less than a year to live. Life was full of the unexpected.

He needed a release. Some way to expend his anxious energy and settle into the idea that he wasn't going to hang out with Hayden again. Not anymore.

She wanted to be left alone. He would leave her alone.

You didn't always get everything you wanted in life. He'd always known that. Now he knew that even better. It was the lesson that kept on giving.

The basketball courts were empty when he arrived. He started shooting, settling into a rhythm, starting from afar and working his way closer in. After ten minutes he pulled his hoodie over his head and dropped it on a nearby bench.

He dribbled and took shots until he was sweaty and out of breath.

He moved to the bench and wiped his face with his hoodie and then turned and drove in a lay-up. The ball swished through the net and he caught it, but held off on another shot as a figure approached him on the court.

"Hey," Beau greeted, shrugging out of his jacket. He dropped it on the bench and joined Nolan, holding out his hands for the ball. "Want to play HORSE?"

Nolan smiled. He couldn't help it. They'd been playing HORSE since they were seven years old. Not so much lately, but it brought back memories. He glanced around, almost expecting to see his sister, but there was no sign of Emmaline. Just Beau.

Just Nolan and Beau shooting hoops. That felt familiar.

"Sure." He passed Beau the ball, watching as he dribbled to his favorite shooting position in the far right corner of the court. He could always nail those corner shots.

Beau moved into position, squaring up, narrowing his gaze before letting the ball fly through the air in a perfect arc. Of course, he made his shot. He never missed. Apparently some things hadn't changed.

Nolan went next. They played in silence, taking turns, and that felt good. *Dribble. Shoot. Dribble. Shoot.*

At least some things stayed the same.

LESSON #36

IF YOU WANT SOMETHING TO CHANGE, THEN CHANGE IT.

x   Hayden   x

Hayden had the place mostly picked up by the time Mom got home.

Her door, of course, was another matter. It would require a handyman. She'd have to come up with the money for that somehow . . . and that brought a fresh wave of bitterness.

She was examining the extent of the damage when Mom sidled up next to her. "Where'd the TV go?"

She blew out a heavy breath and motioned to her door. It was of greater concern to her than their TV. Her door meant security, safety. It meant she could close her eyes at night.

Mom followed her gaze and whistled. "Damn. What happened?"

Her lips worked for a moment until she found her voice. "You happened to it, Mom. Your friend Alex. He robbed us. Took our stuff. Broke into my room and stole all my money."

"Huh." Mom nodded, her expression mild. Which pretty much summed her up: unmoved and unaffected by all the shit that happened to them. Obviously. Because if she cared, she'd be a different person. She wouldn't do all the things she did that rained shit down on them.

With a shrug, Mom went to her bedroom and closed the door.

Hayden leaned against the hall wall and stared at that shut door.

Her life was this. It always had been. She'd accepted it. Took these hits and kept on moving, braced for the next collision. And there would be more collisions. That was without question.

If life was full of hits no matter what she did, she wondered why anything she did mattered. Because all she did was build walls. She erected walls to keep everyone out — and the only people she managed to keep out were the ones who cared about her. The rest, the assholes like Alex, still found the chinks in her armor. They still bulldozed through her walls and hurt her.

She was starting to realize that she didn't want to be alone — a tough realization, considering she had turned away the one person she wanted to be with. Nolan cared about her, and she'd pushed him out of her life.

A knock at the door drew her attention. She stayed where she was, hoping the person would go away. It was probably for Mom anyway.

Then the sudden possibility that it could be Nolan seized her. She jumped to her feet and launched herself to the front door. Yanking it open, hope died a swift death in her throat.

Emmaline and Sanjana stared back at her. Not Nolan.

"Hey!" Emmaline exclaimed. "We thought you might want to do something. We're taking a study break and thought you might want to go get a pizza with us."

Hayden shook her head, ready to tell them no. That she didn't want to do anything. That she wanted to be alone.

Then again, being alone hadn't always kept her safe from her feelings. It hadn't kept her safe from anything. Here she was, miserable.

Maybe she should stop obsessing over what she thought was best for her and start paying attention to what *felt* best.

She could use a friend right now. *Friends.*

If she wanted things to change, she was going to have to step up and try changing things herself. Stop sticking her head in the sand, as Nolan had accused.

Hayden took a deep breath, feeling some of the tension ease out of her body. "Yeah," she said, nodding, a vague idea taking shape in her mind. "Can I borrow one of your phones to call work? I don't feel like going in. I'd love a pizza with you guys . . . and maybe I could get your opinion."

"Opinion?" Emmaline exchanged a look with Sanjana. "Intriguing."

"Yeah." She nodded slowly, the idea becoming less vague. "I could use your help with something."

IT'S ALWAYS BETTER
WHEN THERE ARE GENUINE FEELINGS.

x   Nolan   x

Nolan contemplated staying home the next day. He'd been absent only twice this year. The world wouldn't stop if he missed one day.

He was lying in bed, staring at the ceiling, convinced he wasn't going to school. He'd reached the end with Hayden and that crushed him more than he could have anticipated. It was crazy. Things had hardly even started with her, and yet he felt as though something epic had ended.

The door to his room suddenly banged open.

"Hey! What are you doing still in bed? Let's go."

He sat up and glared at his sister. "You're taking rides with me again?"

"Yeah. I'm taking rides with you again. Just like you're playing basketball with Beau again."

"Knew about that, huh?"

"Of course I knew. I know everything."

Nolan stared at his sister. She was . . . different. Confident and assertive. It was a good thing. Their father would approve of this side of her.

Emmaline yanked the covers off him. "So let's go. And don't worry. Beau will bring me home." She winked and walked back out of his room, shouting. "C'mon. Get a move on!"

Groaning, he climbed out of bed and got ready. At least his sister was talking to him again. There was that. In fact, she talked to him the entire drive to school. She was peppy. Perky. Happy again. Maybe even happier than before.

Beau was waiting for them in the parking lot. Nolan schooled his features not to reflect his disgust when they hugged and kissed. Just a peck, but it was still something he was going to have to get used to seeing. A bit like exposure therapy, he'd need to ease his way in.

"Hey, man," Beau greeted.

Nolan nodded and bumped fists with him. "Hey." It was a start.

He fell in beside them and they all walked toward the school entrance with dozens of others streaming in from the senior parking lot.

"Hey, hold on." Emmaline's hand circled Nolan's arm, stopping him on the bottom step leading up to the entrance.

Nolan paused and looked down at her. "What?" She and Beau exchanged knowing looks. "What?" he repeated.

Smiling, they both looked toward the front of the school. He did the same.

His gaze swept over the building. He didn't notice anything amid all the other students at first. But then someone — or something — was walking out of the double doors. Everyone was stopping to stare, point, and pull out their phones.

He stared too. It wasn't just anyone. It was a zombie. Holding a sign.

Specifically, Hayden was the zombie holding a sign.

He squinted like that might help him understand what he was seeing.

She wore ripped and dirty clothes. Her eyes were red, her face pale . . . except in the places where it was gouged and bloody and rotting. She looked amazing. Incredible. Like something from one of her movies.

A crowd formed around them, murmuring and watching raptly.

His gaze dropped to the blood-speckled sign she held and the words written there.

Even during a zombie apocalypse I choose you . . .
Will you go to the winter formal with me?

His heart seized, constricted right there in his chest. "Hayden?" he whispered, taking the steps necessary to reach her. He stopped in front of her. "What are you doing?"

"I'm asking you to the dance."

He shook his head, ignoring how his heart unclenched itself and started to race. "You hate this stuff."

"Yeah." She looked up at him in her red lenses. He wished he could see her real eyes right then, but he appreciated the lengths she had taken. She was making a spectacle of herself — over a dance. Over him. "But I don't hate you, and you know. I thought it might be nice if a girl asked you for a change." Her lips wobbled in a smile. "Like we talked about."

Yeah. He remembered.

His heart swelled then, beating faster and harder in his chest. He brushed a finger against the desiccated flap of skin hanging off her cheek. It was impressively gross. "You're kind of obsessed with me, aren't you?"

Her red-eyed gaze held his. "Yeah. I am."

"Yes, Hayden. I choose you, too."

A happy, broken little laugh escaped her then. He leaned down and kissed her, vaguely aware of the applause erupting around them.

He came up slightly, his lips a scant inch from hers. "You know this is the best dance proposal in the history of dance proposals."

Her voice was smug. "I know."

"I'm going to have my work cut out for me when it's my turn to ask you."

Her red eyes seemed to glow brighter. "I have faith in you."

LEAVE THE HORROR FOR ZOMBIE MOVIES, NOT YOUR RELATIONSHIP.

Hayden settled into the comfortable movie theater seat. She'd never been to this cinema before. It was too nice, too expensive, but Nolan insisted they go somewhere special. She'd been waiting to see this movie forever and they should watch it in style. His words.

"Excited?" Nolan leaned in and pressed a kiss to her lips. They did a lot of that. Over the last few months, she'd gotten to know the texture of his lips better than her own, and yet she didn't think she would ever get enough of him.

"Yeah." She smiled.

"I don't like zombie movies," Monica complained as she crossed in front of them, her fingers laced with Lia's.

"No one made you come," Emmaline shouted, tossing some popcorn at Monica from the tub she shared with Beau.

"For real," Sanjana seconded. "Stop complaining. It's supposed to be good."

Someone from several rows behind shushed them as the theater went dark and the first trailer began playing.

In the darkness, Nolan found Hayden's hand. His fingers wrapped around hers and she felt like she always did when he touched her.

She felt good. Strong and full of hope. The walls were gone.

She had Nolan. She had friends. She had so many things now. This was so much better than being alone. That was the greatest lesson of all. Better than anything she had ever tried to teach Emmaline. In the end, she was the one who needed to learn. The teacher had become the student, and she was grateful.

As far as she was concerned, the lessons could keep on coming. She would be ready for them.